**Also available from Sarah Smith
and Carina Press**

I Heart SF series

The Close-Up

Also available from Sarah Smith

Faker
Simmer Down
On Location
The Boy with the Bookstore
If You Never Come Back

D1012424

IN LOVE WITH LEWIS PRESCOTT

SARAH SMITH

carina
press

Recycling programs
for this product may
not exist in your area.

carina
press®

ISBN-13: 978-1-335-98488-3

In Love with Lewis Prescott

For questions and comments about the quality of this book, please contact us at CustomerService@Harlequin.com.

Carina Press
22 Adelaide St. West, 41st Floor
Toronto, Ontario M5H 4E3, Canada
www.CarinaPress.com

Printed in U.S.A.

For Sandy and Stefanie.
You absolute gems.

IN LOVE WITH LEWIS PRESCOTT

Chapter One

Harper

There's nothing I love more than slicing a grown man at the knees and watching him fall to pieces—metaphorically speaking.

It was a pleasure I indulged in on a regular basis in my old job as a corporate architect. Those guys never saw it coming, I suspect since I'm a small and unassuming woman who wears thick-rimmed glasses that make me look more like a grad student than the thirty-three-year-old professional I actually am. They didn't expect me to verbally lay them out when they talked down to me or mistook me for an intern and spewed their coffee order the second I walked into a conference room.

As soon as it registered that I was actually the person in charge of their project—which meant I was technically their boss and they'd have to answer to me for literally everything from that moment on—their eyes would bulge in horror. Sometimes they'd stammer an apology, but it was no use. They knew they were beyond screwed and that I was going to be a monster to work with because of the way they treated me—and I freaking loved that.

Right now I'm aching to hack Vlad the contractor

into a million pieces, but there's zero satisfaction in this endeavor. Just anger and rage. Because this guy is ruining the one thing that means most to me in the world.

Ever since walking into my late grandparents' house minutes ago, I've barely been able to look at the shoddy lighting fixtures, the flooring installed in the wrong direction, and the walls painted puke green without wanting to rage scream.

Instead I bite my tongue. I force myself to take a deep breath. I unclench my jaw. I press my eyes shut for a long second before eyeing the barrel-chested contractor who's glancing down at me, eyes glazed over with boredom.

"Vlad. What the hell happened? How did you manage to mess this up so much in just two weeks?"

He frowns. "I don't know what you mean, Harper. Everything looks fine to me."

I start to point out everything that's wrong in the open-concept space, but he cuts me off.

"Sorry, but I'm not going to be lectured by someone who doesn't know what they're talking about."

His curt words are like lighter fluid splashed onto the bonfire of frustration inside me, but it's the "sorry" spoken like an afterthought that steamrolls my insides. That is the least sincere "sorry" I've ever heard in my life—and I used to work with self-important ego maniacs on a daily basis.

I hold up a hand. "First of all, do not speak to me like that. I may not be a contractor, but I'm an architect, and I oversaw the first stage of this renovation—the phase you weren't even part of. I planned the addition of the master bathroom, the half bath, and the veranda. I know what I'm doing. I know what quality workmanship looks like, and this isn't it—not even close."

I gesture to the living room of my *Apong* Vivian and *Apong* Bernie's bungalow in Half Moon Bay, California, which they left to my parents and me.

"Look at the flooring." I stab my index finger at the ground. "I wanted the hardwood planks to run parallel to the fireplace. You installed them perpendicularly, which looks awkward as hell. And Jesus—the fireplace."

I march over to the once beautifully rustic fireplace that is now painted the starkest shade of white. I can barely look at it without wincing. Stunning, earthen-hued Mediterranean tiles covered by that blinding coat of white.

"I left you a voice mail *and* email last week telling you that I changed my mind about painting it over," I say. "But you did it anyway."

I go off about how all the doors he installed creak and wobble, how the tile in the master bathroom shower was placed in the incorrect pattern, how every new cabinet door he put up in the kitchen feels loose.

Vlad crosses his arms and slow-blinks, unfazed by what I'm saying. He couldn't give less of a shit about *his* fuckups.

After a few seconds, he finally twists his head to blink at the fireplace. He hacks, not bothering to cover his mouth. "Okay, maybe I messed up on the fireplace. But hey, I'm just doing my best here. You weren't even around these past few weeks to give me any guidance. That's on you."

I grit my teeth and curse the awful timing of this disaster. I was supposed to be here when the interior remodel kicked off last month, but my great-uncle got sick with pneumonia, so I stayed with my parents at their house just outside San Francisco to help take care of him after he got out of the hospital. He's thankfully recovering, but that meant I couldn't keep tabs on the renovation. I had to trust that Vlad—whom I had met only once before, when we went over the plans at the house and signed the contract—would do his job competently. Clearly that was a monumental mistake.

Today was the first chance I had to check on the progress in person...and it's in shambles.

I step forward into Vlad's space. "Don't you dare pin this on me. This is your fault and you know it."

His leathery brow lifts as I straighten up to my full height, which isn't saying much, given I'm five foot two. But I don't care. I've gone toe-to-toe with guys twice my size and have never once backed down. If this sloppy contractor thinks I'm going to cower in front of him, he's dead wrong.

"You've been half-assing this remodel the entire time," I bark at him, ignoring how the handful of contractors working around us suddenly stop and peer over at us. They've done an impressive job of keeping their heads down and pretending like Vlad and I haven't been snapping at each other for the past few minutes, but I guess you can only ignore a train wreck for so long.

"You need to fix this."

"Not unless you're gonna pay me more money."

The audacity of his demand turns my blood to lava. Not a chance.

"You're fired. Get the hell out of my house."

Vlad lets out a choking sound and hunches forward slightly, like someone has just shoved him. "Y-you can't fire me!"

"I just did." I point to the front door. "Leave."

Vlad's four-man crew seems to understand my command just fine as they quickly pack up their equipment and file out of the house in less than a minute. Vlad glances around at the movement, clearly dazed. When he turns back to me, recognition flashes across his face, then a scowl.

Muttering curses under his breath, he stomps out the door, tripping and nearly falling down before quickly righting his footing. Not cut off at the knees, but good enough.

I stand in the empty space and listen to the sound of his truck engine fading in the distance, my head spinning as I process what just happened. I just fired the contractor remodeling my grandparents' home without a backup plan. I don't have enough money to hire a new crew to fix the mess Vlad made *and* continue with the rest of the remodel.

What the hell do I do?

Shame and panic converge at the center of my chest, making my heart pound like an out-of-control drumbeat. It was my idea to quit my job in San Francisco months ago, give up my Nob Hill apartment, and move out here to Half Moon Bay to renovate my grandparents' home—the first and only home they ever owned after immigrating to the US from the Philippines. I promised my parents I'd honor the memory of *Apong* Vivian and *Apong* Bernie by redoing their house the way they'd always wanted to but couldn't afford. I thought this would be the perfect break from years of working my demanding corporate job.

And because I hired a shitty contractor—because of my lack of foresight due to being burned-out from years of seventy-hour workweeks—I've gone and screwed it all up.

Hot tears prick at my eyes, but I blink them away. I pull my phone out of my jeans pocket to call my cousin Naomi, but I stop myself when I pull up her name in my contacts list. I called her enough times when I was overseeing the addition of the bathrooms and veranda to the house the last few months. Even though I know she'd happily listen to me vent because she's my best friend and has been there for me since we were in diapers, something about this failure feels different—more raw and painful.

I tuck my phone back in my pocket and press a fist to the back of my neck, releasing a smidgen of the tension riddling me. I lock the door and walk down the driveway to my car. A dull pain shoots up my skull. I'm gonna need caffeine before I attempt to figure this out.

I head downtown and grab an Americano from the first coffee shop I see, then wander the streets in an attempt to clear my head. Between sips I breathe in the crisp, salty ocean air that whips gently around me. I take in the mixed architecture of the buildings—some stucco, some all brick, a few Spanish-style. It distracts me for a minute, but my thoughts circle back to the dreaded question that I have no idea how to answer: How the hell am I going to finish the renovation?

The thought of my grandparents' house remaining a half-finished disaster because of my mistake has me on the verge of tears once more. I blink quickly as I turn the corner, nearly running into a tall, broad body clad in a leather jacket and dark jeans, traveling at jogging speed. I dart to the side so quickly I lose my balance. My coffee goes flying.

"Shit," I blurt as I glance down at the sad pool of liquid gold seeping into the sidewalk.

And that's when the dam inside me finally bursts and a tear tumbles down my cheek. I quickly wipe it away. Can't one fucking thing go right today?

"Are you okay?" a gruff voice above me asks.

I'm thrown by the irritation in his tone. Usually a question like that is spoken with concern.

I look up and see a tall, scruffy, thirtysomething blond guy in a baseball cap. When he whips off his shades, a worried frown twists at his face.

"Um, yeah." I squint at him. "Are you?"

He nods, his hazel eyes lingering over my face before scanning over me, like he's making sure I'm telling the truth and not, in fact, hurt. It's weirdly off-putting—almost as off-putting as the fact that he hasn't yet apologized for almost running me over or knocking my oh-so-necessary coffee to the ground.

He glances around, like he's looking out for someone. Then he starts to step away before stopping and turning back to me.

I scoff. "You in a hurry?"

"Kind of," he mutters.

I pick up my now-empty coffee cup and toss it into a nearby recycling bin. "Well, I don't want to keep you. You must have a slew of people you're late for mowing over while blindly turning corners."

His expression softens. "I'm sorry." He peers down at the coffee staining the concrete between us. "Really. Let me buy you another cup."

"Don't worry about it."

"I insist. I could use some caffeine too. Clearly."

The corner of his mouth quirks up in a sort-of smile while he scratches the thick wheat-gold scruff that poorly disguises his sharp-as-hell jaw. I wouldn't normally let a stranger buy me a cup of coffee, but he's at least being friendly now. And he sounds truly sorry. And I still need caffeine. What the hell, why not?

He points to a nearby coffee shop, and I follow him inside to the register. I order another Americano, then step off to the side to grab napkins from the counter by the wall. I walk the few steps back over to him, and when the barista, who can't seem to stop staring at him, turns away to make our drinks, I notice he drops a twenty-dollar bill in the tip jar.

"Wow. Big spender."

"I used to work in food service. I always try to tip more than average to make up for all those stingy jerks."

That voice.

Okay, I've definitely seen this guy before. But where?

He tugs the bill of his baseball cap lower while his gaze bounces around the space.

Is this guy looking for someone? Or being followed? Or just paranoid?

"Hey, are you okay?" I ask. "Are you expecting someone or..."

He frowns and shakes his head before pulling at the sleeve of his jacket and rolling his shoulders back. His fidgety movements remind me of a restless zoo animal pacing in its cage.

"No, yeah, I mean... I'm fine."

As we stand off to the side and wait for our drinks, I do a mental inventory of recent gatherings I've been to where I might have seen him. Nothing. I think of the last work event I had, which was over a year ago. Still nothing.

A more natural smile tugs at his lips. "I like your glasses," he says, his smile turning crooked as he looks at me. "Very cute."

An unexpected ping of excitement hits me. Damn, is this dude flirting with me? What a random turn of events.

Heat flashes across my cheeks as I flash what I'm certain is a cheesy smile. Nah, he's probably just being nice to make up for making me spill my coffee and being so standoffish earlier.

"When I picked out the frames, I was going for Jess from *New Girl*, but I feel like I'm giving off more Velma from *Scooby-Doo* vibes."

He quirks an eyebrow. "I always had a thing for Velma."

My lips part in shock at that flirty comment. Before I can muster a response, the barista calls my order and the door to the shop swings open. His eyes go wide, and he looks in the direction of two teenage girls chatting and giggling as they gawk at their phones and make their way to the counter.

He whips his head to me. "Gotta go."

"But what about your coffee?"

He doesn't answer me as he darts out of the coffee shop. Then I hear the barista squeal.

She's gone starry-eyed as she looks toward the door. Then she looks at me. "Oh my god, I can't believe you know him!"

"I—I don't. He just almost ran into me on the street and made me spill my coffee, then offered to buy me another one."

Her jaw plummets to the floor as she clutches her chest with her hand. "You are so lucky to randomly run into Lewis Prescott!"

I nearly choke on my coffee. *That's* why he looked so familiar.

Lewis Prescott is the star of the hit TV show *The Best of It*, a fish-out-of-water comedy about a hot veterinarian from New York City who moves to rural New Mexico to take over an animal clinic he inherited. Even I, someone who doesn't seek out celebrity or gossip news, know about him because he's been on every magazine cover and talk show over the last year due to the success of the show.

He's also intensely private. His trademark move is to flip off paparazzi when they tail him, and he's known for telling interviewers to mind their own business when they ask about his dating life. Sometimes he just walks off midinterview.

What the hell is he doing in Half Moon Bay?

The teenage girls suddenly perk up. "Wait, did you just say Lewis Prescott was here?"

The barista nods and points to the door. "He was the guy in the leather jacket. He just left."

The girls dart out the door, and I'm left standing with my mouth open, my head spinning for a totally different reason.

Lewis Prescott just bought me a coffee. Holy shit.

Chapter Two

Harper

"So…what are you going to do?"

My cousin's hesitantly spoken words hit me straight in the chest. I've just filled her in on how I fired Vlad yesterday. As I sit in the corner of the same coffee shop I visited yesterday, I squint at the spreadsheet on my laptop screen.

"Honestly, Naomi, I have no freaking clue." When I exhale, my shoulders fall forward, like I've been shoved over.

I barely got any sleep last night. I tossed and turned as a million worried thoughts flashed through my brain. I take another gulp of coffee, ashamed of how defeated I sound. I can't remember the last time I felt this dejected—not even at work when I was regularly facing off with mansplaining jerks who doubted my abilities because I'm a young woman. Those moments were actually enlivening. I'd get this hit of adrenaline every time I verbally laid them out in a meeting or on a jobsite.

But this? This is something else entirely. This is my whole chest aching at the thought that I've screwed up the most precious thing my grandparents left our family.

I contemplate blurting to Naomi that I had a random interaction with a TV star yesterday at this very coffee shop, just to change the subject, but when I open my mouth, all that comes out is a soft croaking noise. I can't even get the words out, I'm too upset.

As wild as it is that I literally bumped into Lewis Prescott, the shock of our brief encounter proved to be only a fleeting distraction. When I drove back to my grandparents' house, the gravity of my situation lingered over me like the weight of a thousand cinder blocks. I couldn't escape that sense of failure then, no matter what I tried to distract myself with. I still can't.

While Naomi reassures me that it'll all end up okay, I pull up the news on my laptop. I don't have the heart to tell her that her well-intentioned words of encouragement are doing little to ease the dread pooling at the pit of my stomach. So instead I hum affirmations to her every few seconds while skimming my news feed. When I come across a photo of Lewis flashing double middle fingers, his mouth open and his face beet red like he's mid–angry scream, I make a choking sound.

"You okay?" Naomi asks.

"Um, yeah…just gimme a sec."

I quickly skim the text in the article.

It's been a rough month for disgraced TV star Lewis Prescott. First, he gets canned from his hit show, The Best of It, *after threatening the showrunner during a heated argument. Then his Victoria's Secret model girlfriend breaks up with him that same night at Chateau Marmont, in full view of paparazzi.* Comme c'est tragique! *And how can we*

*forget our favorite hunky veterinarian's infamous
meltdown that followed?*

I click on the video clip beneath the paragraph, my
mouth open in horror as I watch a dozen paparazzi shouting at him.

*"How's it feel to lose your girlfriend the same day you
lost your job, big shot?"*

*"I heard you punched the showrunner because he
called you 'bimbo pretty boy.' Is that true?"*

*"Lewis, come on! Stop and give us a photo, man. Just
this once!"*

I feel my pulse race as I watch them swarm him like a
pack of wolves zeroing in on a deer. He tries to maneuver
around them but is constantly stopping and backtracking
as they push closer, shoving their bodies and their cameras in his space. It's clear he's about to lose his shit—his
skin turns redder and redder by the second, and his jaw
muscles look like they're about to rip through his skin.

"Aww, come on, pretty boy," someone taunts. *"You
can't give us one picture? Answer one question?"*

I wince as Lewis stops dead in his tracks and turns
around to address whatever cruel jerk just goaded him.

*"You want a picture, you fucking low-life pieces of
shit?"* His voice booms so loudly, I jerk back against the
couch. I turn down the volume on my computer and look
up, grateful that there's no one else in hearing range.

Lewis's hazel eyes are wide and wild with fury as he
steps forward, causing a handful of the photographers
to stumble back. *"Here! Here's your motherfucking picture!"* He flips double middle fingers. *"Fuck you all.
Go to hell."*

My jaw falls to the floor as the video ends, and I skim the rest of the article.

Prescott hasn't been seen since the night of his profanity-laden tirade. It's a far cry from the intensely private actor's cool, calm, and charming demeanor. He famously refuses to answer questions about his personal life, sometimes walking off midinterview whenever a reporter presses about his romantic life or his family. Looks like this rising star finally hit his tipping point. Is he gone forever? Is he keeping a low profile to quell all the bad press? Is he planning a comeback? Let us know what you think in the comments section! And if you spot the hunky star, snap a photo and tag us!

No wonder Lewis was so skittish when I ran into him yesterday. He's being tailed by the paparazzi *and* the public. On top of that, gossip news is treating his personal and professional hardship like it's an amusing clip from a reality show. God, what the hell is wrong with our culture that we think it's okay to treat a human being like this in their lowest moment? I make a disgusted noise.

"You okay?"

The sound of Naomi's voice jolts me. Oh right. I'm still on the phone with her.

"Um, yeah. Sorry. I got lost in my thoughts for a bit."

"I know what you're thinking, Harper," she says. "Don't you dare feel guilty about what happened with the remodel. It's not your fault."

I shove aside all thoughts of Lewis. As bad as I feel for him, I don't even know the guy. I'll probably never see him again. I refocus on the failed renovation and the fact that I still have no clue what to do.

"But it *is* my fault, Naomi. If I had been more careful—"

"Stop. Harper, what you're doing—what you've already done—is amazing. Our grandparents' house has been sitting there for years just waiting for someone to build it up like they always wanted. But none of us in the family had the guts or the money to take it on. You did, though. You quit your job after years of establishing yourself as a brilliant architect and used your skills to honor our grandparents' memory. You've already kicked ass with the additions you've put onto the house. Can you imagine just how giddy *Apong* Vivian would have been to see the veranda? And *Apong* Bernie's eyes would have popped out of his head to see that master bathroom and the half bath you put in. Remember how he always complained about having only one bathroom when all of us girls would come visit for the holidays?"

Naomi's reassurances have my chest tightening in a completely different way now. Because she's right. They would be ecstatic at what I've accomplished so far.

"I know what happened with Vlad is beyond maddening," she says. "And I swear to god, if I ever see that guy, I'm going to kick him in the nuts with my pointiest high heel for being such a dick to you."

I let out a watery chuckle at the thought of sweet and adorable Naomi nailing Vlad in the crotch.

"I should have done more research before hiring him," I mutter. "He must have faked his online reviews or something, because they were all glowing."

"I promise, it'll work out. We'll figure a way."

My throat throbs with emotion. I sniffle and swallow.

"Thanks, Naomi. I just… It's overwhelming to think about where to go from here. I don't even know where to start. I put aside a lot of money for this renovation, and it was already more expensive than I wanted it to be. Not working is making it hard too, because I don't have that source of income anymore. I can't just throw money at stuff when I'm not bringing it in, you know? I had a plan—save money so I could quit work for a while in order to focus fully on the renovation. I was so burned-out from my job too, you know? Seeing Uncle Pedro in the hospital helped me realize how short life is and how I don't want to spend it living like a workaholic."

I swallow back the sudden lump in my throat, thankful that Uncle Pedro is out of the hospital and recovering with my parents.

"Once this house is finished, I'll start working as an architect again. But maybe I should just bite the bullet and start working now? I can't think of another way to pay for everything that's gone wrong."

Naomi starts to talk, but I press on. This is the only way I can make sense of the muddled, panicked thoughts in my brain—to talk it all out.

"Now I have to hire someone else to come in and fix what Vlad screwed up, and it'll probably be double what I budgeted and I don't want to dig into my retirement…"

"No, don't," Naomi quickly says. "Look, I know I tease you about how careful you are with your money, but I also know how important it is for you to save and plan. That would kill you to dig into your retirement. And *Apong* Vivian and *Apong* Bernie wouldn't want you to do anything that would put you out for their sake."

I'm instantly heartened at her words. We're the exact same age, and our families grew up together in the Bay

Area. She knows better than anyone why I'm so careful with money. Our grandparents were immigrants from the Philippines and moved to the US in their twenties, settling in Half Moon Bay. They worked hard to provide a stable life for their family. As a kid, I watched them, my parents, Naomi's parents, and our relatives pinch pennies and budget for everything in order to afford a middle-class lifestyle in one of the most expensive areas in the country.

When I landed a lucrative corporate architect job straight out of college, I held on to it for dear life. And I'm glad I did. I made a lot of money for ten-plus years. I was able to pay off my student loans, finance a healthy retirement fund, buy a one-bedroom apartment in Nob Hill, build a cushy savings account, and help out my family from time to time. I'm grateful for my financial stability, but my experience has also made me hesitant to spend large amounts of money unexpectedly.

It's not like I have an endless stream to draw from. Yes, I'm more financially stable than most, but one unforeseen catastrophe—like a renovation gone wrong— could easily wipe out a huge chunk of my savings, leaving my finances wrecked.

I tug a hand through my hair, pulling me back to the present. "I'll figure out a way through this." I repeat Naomi's reassurance from a minute ago. "It's not like the house isn't livable or anything like that. I'm still fine staying there while I work out what I'm going to do next."

My dream was to settle into that house and for the next year immerse myself in quiet coastal life and do volunteer work as a way to decompress from all the time I spent as a workaholic in San Francisco. I'd be in the house where I spent so much of my childhood. I was so pumped to decorate the newly renovated space with all the special heirlooms *Apong* Vivian and *Apong* Bernie left me and my family. And I was planning to host holidays and family gatherings there too, starting this year, so that my family could come together in the newly remodeled house and celebrate like we used to when my grandparents were still alive.

But the thought of doing all that in a house with a half-finished floor, shoddy kitchen cabinets, and puke-colored walls has my eyes burning. Our grandparents gave our entire family so much endless joy and so many memories with that house, and my attempt to carry on their love and tradition failed miserably.

"Harper." Naomi's voice cuts through the cloud of sad thoughts consuming me. "Do you want to borrow some money? I know I don't make as much as you and so I don't have as much savings, but Simon and I would be so happy to—"

"Nope." I sit up. "No way am I letting my cousin, who's in the middle of planning her dream wedding to her dream guy, give me any money."

Naomi proposed to Simon at their apartment in San Francisco just a few months ago while I was here in Half Moon Bay, overseeing the tail end of the additions to the house.

She starts to insist, but I shoot her down again.

"How's wedding planning going, by the way?" I ask, eager to change the topic of our conversation to something happy. "I still can't believe it's happening so soon."

"We don't want a long engagement. And surprisingly, planning everything has been pretty stress-free. I'm amazed at the number of vendors that have been available on our tight timeline."

I was shocked to hear they were planning to get hitched so soon after the proposal. But it's also a disgustingly sweet testament to how in love they are. They don't want to waste a single moment not being married to each other. Even my cynical, romance-weary self had swooned at that.

She tells me about how they're writing their own vows and how they're going to have a dessert bar in lieu of a wedding cake with cupcakes and egg tarts. She lets out a breath that sounds the exact opposite of my stress-ridden exhales: light, airy, and delivered through a giddy smile.

"I'm so freaking happy, Harper. I can't wait to marry Simon." She's full-on beaming now, I can hear it.

"Look, I know I'm in the middle of a shit show, but I want you to know that it absolutely will not affect my ability to be a stellar maid of honor."

"I know that."

"You sure you don't want to have an engagement party or a bridal shower? It's not too late for me to set something up."

"You know we're not into all that traditional wedding stuff. I mean, I proposed to Simon."

"Okay, fair enough. But thank god you still want a bachelorette party. There's no way I'd let you get away with forgoing that."

"Simon actually suggested having a bachelor-bachelorette party. That way we wouldn't have to hire a male stripper, since, you know…he'd do it."

I roll my eyes and laugh. "Of course he'd suggest that."

My cousin's future husband is a cam guy turned relationship therapist with progressive views about everything. He's also an insanely romantic guy who lives to make her happy, and nothing would make Naomi happier than seeing her fiancé perform the striptease at her bachelorette party. I'm sure Simon would absolutely nail it, given that he won an amateur strip club night when they were just work colleagues, before anything romantic happened between them. It was supposed to be strictly business, a fun scene for the online series she was filming about Simon's work and life. But the dance must have knocked her socks off, because the professional lines blurred and they started hooking up. I'm convinced that seeing Simon in all his *Magic Mike* glory marked the beginning of when she started to fall for him.

"I'll plan something amazing for your bachelorette party, promise," I tell her. "When are you…"

When I glance up, my eyes go wide at the sight of Lewis Prescott walking into the coffee shop. Damn, what are the odds of seeing him again?

His chest heaves as he takes a breath, his head pivoting as he glances across the room. His eyes lock on me before he throws a quick look at the counter, which is now empty, since the baristas are currently rummaging in the back room. He darts over to me.

"Hey." His voice is a low, breathy whisper as he plops onto the couch I'm sitting on. "Harper, right? Can I use you as a hiding spot?"

"Um, what?"

"Who's that?" Naomi's asks.

Before I can say anything, Lewis yanks off his jacket, turns it inside out, stretches his long body over the couch, curls into the fetal position, and rests his face on my lap before throwing the jacket over his head. My thigh muscles twitch at the sudden feel of his face against my body.

"When they come in, say I'm your husband. Say I'm sleeping," he whispers.

The warmth of his mouth as he breathes against my denim-covered thighs turns my brain to slop. Fire flashes up my chest and my cheeks. Well, that was unexpected.

Was it really, though? It's been a solid three years since I've been in a relationship, thanks to my workaholic lifestyle. And the last time I cozied up to anyone was over a year ago, when I flirted with a random guy at a bar and made out with him at the end of the night. When we sobered up the next day, we realized we didn't have anything in common, and our flirty texting petered out after that.

So yeah... I guess it makes sense why the feel of a sexy TV star's face pressed against my leg would cause a full-body hot flash.

Thankfully Lewis doesn't seem to notice the reaction I'm having. He hasn't said a word in the twenty seconds he's been tucked into me.

I dry swallow and clear my throat. "Naomi, I, uh, I'm gonna call you back, okay? Something just came up." Or dropped down...

When I hang up, a trio of college-aged women strolls into the coffee shop, their heads pivoting as they gaze around the space. The movement reminds me of a flock of flamingos darting their beaks in every direction in search of insects to eat.

They peer over at me. "Hey!" one of them says. "Have you..."

She drifts off when I press my index finger to my lips. "I'm sorry, but can you please keep it down?" I ask in a gentle voice. "My husband has a migraine. If you talk too loudly, it'll aggravate his pain and he'll spew chunks everywhere."

All three of them grimace in unison before quickly

backing away and heading out the door. I count to ten to make sure no one else walks in before tapping Lewis's shoulder.

"The coast is clear."

I expect him to dart up instantly, but when he keeps his head nestled in my lap for the next several seconds, my breath catches. Did he fall asleep?

But then the low rumble of his laugh hits my ears.

"Migraine-induced vomiting, huh?" he says, his head still covered by his jacket. He gives my knee a light squeeze, and I almost gasp at how playful it is.

"Best I could come up with on such short notice."

He pulls off the jacket and sits up, the most adorably sheepish look on his face. I nearly stutter out loud, but I catch myself. I'm blown away at just how playful he's being in this moment. Even though I'm not an obsessed fangirl, I've watched a good chunk of his movies and a few episodes of his show, and I've caught some of his interviews. I've only ever seen him as the cool, collected TV star. And the skittish grump from yesterday.

I shake my head slightly. I'm being ridiculous. He's a human being. He can have different facets to his personality, just like we all do.

"Thanks for helping me out," he mumbles. "Sorry too. That was pretty intrusive of me to put my head in your lap like that. We barely know each other."

I shrug and try my best to play it cool, but it's a hell of a task. Because as I gaze up at Lewis's impossibly handsome face, I can't help but notice the warmth of his body as he sits next to me...specifically the warmth of the side of his ass that's pressed against my hip.

"It's all good." I immediately down the rest of my

coffee, offering him my untouched glass of water when I notice how hard he's still breathing.

He drains the glass, then sticks his hand out to me. "I'm Lewis."

"I know."

His eyes widen, and I'm taken aback at the horror in them. It lands hard, like a shove. It takes a second to process why, but then I realize it's because he's afraid I'm going to go after him like a crazed fan too.

"Don't worry, I haven't told anyone about running into you. I'm not planning on it either."

He exhales, looking visibly less stressed. He opens his mouth to speak but then stops himself before darting his gaze around the space again. The door opens, and an elderly couple walks in. I take note of how Lewis's broad shoulders lower to a relaxed position as he takes in the couple. Clearly, they have no idea who he is and he's relieved.

"You wanna get out of here?" I ask. "I can give you a ride to wherever you're staying. I'm parked right out front."

Instantly I wish I could take back what I've just said. Like Lewis Prescott needs a ride from me, someone he barely knows. I'm sure that's the last thing an intensely private celebrity wants, for a stranger to learn where he's staying. And I'm also sure he's got a sports car parked around the corner and can make a speedy getaway on his own. I probably sound like a weirdo for even offering.

"Er—never mind, I—"

"Yeah, I'd love that," he says quickly as he hops to his feet and grabs me by the hand to help me stand up. Once again, I'm left making barely audible sputtering noises at such a friendly touch and his immediate acceptance of my offer.

He points to the laptop on the coffee table. "That yours?"

I nod, and he scoops it up along with my power cord. I grab my purse, and together we walk out to my car.

"So. Where am I taking you?" I say once I pull out of the space and roll through the main drag downtown.

"The Sandy Shore Motel on the edge of town."

I almost laugh. The Sandy Shore Motel is the seediest motel in all of Half Moon Bay. He probably just wants me to drop him there so he can throw me off the trail.

"That place is a dump."

"I'm aware," he mumbles while staring straight ahead.

I slow to a stop at a red light, wondering just how much I'm allowed to pry in this odd situation where I'm giving a television star an impromptu lift in my cluttered hatchback. Probably not much at all, given that we barely know each other.

"Sorry, I should haven't said that about the motel," I say in a quiet voice.

"It's fine."

When I glance over at him, I'm thrown by the slight smile on his face, but after a second his stare turns focused and serious.

"I'm assuming you know...what happened...with me," he says after a moment.

"I have an idea," I say, my gazed fixed on the road ahead. "Sorry for what you're going through. And for how you lost, um, your job."

I bite my tongue. Why did I bring that up? He probably doesn't want to be reminded of that awful moment.

Despite knowing better, I start to wonder why exactly Lewis got fired. Did he and the showrunner just not like each other? Did Lewis do something to get on the showrunner's nerves, like arrive late to set one too many times? Or did he do something outrageous?

I quietly scold myself for speculating. He's sitting right next to me while I'm thinking such intrusive thoughts about him. It's none of my business why he got fired—it's none of anyone's business. That's exactly why he's here, to hide out from all the nosy people trying to pry into his life. I've got zero right to speculate about any of this right now.

"Yeah, well. It is what it is," he says gruffly. "Just trying to lay low till the bad press dies down."

"Why'd you tell me that?" I ask when I can't hold in my curiosity any longer.

"What do you mean?"

"Aren't you worried that I'm going to tip off the paparazzi? Or chase after you once I know where your motel is? Or take a photo of you and send it to all my friends?"

His light chuckle completely throws me, as does the very tempting dimple in his right cheek. It's such a wholesome and adorable feature on his otherwise ruggedly handsome face. I have to look away—it's almost too beautiful, too arresting for my brain to handle. A beat later I glance back over and catch his sparkling hazel eyes scanning over my face. For a millisecond it looks like his gaze is lingering over my lips, but he's back to my eyes before I can be sure.

"No. I'm not worried about you ratting me out."

I'm speechless as I pull into the pothole-ridden parking lot of the motel, astounded that this guy comes off as so trusting given everything he's going through.

"Why would you trust me? We don't even know each other."

"Because you're treating me like a regular person, not a celebrity. That counts for a lot in my experience. Plus, you haven't told anyone about seeing me."

Damn. The way Lewis can quickly read a person he barely knows is impressive. I wonder if that's a skill he's had to develop as a celebrity, sussing out trustworthy people in a sea of folks who are constantly after you for your fame, your money, or some other nefarious reason.

He points to the far end of the single-story, L-shaped motel that's swathed in a drab adobe shade. "Right there is fine."

I drive over and park. "Wow."

"I know, it's a shithole."

I burst out laughing. "This is the perfect hideout. I'd never expect a celebrity to stay within a hundred miles of this place."

He chuckles as he moves to open the door. "Thanks again for hiding me earlier. And for the ride."

"No problem. Good luck with…" My phone buzzes, and I glance down to see another text from yet another contractor quoting me an insane price to finish the re-model.

I grit my teeth and before sighing sharply.

"Everything okay?" Lewis asks.

"Not even close."

He opens his mouth like he's not quite sure what to say to that.

"Sorry, I'm just trying to salvage the remodel from hell. It looks like it's going to be hell on my bank account too."

He winces. "Shitty contractors?"

I let out a sad chuckle. "How'd you know? I fired the contractor yesterday because he screwed up everything from the flooring to the light fixtures."

I quickly explain that I've quit my job and moved to Half Moon Bay to fix up my grandparents' old house.

"I used to be a contractor before I was an actor," Lewis says.

"Really?"

He nods. "It was only a few years ago that I gave it up completely. I'd do house flips while auditioning and when I nabbed small parts here and there."

"Damn. Too bad you're not available to work on my run-down bungalow." I'm cleaning my glasses lenses on the hem of my long-sleeve T-shirt when I look up and notice that Lewis's brow is lifted slightly, like he's actually considering what I've said.

I laugh and wave a hand before focusing back on my smudgy glasses. "I'm kidding. But hey, if you ever need a place to hide out where no one will ever think to look for you, check out the Ellorza family residence on the south side of town, right next to that rocky hillside the city council zoned against any new construction decades ago."

I expect Lewis to chuckle a thanks or a good-natured "okay then" at my terribly long-winded joke before hopping out of my car. But he doesn't move to leave, or even say a word. I slide my glasses back on and glance up at him. His mouth hangs half-open, and there's a gleam in his hazel eyes as he gazes off to the side.

"Okay. Yeah. I wanna do that."

"Do what?"

"I wanna move into your house."

"Um, what?" I laugh but immediately stop when the focused expression on his face remains.

"No one knows I'm staying at this motel, but it's only a matter of time before they find out. Someone—one of the receptionists or the housekeeping staff or another guest—is bound to notice me. Or one of the people who've been trying to chase me down in town will catch up to me and my hideout will be blown. But no one will know I'm staying with you."

I'm speechless as he gazes at me expectantly. Is this guy serious?

"It can be a work trade. I help you renovate your house in exchange for safekeeping."

My mouth hangs open as I soak in everything he's saying. He's serious.

I hold my hand up. "Hang on a sec. I was kidding, Lewis. I don't actually think you should hide out in my grandparents' home."

"Why not? It's a pretty brilliant plan. Plus, it's a win-win—we both get what we need."

I sputter at what is happening right now—this TV heartthrob is seriously making a case for hiding out at my house.

"First of all, it's a mess," I say. "It's just me in that house right now, and even I'm having a hell of a time trying not to hurt myself by tripping over paint cans and errant light fixtures."

He shrugs. "Like I said, I used to be a contractor. I know what it's like to navigate the mess. I could do it in my sleep."

I'm stunned speechless yet again.

"What if I paid you?" Something behind his eyes turns fiery, pleading almost. "A million bucks to let me stay at your house, just for the next three months. Until the bad press dies down, then I'll head back to LA and I'll be out of your hair. You'll never have to see me again."

My jaw unhinges as it falls open. "What the— Are you seriously trying to bribe me?"

He jerks back at my response. "No! God, no. I'm so sorry, I didn't mean it like that, just that... I'd be more than happy to pay you to let me do this. I would never expect you to do this for me without being compensated."

Compensated.

Something about that word sits like a rock in my stomach. Is this how he lives his life as a rich and famous celebrity—offering insane amounts of money for random favors? I could never fathom doing that, even if I had that much money.

"I'm not taking any money from you."

He holds up both hands, palms facing me. "How about I fix up your house, then? Free of charge."

I sputter out a laugh. "This cannot be real."

"I'm one thousand percent serious, Harper."

"Even if I were to say yes to such an outrageous proposition, there's no way you could do the reno job yourself. The place is a disaster."

"I've worked on skeleton crews that did the work of twenty people in half the time. I've worked from sunup to sundown on jobsites to finish houses in record time."

He speaks with that sure, resolute tone once more.

"At least show me the place—let me see what state it's in," he says, his tone softer. "Please?"

The words *no way* dangle off the tip of my tongue, but against every instinct I have, I swallow back the words and actually think about what he's proposing. There's no way I'm taking any money from him, but I can't deny that his offer to fix up my grandparents' house would be freaking awesome. I should at least think about it.

I face forward and put my car in gear.

"Okay, I'll show you. But no promises."

Chapter Three

Harper

Lewis Prescott paces around my grandparents' living room, and I have to fight the urge to pinch myself.

How the hell is this my life? Twenty-four hours ago I was standing in this very spot as I fired my contractor. Now I'm observing the man that *Cosmopolitan* voted as having the sexiest six-pack in Hollywood while he studies the gaps between my floorboards.

I shake my head as if to magically reset my thoughts, my vision, my reality. But nope. The scene in front of me remains. This must be what people mean when they say "mind fuck."

Lewis trots over to the kitchen and opens one of the cabinet doors, wincing when it squeaks. "That Vlad guy definitely half-assed this cabinet installation. Christ, they're not even level, and all the hinges are loose. The veranda and the added bathrooms are incredibly well done, though."

He steps over to the hallway leading to the three bedrooms and sticks his head in the half bathroom that I designed.

"The materials in here look really high quality, and

the design is perfect. It's a small space, but you utilized it well with the kind of fixtures you chose and how you oriented the sink and the toilet."

I know the smile I'm flashing is cheesy, but I can't help it. I worked so hard on that bathroom, and it feels so damn amazing to be complimented on it.

"And the veranda is just...damn." He walks back to the kitchen and through the French doors that lead to it. "It's a gorgeous wraparound," he says while standing in the open doorway.

"Thanks," I say. "It took a while to get just right, but I think it was worth it."

"You worked hard on the first stage of this renovation, and it shows."

Lewis finishes his walk-through after commenting here and there about the other problems he notices with Vlad's remodel.

He turns to me and rests his hands on his hips. "My honest opinion?"

"Please."

"I can easily fix all of this and do the last couple of projects you mentioned in three months, max."

"Seriously? By yourself?"

"If you're willing to help me out with stuff when you're free, it'll go faster."

I was fully expecting Lewis to observe the disaster zone that is currently this house and admit that he'd need at least a ten-person crew to take on this mess. It takes a few seconds of me standing there staring at him to fully process that this is actually doable.

"Okay...maybe I could do that."

"So does that mean I'm hired?" Lewis flashes a half smile that has me chuckling.

"Not so fast. Can I see some of your past work? I know that might be super annoying for me to ask, but this house means everything to me, and someone already came in and screwed it all up. I don't want to risk that happening again. I need to know you have the skill to fix what's wrong with this house *and* carry out a quality remodel."

Even as I say it, I have no idea how he'll be able to quell my worry. But he flashes a boyish smile, like he expected me to say all this all along. "Absolutely."

He pulls out his phone and for the next few minutes shows me photos of a sprawling mid-century modern home.

"This is my house in LA," he says. "I bought it just over three years ago. It was a foreclosure and a total dump. Structural problems, mold in the ceilings, fire damage, the works."

He flips through a dozen photos showing discolored ceilings and crackling walls pocked with holes.

"I spent almost a year fixing it up whenever I had time off between roles."

My mouth hangs open as I take in the stunning transformation: the open-concept design, post-and-beam construction, clerestory windows all along the entire first floor. If he was able to turn his house into a freaking palace, I know I can trust him with this remodel.

"Whoa. That's gorgeous." I look up at him. "Okay. You've clearly got some serious skills. But there's one more thing that you need to be okay with. Given the fact that I live in this house, I'll be here pretty much every day until this renovation is done, so…"

"You want to micromanage me." He says it so casually, like he doesn't mind at all, I'm a little shocked. What I'm suggesting is a contractor's worst nightmare.

"Pretty much, yeah," I say. "Look, I know how annoying that's going to be, but this is my grandparents' house. It was their first and only home in the US after moving from the Philippines decades ago. When they passed, they left it to my parents and me to take care of. And we…well, we let it get a bit run-down over the years."

My gaze falls to the floor as a pang of sadness hits my chest. God, I miss *Apong* Bernie and *Apong* Vivian so much.

"Even though they're not here anymore, I want to make this house as perfect as I can to honor them. They deserve that."

Lewis's gaze turns thoughtful as he looks at me. "I get it. I promise, if you let me do this renovation, I'll bust my ass to make it exactly how you want it. I'll run every single detail by you, no matter how small. No complaints whatsoever. You say jump, my response will always be, 'how high?'"

I'm heartened at the confidence and conviction in his tone. Combined with his unwavering eye contact, it comes off so intense, so sincere. I believe him completely.

A few quiet moments pass as I cross my arms and gaze around the space. If I say yes to Lewis's offer to fix up the house, I'll be saved. I won't have to shell out tens of thousands to fix Vlad's mistakes and hire a new crew. Lewis will do it all for free, and the renovation will turn out exactly how I want it.

This time the word *yes* dances on my tongue, but before I can say it, he speaks.

"If you say yes, I'm gonna need to give you something for letting me stay. You're letting me hide out for the next three months, which is a million times better than that roach motel I was planning to hunker down in."

I open my mouth to object, but he shakes his head.

"You're saving me, Harper. I'm not going to let you do that for nothing."

"Lewis, I'm not accepting money from you. You offering to fix and finish this renovation for free is payment enough."

He crosses his arms over his chest and takes a step toward me, closing the space between us to just a couple of feet. It would be intimidating if he didn't have the most playful smile on his face, like he's more amused than frustrated at my stubbornness.

As we stand and stare at each other, I can't help but chuckle at this stalemate.

Suddenly an idea pops in my head. "Okay, wait. There's no way I'm taking your money, but if you're hell-bent on giving away your cash, there's this amazing nonprofit that I volunteer for. They're grossly underfunded and always in need of donations."

I tell Lewis about Glad You're Here, how I started volunteering there in college and whenever I had free time at my old job, and how I'm planning to volunteer there more now that I'm not working.

"They provide services for immigrant and refugee families here in the Bay Area. They have a small office between Half Moon Bay and San Francisco. You can donate the money you wanted to give to me to them instead. Then we'll have a deal."

Lewis beams and steps closer before sticking his hand out. I shake it, relishing the warm feel of his hand, how his skin is somehow soft and firm at once.

"It's a deal."

"So we're really doing this?" I say, my hand stilling in his.

"Yup. Just one thing—you can't tell anyone I'm staying with you."

I tilt my head to the side. "Of course I won't."

"I don't plan on leaving the house much," he says. "I don't want to draw any attention to myself. I know that'll make for us spending a lot of time together…"

"Well, whenever you annoy me, I'll just head to San Francisco to check on my family," I tease.

"I guess you'll be spending a lot of time with them, then," he jokes back. "Hey, would it be weird if I made another request?"

"Such as?"

"No one other than you and me can be in the house while I'm here. I just can't risk someone recognizing me and giving away my hideout."

"That's completely reasonable. I promise that for the next three months, the only two people who will ever know that you're staying in these luxury accommodations will be you and me."

He visibly relaxes.

"You sure you'll be okay hiding out here? It's nowhere near as nice as your palace in LA," I tease.

"This house is beautiful, Harper. Don't sell it short."

There's a sincerity in his tone that softens me. It's then that I notice our hands are still joined in the handshake.

One of his eyebrows quirks up along with the corner of his mouth. "Excited to move in with you, roomie."

"Just don't leave the toilet seat up and we'll be fine," I joke. But when we release our hands, I realize that I'm a little more excited than I should be.

I drive him back to the motel to collect his things, ignoring the somersaults happening in my stomach. For the next three months, I'll be sharing a house with Lewis Prescott.

My stomach dips. Are those nerves? Butterflies? A mix of both?

I guess we'll find out.

Chapter Four

Lewis

I pound the pavement as hard as I can, my lungs on fire.

It's a half hour before sunrise as I finish the last mile of my predawn jog, and judging by the zero cars along the road, not a single soul is awake other than me. Just as I'd hoped.

The sound of waves crashing echoes in the distance. I knew coming to Half Moon Bay was the right call. I've only ever driven through this sleepy coastal town, but I always wanted to stay and visit. I just never had the time with my schedule. Now I do, though.

As I pick up the pace the final half mile back down the quiet, darkened street to where Harper's family house is, I start to smile. Even though my chest is about to explode, sweat's dripping in my eyes, and my legs are aching, I'm happy.

This is the first time I've felt happy in weeks—pretty much ever since the day I got shitcanned from *The Best of It*.

Just the thought of what happened that morning has my stomach churning. I pick up speed, full-out sprinting just to drown out that sickening feeling.

No way do I want to let that god-awful moment occupy another millimeter of space in my brain. I've spent enough time obsessing over that day.

I gasp for air as I cover the last stretch of my run. But despite how hard I focus on the fire in my chest and legs, unwanted memories creep in. I blink and see the rage on Darren's face when I confronted him. I blink again and see his eyes widen when I call him a predatory piece of shit. I see the bulging vein in his neck when he yelled that I was fired and demanded that I get the hell off his set before he called security. I see the stricken faces of half the crew standing outside my dressing room, having overheard the whole argument.

I see the look of disgust on my ex-girlfriend Natalia's face that evening when I told her at Chateau Marmont that I had gotten fired after I confronted Darren for sexually harassing half of the crew on the show. I see her roll her eyes before berating me for blowing her chance of a guest appearance, not at all concerned that the showrunner was a sorry-ass excuse for a man.

I see the horde of paparazzi crowding our table as she broke up with me right then and there, taking photo after photo, aiming their cameras at my face so they could document one of the lowest moments of my life.

And then I see the exact moment when I lost my shit on all of them, calling them every cussword in the book while flipping them off.

Sure, I've cursed at scumbag paparazzi and disrespectful reporters before, but never like that. I was rabid that night. I had just lost my job and my girlfriend, and every tabloid photographer in the vicinity wanted to document my humiliation and sell it—they wanted to profit off my misery, and I couldn't take it anymore.

I slow to a walk and stumble forward before catching myself, every muscle and limb in my body shaking and aching. Lungs burning, I rest my hands on my head and walk up and down Harper's block, chest heaving as I gasp for air.

The happiness I felt moments ago is gone. Instead that knot of anxiety is back, lodged right at the center of my chest. But when I stop at the end of Harper's driveway and fix my gaze on her house, a sense of calm moves through me. My breathing begins to even out; my heartbeat slows from frantic to just speedy.

What happened all those weeks ago doesn't matter, not now. There's nothing I can do about that piece of shit Darren, about my selfish ex, about being blacklisted from Hollywood. I'm thankfully hundreds of miles away from that shit show because of the kindness of a stranger— and for that I'm grateful and relieved.

I press my eyes shut. Instantly, Harper's angelic face fills the darkness behind my eyelids. I feel my lips curving up. As sweet as she looks, she's feisty. I barely know her, but I like her. She's no-nonsense and blunt while at the same time genuine and sincere—a killer combination of qualities that I haven't observed often. Such a far cry from the Hollywood types I've been surrounded by the past ten years. As much as I love acting and performing, the industry attracts a certain type of personality. Shallow. Superficial. Self-serving. Fake.

Even though I've only known Harper for a couple of days, already I can tell she's not any of those things. Just the fact that she quit her job to remodel her grandparents' old home in their memory shows what a thoughtful and true person she is. She's on a completely different level than so many of the people I've met and worked with.

My phone buzzes, and I see a text from Katie, one of the makeup artists from *The Best of It*, who's also one of my closest friends.

You better not be jogging this morning. Please tell me you're using your time away to sleep in at least.

I chuckle.

Me: Of course I'm jogging, sorry to disappoint.

Katie: JFC you're too fit for your own good.

Katie: But seriously, hope you're doing okay.

Me: I'm good, just laying low. How are you holding up?

When she doesn't answer right away, dread creeps in. Katie was one of the people that asshole Darren was sexually harassing. When she confided in me about it, she also told me he'd been doing this to multiple female crew members ever since filming started. I instantly saw red. With their permission, I confronted him, hoping it would make him stop…but instead everything went to hell.

The show is currently on hiatus since my firing, which means none of the crew are working or getting paid, and that thought morphs my dread into guilt. It settles like a giant thorn at the pit of my stomach.

Katie finally texts back.

I'm hanging in there. We all are.

I've worked with Katie on and off for the past handful of years. She's one of the few genuine friends I've made

in this business. To think that she and everyone else on
the show could lose their jobs as a result of me going after
Darren makes me sick to my stomach. Katie has a wife
and a daughter. Almost all of the crew have partners or
children or both to support...

I start to type a response but stop when I can't think
of anything helpful to say. A second later she texts again.

Katie: Don't feel bad, okay? It's not your fault things
turned out this way.

Katie: You stood up for us—you defended us. That
means a lot. We all think so.

Thanks. That knot in my stomach loosens. Katie always seems to be able to read my mood over text, and
I'm grateful for it. But it doesn't erase that feeling hanging over me like a cloud—the feeling that I tried to help
them and failed miserably, and that Darren is still getting
away with every horrible thing he's done.

Me: How's the rest of the crew doing?

Katie: Okay for the most part. Everyone is putting feel-
ers out to see what kind of work they'd be able to get
in case things at the show don't pick back up, but we're
kind of in a holding pattern until the higher-ups make
a final decision about the hiatus.

Katie: We've met a couple times to see what options
we have about reporting Darren's behavior, but no one
feels comfortable enough to do anything right now, especially after what happened with you.

Me: I get it. I'm sorry.

Me: I know I'm technically MIA, but whatever you all decide to do, I'm here to support you.

Katie: Thanks, Lewis. That means a lot.

Katie: How's the hiding out going?

Me: So far, so good. I ended up some place quiet near the ocean.

Katie: Sounds pretty.

Harper's beautiful face materializes in my mind. Those inquisitive dark brown eyes, the way she gestures when she talks, the way her mouth always looks like she's fighting a smile. When I open my eyes, I realize that I'm smiling now too.

I type a response.

It's really pretty actually.

Sure, camping out in the home of a person I met two days ago for the next three months is beyond nuts. If someone had told me a week ago that this would be my living situation for the foreseeable future, I'd have laughed and said they were full of shit. I'm the kind of guy who takes forever to warm up to a new person. But with Harper, it just *feels* right. It feels comfortable to be around her. And that counts more than anything else right now. She's honest, she doesn't have an agenda to push—all she cares about is fixing up her grandparents' house and volunteering. That makes her a damn angel in my book. Around her, I don't feel on edge or like I have to have my guard up, like I do with so many of the Hollywood types I'm surrounded by. And because of that, I trust her.

As much as I wish I weren't in this mess, I'm grateful for the reprieve that Harper is giving me. Spending the next three months fixing up this house is the perfect way to keep myself busy. No one knows that I'm here, not even my agent, Trent. It's the perfect hiding spot and the perfect amount of time for people to mostly forget about my firing and my drunken tirade without slipping into oblivion completely.

I start to walk up the driveway and see another text from Katie.

I know it's tough right now, but your adoring fans still love you. Have you seen all the love you've been getting on social media?

She sends me screenshots from Twitter.

Paparazzi are scum. #teamlewis all the way #welovelewisprescott

Lewis was totally justified in going off on those paparazzi a$$holes for harassing him. They're the lowest of the low #teamlewis

Sad that Lewis is gone from The Best of It, but I'm a fan of his forever! Can't wait for his next project! #teamlewis4eva

Hope Lewis is doing okay on his hiatus. Can't wait till he's back, love him soooo much <3 #lovelewis #teamlewis

By the time I finish skimming the tweets, I'm smiling so wide, my cheeks hurt. This business is killer with the inconsistent work, long hours, sporadic filming schedules, and dealing with intrusive reporters and paparazzi. But the one bright spot has been my fans. They've been so supportive of me and my work over the years, and it's meant the world. Social media is my favorite way to connect with them—I have accounts on both Twitter and Instagram so I can like and comment on their posts.

Even though my agent advised me to refrain from interacting on social media to keep my profile low while I wait out the bad press, I go ahead and like a dozen tweets and Instagram posts. I almost reply to a few comments, but I stop myself. Trent said to keep a low profile, so I should do that.

I'm about to put my phone back in my pocket and walk into the house when my phone buzzes. When I see it's my agent calling, I stop and answer.

"Hey, Trent," I say through a breath.

"Whoa, hey there, champ. What, you having a heart attack or something?"

I roll my eyes. "Funny, Trent. It's called running. You should try it."

His throaty cackle hits like a slap to the ear. I have to hold my phone away from my face until his laughter fades.

"You know I like to stick to running my mouth, my man."

"So what's got you calling me at the crack of dawn?"

"Just wanted to give you an update on how things are going with you ever since you left town. Your incident at the Chateau Marmont is no longer trending on social media. That's a good sign, my man."

I grit my teeth. Ever since I left LA, Trent has called me nearly every day either to remind me not to have another profanity-laden outburst or to update me on the news coverage of my meltdown.

"Last night some teen star got into a drunk-driving accident with her much older producer riding shotgun. She crashed the car right in front of The Grove, so that's got everyone in a frenzy. No major injuries to report, which means the public's attention won't last long."

The acid in my stomach bubbles at the joyful lilt in Trent's voice.

"That said, people are well on their way to forgetting about your little display at the Chateau, my man. And that's good. G-O-O-D, good."

I try not to groan. One of his quirks is to spell out whatever word he wants to emphasize. He's done it in almost every conversation I've had with him in the five years that he's been my agent, and it hasn't gotten any less annoying.

"That's great," I mutter. "It's so very you to take pleasure in a drunk-driving accident."

He cackles once more, like he thinks I'm joking. "What's your status? You still okay hiding out?"

"Yup. Staying at a secluded place for the next few months. I won't be out much, so that should lower my profile."

"That's good, my man. Real good. Like I said, lay low for a few months, just long enough for people to forget about your little incident and miss you. Then—bam!

You're back! Looking refreshed and refueled, flashing that pretty boy smile. Everyone loves you again! I mean, L-O-V-E-S loves you! Directors and producers will be knocking down my door begging to work with you..."

I tune out Trent's voice as my head starts to ache. He sounds like a radio DJ mixed with a sleazy car sales-man. It's full-on fake and he knows it, but he doesn't care. That's how he is. One thousand percent superficial in almost every interaction with almost every person he comes in contact with. I've witnessed him fawn over a client and then shit-talk them the second he ends their call. I don't even like the guy. But he's an in-demand agent who got me a string of parts in major movies and shows—including the starring role in *The Best of It*. His obnoxious habits are worth putting up with as long as I keep getting good roles through him.

"I'm telling you, my man. They'll be all over you once you're back on the scene. They'll want to cast you as the bad boy hunk in their show or movie—"

"I told you, Trent. I want to transition out of those roles."

"Huh?"

I grit my teeth. I've been telling Trent for years that I want to do meatier parts, but half the time when I bring it up, he acts like it's the first time I've ever mentioned it.

"I've played the pretty boy, the bad boy, the male bimbo enough times. Don't get me wrong, they were all a blast, and I'm thankful for the exposure they gave me. But I want to do something more serious. I've told you this, Trent."

"Whoa, whoa, whoa, my man. No need to get upset. Besides, one thing at a time, all right? First, let's focus on moving past your little potty-mouth outburst. And the best way to do that is to play up your strengths—play up what people love about you. And what people love about you, my man, is how you look. You're a hottie. H-O-T-T-I-E hottie. Don't discredit that—it's gotten you this far. Flaunt it while you've got it, eh?"

I muffle a groan. I'm not in the mood to argue with him about this again.

"Okay, well, thanks for the update. Gotta go."

I hang up and walk into the house just as the sun starts to rise. As quietly as I can, I toe off my running shoes and step to the hallway bathroom, careful not to wake Harper, who's sleeping in the master bedroom.

As I let the stream of hot water soak me, I make a mental list of everything I need to order from the hardware store and online to get started on this renovation. Today I'll start small with repairing the kitchen cabinets and looking up paint swatches for her to choose from for the walls.

I step out of the shower, dry off, wrap the towel around my waist, and open the door. To completely collide with Harper.

She makes an "oof!" sound as I mutter a curse and an apology, then reach down to grab her arm as she wobbles. I notice she's not wearing her glasses. Can she even see me clearly? Before I can grab her, she reaches out and her hand clutches between my legs…right on the money.

I instantly still. My eyes go wide as I gawk down at her while she blinks up at me. For the first second her face is groggy…but then recognition sets in. I see it play out in those burnt-umber eyes that are wide as saucers. Her gaze flits from my face to my crotch, back to my face, then my crotch again. When she looks up at me, her eyes are practically bulging out of her head. Then she yanks her hand away, her jaw drops, and a look of horror sets in. She's fully alert now.

"Oh my god, oh my god, oh my god, Lewis, I'm so sorry. I'm so, so sorry, I didn't mean to touch your dick—I mean you!"

She covers her face with her hands and stumbles backward down the hallway. My skin is hot enough to melt an iceberg. Well, this is awkward as fuck.

"It's, um, fine," I mumble.

As we stand in the hallway facing each other, a handful of feet apart, invisible flames of embarrassment engulf me from head to toe. I must clear my throat a dozen times as she continues to sputter and stammer.

"I just—I'm sorry, I forgot to grab my glasses when I walked out of the bedroom." She wrings her hands, like they're wet and she's frantically trying to dry them.

The movement makes her chest, which is barely contained in the tight tank top she's wearing, jiggle slightly.

Shit.

I immediately dart my gaze to the floor and think of dirt, rocks, paint, turtles—anything to take my mind off how cute and sexy Harper looks in her pajamas, her boobs almost spilling out of her top…

And that's when that bastard between my legs starts to act up.

"I should have been more careful," she says quickly.

I hold up both of my hands at her, forcing a chuckle that sounds more like I'm choking. "Hey, it's…uh…it's totally fine."

I try to smile, but I'm sure my expression looks more deranged than friendly.

With one hand I grip the towel at my waist, as if that's going to keep my boner from rising up against the flimsy cotton material. I dart my free hand over my crotch, but not before Harper gets an eyeful. Her unblinking stare tells me she definitely saw it.

"I'm just…gonna…" I scurry past her to the bedroom I'm staying in, shut the door behind me, and collapse against it.

And then I stand there, a mix of embarrassment and disbelief whipping through me, freezing me in place. Did that…did that seriously just happen? Did Harper accidentally grab my dick? Did I get hard in front of her, giving her an up close view of my erection?

The pressure below my waist builds. I glance down. Jesus Christ, still? I force out a breath as the ache intensifies. I'm hard as a fucking rock.

I guess I can't be too surprised. This is my body having a physical reaction to what just happened—to the sight of Harper looking sexy as hell after just rolling out of bed. To the feel of her hand gripping my cock…

I force out a breath through gritted teeth. Fuck. There's only one way to deal with this.

I yank off my towel, close my eyes, and grip the base of myself. I tug hard at first, as a sort of punishment to myself for being such a goddamn caveman in this moment. That surge of pain in my lower abdomen immediately morphs to pleasure. I bite back a groan. Leaning against the door, my breath catches. This is gonna be quick—as quick as I can make it.

Turns out, it doesn't take long at all when I replay the image of Harper's pretty face puffy with sleep, the curve of her ass and hips, the bounce of her perfect tits in my head over and over, like some pervy highlight reel. The deviant part of my brain kicks in, and my mouth waters as I let myself imagine what her nipples taste like. Like heaven, I'm sure.

I tug faster and harder, my breathing turning to desperate pants that I'm trying like hell to keep quiet. When I recall the feel of her gripping me, how silky her skin felt when she crashed into my bare chest, I'm instantly on edge. Soon my mind wanders to a place I know it shouldn't go... I wonder if those soft and delicate hands of hers would be this rough with me. Christ, I fucking hope so.

That thought is what does it. I spill all over on the towel already on the floor. I bite down as hard as I can, swallowing back the groan begging to rip from my throat. But I can't. No way in hell can I make a single sound right now. I'd die if Harper overheard what I'm doing, if she knew that I was jerking off to her accidentally touching me. Without a doubt, she'd think I'm a freak. Or a deviant. Or both.

When I finally open my eyes, I lean down to pick up the towel and clean up. My skin ignites, a blend of shame and embarrassment hitting me at once. Did I really just do that?

Yup.

I back up to the door once more and let my head fall against the wood, shut my eyes, and groan. It's not even a full twenty-four hours into living together, and already I've embarrassed myself in the worst way.

We've got three months of this to go... How the hell am I going to look Harper in the eye after this?

Chapter Five

Harper

No. Dear god, no, no, no. This absolutely cannot be happening.

But it is.

I just grabbed Lewis Prescott's dick.

As I hole up in my bedroom, leaning my back against the closed door, my hand falls against my chest. My palm absorbs the frenzied beats of my heart. I press my eyes shut, but no matter how hard I try, I can't stop envisioning the generous length between his legs.

I can't stop envisioning *him*.

Bare chested, skin wet and tan, that mop of dirty blond hair damp and tangled, his muscles bulging everywhere. *Everywhere*. And not the bulky kind...the long, lean kind that's my weakness.

My throat goes dry as I recall how perfectly sculpted every inch of him is. I mean, that's not breaking news. I've seen him shirtless plenty of times—on TV and in movies, though. There's something shockingly different about seeing that flawless physique half naked just inches from me. Like looking at a photo of a gorgeous mountain range and then seeing it in person and having your mind blown because nothing compares to observing pure, raw beauty with your own eyes.

Nothing compares to touching it either.

The hand on my chest—the hand that I accidentally fondled Lewis with—is now tingling. I yank it from my body and shake it until my fingers feel like they're going to fly off my wrist. It's no use, though. The sensation doesn't go away. It's getting worse, actually. That tingling is now flashing all over my skin, and a faint ache hits between my legs.

You have got to be freaking kidding me.

Are you serious right now, body?

I close my eyes, the answer to that question clear as day. Yes. My body is seriously turned on because I just felt up one of the hottest dudes on the planet…and there's only one thing that will make it go away.

I slide my still-tingling hand down the front of my pajama shorts, under my panties, and lightly touch the spot that's causing all this trouble.

"Fuck," I hiss out in a whisper, then immediately clamp my mouth shut.

I cannot be loud when I do this. If Lewis were to overhear me as I touch myself to the thought of him, I'd die a million deaths of humiliation. So if I'm going to actually do this, I need to be quiet as a mouse.

My chest heaves as my fingers hover over my mound, not yet touching. But just the anticipation has me vibrating. Despite how badly I want to moan, I'm quiet. My mouth is practically wired shut as far as I'm concerned. God, Lewis was so insanely hot. All those droplets of water dotting his perfect skin, all over his perfect body. My mouth waters. What I would have given for the chance to lick his skin, to press my nose against his bare chest and inhale his heavenly fresh-from-the-shower scent of spicy soap and hot water. My mouth waters. I'd lick him all the way down to the good part, the part covered by the towel, the part that—judging from what I felt in my hand—is one hefty package.

I press my fingers gently against my clit, biting my lip to keep that moan at bay. God, I'm an absolute deviant for doing this. This is so naughty, so wrong…

Wrong.

That single word stops me dead in my tracks. My hand stills. My eyelids fly open, and I stare at my offending appendage, now raised above my head.

I absolutely cannot do this. I cannot touch myself to the thought of Lewis. He's my roommate and my contractor, and I should only ever be thinking of him in that way. Nothing more.

I tug both hands through my hair, blown away at what I've almost just done: objectified the guy who's kind enough to fix up my grandparents' house for free.

"Jesus," I mutter. This time it's shame and embarrassment, not tingles, flashing across my skin. I am a pervert. Even though we've got a full day of working on the house planned, there's no way on God's green earth that I'm going to be able to look him in the eye anytime soon. But I can't just hide away in my bedroom either.

"I've gotta get out of here," I mutter to myself.

I've got to clear my head and get some air so I can figure out how the hell I'm going to face Lewis after I just almost violated him in my filthy sexual fantasy.

I hop up, throw a hoodie on, grab my purse and keys from the floor of the bedroom, then crack open the door. When I peek through the inch-wide gap, I notice the door to Lewis's room is shut. I say a silent thanks and dart out as quickly and quietly as I can, run through the front door, and hop into my car.

Caffeine is what I need. I was just groggy as fuck, waking up early to get ready for our early-morning renovation kickoff, and hadn't had coffee yet. Everything will be just fine as soon as I chug a cup of the good stuff.

As I zoom to the coffee shop, I check the time. It's barely 7:00 a.m. Dammit.

I've never needed to talk to my cousin more than I need to in this moment, but it's Saturday and she cherishes her weekend sleep-ins. I dial her number anyway, because fuck it, this is an emergency and I need her to help me figure out what to do next.

Her phone rings for so long, I assume I'm about to get her voice mail, but she picks up.

"Hello?" she croaks.

"Naomi! Oh my god, you're not gonna believe what I just did. Er, almost did."

Instead of answering me, I hear the muffled sound of mumbling. She must be talking to Simon, which means my phone call probably woke him up too.

"I'm sorry, I know there's nothing you hate more than an early phone call on a Saturday morning, but I promise, this is an emergency. I need your help."

"Crap, are you okay?"

"I'm fine. It's just…okay, what I'm about to tell you, you absolutely, positively cannot tell a single soul. Okay?"

"Okay…"

She yawns, and I brace myself to break the promise I made to Lewis less than twenty-four hours ago.

"I found a contractor to fix up the house. And it won't cost me anything extra."

"Harper, that's great!"

The sounds of Naomi's coffee maker echo on her end of the line, making my mouth water. I spot a drive-through coffee shop with a line ten cars long and pull up to it.

"Why do you sound so panicked, then?" Naomi asks.

"Because...well, because the contractor is Lewis Prescott. As in, the famous actor Lewis Prescott. He's moved in with me during the duration of the remodel. And I just... I just... I just grabbed his dick. And then I almost got myself off fantasizing about it."

I cover my face with my hand and grimace, even though no one can see me. The sound of Naomi sputtering is the only thing I can hear for five seconds. Then she laughs.

"Okay, very funny. This is your idea of a joke, right? Well done."

"No. Naomi, listen. I'm telling you the God's honest truth. Lewis Prescott, the hot TV veterinarian, the guy who had a very public drunken meltdown in front of the paparazzi last month, is living with me for the next three months—and he's remodeling my house."

"What?!"

Naomi's shrieked question pierces right through my eardrum. I have to hold the phone away from my face for a moment before I explain everything to her: our random run-in, how he used to be a professional contractor before he was an actor, how he offered to resume the renovation in exchange for letting him hide out at the house so he can let the bad press die down before heading back to LA.

"I—I can't believe this," Naomi stutters.

When she squeals, I quickly shush her. "Don't, you'll wake Simon."

"Don't worry, he's just left to go to the gym. Oh my god…just…oh my freaking god! Harper! Do you know how lucky you are? You're living out my fantasy—you're living out millions of people's fantasies, actually. Shacking up with Lewis Prescott!"

"Don't tell Simon. Lewis is super private, and I shouldn't even be telling you about him."

"Of course, don't even worry, I swear I won't…" She stops talking suddenly. "Wait, hold on. Did you say that you grabbed his dick? And then rubbed one out?"

That familiar burn makes its way up my chest, neck, and cheeks for the second time this morning.

"Almost masturbated. But, uh, yeah. I did, um, grab his dick."

I tell her it was a total mistake caused by this morning's early wake-up call and that I was so randomly turned on.

"Okay, well, I'm gonna need details. Very specific details. How did it feel? How big was he? Did he seem kind of into it when you touched him?"

"Jesus, Naomi."

I tell her to hold on while I pull up and order coffee from the barista. As soon as he hands me my drink, I pull into a nearby empty parking spot so I can put my full focus on this conversation.

"Truthfully? He felt…impressive."

Naomi gasps.

"He's six foot three," I say before sipping my café au lait. "I assumed he'd be carrying something impressive. But to feel it…"

"Damn."

We pause and sip our drinks.

"You said he was in a towel, right? How did he look? Give me details."

I lean against the headrest and groan. "So good, Naomi. Like, I guess I just assumed he'd look at least a tad bit flawed in real life. There's stuff like flattering lighting on a TV set and airbrushing on photo shoots to make celebrities look otherworldly attractive. But his body is flawless. He looks just as beautiful in person as he does on camera, like a cross between a Greek god and an Olympic swimmer."

A choking sound emanates from Naomi's end of the line.

"He has eight ab muscles, Naomi. *Eight.* I have never seen a washboard stomach with eight abdominal muscles in person in my entire life. Until him."

"Wow," she says through a sigh.

"How do I move on from this? I sputtered an apology once it registered what I'd done, but I know for sure that didn't do any good. He just ran off to his bedroom." I let out another groan. "God, he's probably so upset and freaked-out by me right now. I pretty much mauled him."

"Come on. I'm sure he doesn't feel that way at all. He probably understood that it was a mistake."

I shake my head, doubting the certainty of her tone.

"There's no magic way to fix this," she says. "You know that, right?"

I tug at my messy bun before yanking out my hair tie. "I know."

"You just gotta talk to him. Tell him that you're sorry and that you want to figure out a way to move on from it."

"I'm gonna pass out from humiliation."

I check the time and see that we're officially one hour

past the planned starting time for the renovation because of the surprise gropefest.

"Get some food on your way home like nothing's weird and you just ran out to get some breakfast. Like doughnuts. Doughnuts make every situation better."

I scoff. "Do they?"

"Of course they do. Everyone loves fried dough and sugar."

I start the car and drive toward a doughnut shop a couple miles away. "I should go. Thanks for talking me through this, Naomi. You're the best."

"Oh, it was my pleasure. As a matter of fact, feel free to call me anytime with similar problems and I'd be happy to give you my complete attention. Morning, afternoon, night…"

"God, Naomi, I get it! But seriously, I know I already said this, but I'm saying it again because that's how important this is—you have to promise me you won't tell anyone about Lewis staying with me, okay? He wants to keep his whereabouts private, and he's doing me a massive favor by taking over this renovation for free while he's hiding out. I don't want to betray his trust. Or his privacy."

"I swear, Harper. I won't tell a soul."

The conviction in my cousin's tone eases the ball of anxiety in the pit of my stomach. She's never once broken a promise to me, and I know she'll keep this secret forever.

We say goodbye, and I park in front of a doughnut shop, staring up at the neon sign that reads Dimple's Doughnuts in neon-pink cursive. I immediately think of that sexy-as-hell dimple in Lewis's right cheek and get flustered all over again.

I take a breath. "I hope this doughnut thing works."

Fifteen minutes later, I walk into the house, hot-pink box of freshly fried doughnuts cradled in my arm. Lewis is studying his laptop screen at the kitchen island, and I freeze in place.

What do I say? "Hello"? Or "Good morning"? Or "Sorry I accidentally fondled your genitals! Want a raspberry-filled doughnut"?

But then he does something I don't expect. When he looks up and sees me, he smiles.

"Hey."

"Hey."

Well, we cleared that initial greeting hurdle. Way to go, us.

I kick off my sneakers and walk over to the kitchen island. When I set the box on the counter, Lewis rips into it immediately. He demolishes half of a long john in a single bite, and for a few seconds, I just stare at him, in awe of his appetite. And his ability to act so natural despite the pornographic awkwardness that happened between us less than an hour ago.

He pauses when he notices me staring at him. "Sorry, I figured it was okay to dig in."

"Yeah, absolutely."

I grab him a plate along with a napkin while he digs into a passion fruit cake doughnut next. He mumbles a "thanks" between bites.

I grab a glazed yeast doughnut, take a small bite, then set it on my plate. When I push it away, his brow furrows the tiniest bit.

"You're not hungry?"

I shrug and try for a smile. "I guess I'm still kind of processing what…happened…"

He nods as he quickly chews, then pushes his plate to the side. His cheeks are as pink as the doughnut box.

"Hey, look, it's really not—"

"I'm sorry I—"

We speak at the same time, stammer at the same time, and go silent at the same time.

After a beat, I speak up. "Let me go first, okay? I am so, so sorry for, um, inappropriately touching you. I truly didn't mean to. I was so groggy when I woke up, I wasn't paying attention, and then I bumped into you and lost my balance and…"

I press my eyes shut, annoyed at how it sounds like I'm just making an excuse.

"But that doesn't take away from how awful it was of me to use your—I mean, use *you* to steady myself…" I bite my lip, face hot, and hazard a look at him. "This is the world's lousiest apology."

Lewis's expression is soft. His mouth is a slight scrunch like he's holding back a laugh, and his eyes shine. Then he smiles.

"It's really okay, Harper. I know you didn't mean it. It was an accident. I wasn't watching where I was going either."

The ball of nerves bouncing around my stomach loosens.

"I just don't want you to feel uncomfortable being around me after that," I say. "I know we don't know each other all that well."

"But what a way to get to know each other, though, right?"

I burst out laughing right as he chuckles. The tension in the room breaks. Even the muscles in my shoulders, which have been knotted tight ever since I stumbled into him, loosen.

"I promise, you're not making me uncomfortable." He runs his hand through his unruly mop of hair. "I mean, yeah, it was a little awkward, but it's all good now."

"Really?"

"Really." He smiles, almost to himself. "Not to sound like an insufferable Hollywood douchebag, but I've done love scenes that were a million times more awkward than this morning."

"Seriously?"

"Oh yeah. There was this one movie I did, like, eight years ago where I was a minor side character, but I had a pretty lengthy love scene with the female star. I had to pretend to go down on her and then she had to climb on top of me and…gyrate enthusiastically."

He makes a thrusting motion with his arm, and I burst out laughing again.

"Oh my god, really?"

He nods. "There was another time where I was a guest in an HBO series a few years back. I had a skinny-dipping scene in a pool that ended in a pretty serious makeout with some simulated heavy petting. Since there was implied nudity in that scene, I had to wear this flesh-colored sock thing over my…you know."

I can't help but giggle at the way his cheeks turn fire-engine red.

"I'd wear a robe between takes when we weren't filming, but as soon as the director said, 'Action,' I had to strip it off, and I swear to god, there is nothing more humbling than standing on a set, naked except for a tube sock on your private parts, two dozen crew members low-key gawking at and judging you."

I cover my mouth to stifle my laughter. "That sounds like my worst nightmare," I say when I catch my breath.

He shrugs while smiling, the red on his cheeks fading to pink. "It's all part of the job. And that wasn't even the worst of it. In the middle of the makeout scene, I had to hoist her up around my waist and bounce her up and down so it looked like we were really going at it. The water combined with the material of the sock and numerous takes resulted in some pretty serious chafing."

I hunch over and grip the edge of the countertop, I'm laughing so hard. After several seconds of attempting to catch my breath, I straighten up. "I'm sorry for laughing. That sounds so painful."

He waves a hand like he's not bothered at all. In fact, the gleam in his eyes reads amused as he watches me. "Nah, it's hilarious looking back on it now."

When I finally catch my breath for the second time, I feel my stomach growl. I grab my doughnut and finish the rest.

"Thanks for that. I feel a lot better now." I grimace at my wording. I still sound like I'm making this whole mess about me.

Lewis gulps some water, then wipes his mouth with the back of his hand. "There are worse things in the world than being grabbed in the junk by a cute girl."

He winks at me before turning around to the sink and washing his hands. What feels like a tiny butterfly flapping its wings inside my tummy hits me. That was a smooth-as-hell way to end the conversation. I gulp more water and dial back that giddy feeling in an attempt to refocus. Lewis was just being playful with his "grabbed in the junk by a cute girl" comment. Nothing more, nothing less. And if he knew that I almost pleasured myself after that accidental encounter, he definitely wouldn't be thinking such a sweet thing about me.

"You know, you're not at all what I thought you'd be like."

My out-of-the-blue comment earns me a confused frown followed by a half smile. "I'm not sure how to take that."

I shake my head, just now realizing how awkward I sounded. "Okay, this is probably going to sound obnoxious, but you have kind of a reputation in Hollywood."

His expression falls slightly, and I immediately regret how I've worded things.

"I didn't mean that in a bad way. It's just that you give off this boldness, and I find that really intriguing. You're very private, and you don't take crap from intrusive interviewers. You're not afraid to get in the face of paparazzi when they're aggressive with you. You come off as a total badass with a major case of 'I don't give a fuck.'"

When he starts to smile again, it feels like a win.

"I guess I didn't think you'd be so fun-loving and goofy and sweet too. But that's my own ignorance. I should know better than to take everything that I see portrayed in the media at face value. So much goes on behind the scenes that the public couldn't possibly understand."

His gaze turns thoughtful, and for a second it looks like he's going to say something. But he purses his lips and stays quiet.

My cheeks and chest grow hot as I work up the courage to say this final thing. "It nice, that you're letting me see this side of you. You barely know me."

I study the slate gray countertop, too afraid to look at

him. It was such an unprompted confession. I have no idea how he'll take it.

"Harper."

I look up when he says my name, dizzy at the expression on his face: warmth and affection all at once.

"I may not know you very well, but I like you," he says softly. "You're honest and genuine. I felt that from you right off the bat when I met you. That makes it easy to be myself. I don't always get that opportunity in my line of work."

I'm blown away at the caliber of his compliment. "That means a lot, to know that you feel like you can trust me."

His focused gaze lingers on me for a long moment before he turns back to the sink to refill his glass.

"Okay, should we get started?" he asks.

"Definitely."

I grab my laptop from the kitchen counter and walk over to his side of the island. He shows me his laptop screen and goes over the ideas he's come up with.

"Based on the walk-through you gave me yesterday and everything you told me you wanted to complete in this renovation, this is the schedule I came up with," he says. "I broke down each project and the approximate number of weeks I think it'll take me to finish each one. I highlighted the projects that I'll need your help on."

"Wow, this is really well thought-out."

He blushes. "It's been a while since I've gotten to work on an overhaul like this. I got kind of excited to dive in."

I quietly take note of how adorable he is when he's enthusiastic.

When we finish up finalizing the schedule, I show

him out to the garage, where all the raw materials I pur-
chased for the remodel are splayed out.

Lewis's gaze lands on the multitiered brass chandelier sitting in the middle.

"Vlad said he reinforced the ceiling for the chandelier,
but would you be willing to double-check it?" I asked.
"After everything he messed up, I'm reluctant to take
him at his word."

"Understood. Yeah, I can do that."

"I'd like to be able to hang crystals on the chandelier."
I point out the rectangular box of crystal accents sitting
on a shelf along the wall.

"I was thinking I could start with the kitchen today,"
he says. "Tighten up all those loose cabinet doors, then
start pulling up the flooring in the living room tomorrow. I'm definitely gonna need your help for that. It'll
be tedious as hell, especially since you wanna reuse the
hardwood."

"I'll be ready. Do you need me to help you with the
cabinets?"

He shakes his head. "Nah, I got it."

I head back inside while Lewis grabs my grandpa's
old toolbox from the garage. I get ready for the day in
my bedroom, thinking about how in this way Grandpa
Bernie's tools get to be part of the renovation he dreamed
of even though he's not here. The sound of Lewis drill-
ing in the kitchen echoes through the house.

I check the time to make sure I'm not late heading to
the Glad You're Here office to volunteer for a few hours.
When I head back into the kitchen to let Lewis know
I'm leaving, he twists around and flashes a grin at me.

"See you when you get back."

I have to swallow back a gasp at how delicious he

looks in this moment. White T-shirt spotty with his sweat, ripped jeans tight around his tree-trunk legs, the muscles in his shoulders and back swelling under that thin cotton fabric.

I blink and silently tell myself to get my shit together.

But of course I'm losing my shit around this guy. I'm used to seeing him on TV, not in my house all sweating and grunting, fixing it up for me.

I mumble a "sounds good" and flash a thumbs-up at Lewis before scurrying out to my car. Before I pull out of the driveway, Naomi texts me.

How did it go? Did you talk it out like adults like I suggested?

I call her and put her on speaker while I reverse out of the driveway onto the street. As soon as she answers, I give her an update.

"I did end up taking your advice. We talked it out, and once we got past the awkwardness, it actually wasn't that bad. I think we're good now."

"Yay! How great!"

"Yeah. Great."

"What's up with you now?"

I scramble to think of an eloquent way to put this but fall short and decide to just go with the truth.

"He's hot, Naomi. Like, ridiculously, obnoxiously hot."

She barks out a laugh. "You're just now realizing this?"

"Of course not, I just…" I shoot out a breath as I drive out of Half Moon Bay, taking the highway to the freeway. "I just don't know if I can handle being around his hotness 24-7, you know? Like, it's been ages since I've shared space with another human being, other than when you lived with me before moving in with Simon. And I've never lived with a guy before. I just don't know how I'm going to handle myself for the next three months if I can barely keep my cool and we're not even one day into this setup. I mean, I almost masturbated to the guy this morning...it's not even been twenty-four hours."

I can hear Naomi stifle a chuckle. I roll my eyes.

"Okay, valid point," she says. "I'm sure I'd be freaking out too if I were living in the same house as a sexy celebrity."

"It's more than that, though. Right after we talked out the awkwardness of this morning, things felt fine. Comfortable, even. We went over the projects for the renovation, and it felt totally normal. And then I saw him. Standing in the kitchen, reaching up to tighten the hinges on the cupboard doors, and I swear, my eyes nearly popped out of my head. He was all muscle-y arms and sweat and grunting noises. It threw me off completely. I pretty much ran out of there so I wouldn't—"

"Lunge at him?"

I scoff, even though she's right. I'm just too embarrassed to admit it.

"It's okay for you to admit you're attracted to a guy, Harper. I know you spent the last several years putting relationships on the back burner to get ahead in your career, but you're a human being. Hotness is hotness, and we all have a weakness for it."

I sigh. "You have a point."

"Seeing a sexy guy work with his hands has got to be some sort of attraction trigger for our lizard brains. Like, if we were cave women, that's the guy we'd go after—the hot one who can fix stuff for us."

I roll my eyes and laugh as I merge onto Interstate 280. "I'd like to think we're a little more evolved than cave women."

"We are. And we're not. That pulse you get in your lady bits when you see someone you find attractive is as Neanderthal as it gets. And there's nothing wrong with that."

"There is if you're living together in a strictly business setup and aren't supposed to look at each other that way."

"Come on. Beyond the awkwardness of your run-in this morning, I bet Lewis didn't totally hate you running into him, and that might have something to do with those tiny tank tops you wear to bed."

"Ha. Get real, Naomi. The guy was dating a Victoria's Secret model before he met me."

The sound of her laughing makes me roll my eyes yet again.

"Of course you'd say that. Because you're completely unaware of how adorable and sexy you are. Maybe he got a little handsy with himself, just like you almost did."

"He did say 'there are worse things in the world than being grabbed in the junk by a cute girl,'" I blurt. "He was clearly joking, but…"

"He liked what he saw this morning, Harper. That's ironclad proof right there."

"Lewis is a movie star. He's dated supermodels, actresses, other celebrities. There's no way a girl like me would even be a blip on his radar."

As confident as I am, as much as I've accomplished in my life, being around Lewis throws me for a loop. He's from an entirely different world—he's a celebrity who's constantly surrounded by beauty, glamour, glitz, and riches. I'm as regular girl as they come, with my working-class background and normal life. I'm such a far cry from what I'm sure he's used to.

The scoffing noise Naomi makes catches me off guard. "Harper, don't you dare talk yourself down. You are the most successful and accomplished person I know. You've designed skyscrapers. You were the youngest senior architect at one of the most prestigious firms in the Bay Area. You own your own place in Nob Hill that you're now letting our college-age cousins live in for free while they finish grad school because you're a saint. And you're beautiful. This guy plays pretend for a living. I don't say that to disparage him—I just want to make it clear that just because he's famous doesn't make him any better than you."

Hearing my cousin sing my praises warms me from the inside out, but then I shake my head. This conversation has gone way off track. I initially called her to vent about how awkward it is to live in the same house as a celebrity dreamboat. Now we've veered into this bizarre discussion where she's insisting that Lewis Prescott has jerked off to me and would be lucky to have me.

"Okay, enough. This isn't even why I called you in the first place. I just need to figure out how to navigate living with him."

"Try not to read too much into it. At the end of the day, he's just a hot guy you're sharing a house with."

Naomi's simple, straightforward words cut right through the muddled thoughts in my brain.

"You're right. I can do this."

We say goodbye and hang up. As I drive the rest of the

way to the Glad You're Here office, I repeat what Naomi told me.

"He's just a hot guy. A hot guy I'm sharing a house with. It's no big deal. No. Big. Deal."

Chapter Six

Harper

When I pull into the parking lot and walk inside, I'm greeted by Diana, one of the cofounders of Glad You're Here, working the front desk.

"Harper! It's so good to see you again!"

She hops up and wraps me in a hug. She's a full head taller than me and squeezes so tight that I lose half the air in my lungs. But I love it. Diana is the definition of warm and welcoming, and when I started volunteering for the nonprofit in college, she greeted me just as enthusiastically almost every time she saw me.

"Well, just look at you." She holds me by the shoulders, her deep brown eyes bright. "Adorable as ever."

I chuckle. "You're too kind, Diana."

She releases me, then steps over to the coffee machine sitting right next to the reception desk and pours me a cup. "Not even. Just ask my husband and my daughters."

I let out a laugh and thank her for the coffee. I take a sip and ask her about her kids.

"Good lord, this teenage phase. I thought I was ready. I wasn't. Moody and mouthy, that's all my kids are at this stage." She rolls her eyes, which looks so unnatural on her. She always looks like she's on the verge of a smile—it's one of the things I love about her.

"At least ten times a day I have to stop and remind myself of how adorable and precious and sweet they were as babies," she says. "That's the only way I can keep from losing it on them when they pull attitude with me."

Her black-brown curls bounce as she shakes her head, a few strands of silver shining through.

"As a former angsty teenager, I apologize on behalf of your daughters. They'll grow out of it and appreciate how patient and loving you were with them."

"Oh, I know." She waves a hand, the gold bangles on her wrist lightly clanking. "I was like that too at that age. This is payback for what a little witch I was to my mom and dad."

I chuckle. "Still covering the front desk on Lupe's days off, I see?"

She nods. "I'd love to hire an additional person, but that's just not in the budget, unfortunately."

I nod my understanding as she leads me to one of the offices in the back, where I'll be helping clients fill out job and apartment applications today. As a former social worker, helping others is Diana's passion. Her dad is from El Salvador, and starting this nonprofit to help other immigrants establish themselves in the US is something she's always dreamed of doing. But I've seen just how much of a struggle it is to keep Glad You're Here running over the years. They receive grants and other government money, but a good chunk of what keeps them operating are donations. When I was working at my old job, I donated a percentage of my income, but now that I'm taking time off, I have to temporarily pause on giving money.

Even thinking about it now sends a wave of guilt through me. That's part of the reason I want to volunteer more now—if I can't give monetarily, I want to give in some other way, and I figured my time was the next most valuable thing I can offer.

"Are donations down again?" I ask reluctantly.

She nods. "Times are tough for people. It seems like every year, the cost of living goes up and up. Most people's incomes can't sustain that, so donating to charity isn't something a lot of people can do. I get it. I really do. It just makes things hard for us."

As I follow her into a small room in the back and she gets me set up on a laptop, I think of the money Lewis promised to donate and know I made the right ultimatum. I wish I could tell Diana that relief is on the way, in the form of one million dollars, but I have to wait until my bargain with Lewis has been fulfilled.

Once I'm set up on the computer, Diana tells me that the first person I'm helping is due to arrive in ten minutes.

After that, it's a busy few hours of helping people fill out forms online, printing documents, and answering questions. I'm finishing up with someone when I hear Diana's voice boom from down the hall.

"Oh my god!"

I pop up out of my chair. "Just one sec," I say to the person sitting next to me.

When I walk out to reception, Diana is standing up, covering her mouth with her hands, her eyes wide as saucers as she looks at the screen of her computer.

"Are you okay?" I ask as I rush over to her.

A beat later, her hands fall to her sides and she beams

at me. "We just got a one-million-dollar donation! From an anonymous donor! Can you believe it?"

She jumps up and down while squealing. I run over to hug her, stunned. Holy shit. It was like Lewis read my mind.

Diana's speaking so quickly in her shock and excitement that I can barely understand her. Something about updating some of the computers and hiring another employee and using a chunk of the money to help with things like apartment security deposits, down payments for cars, school supplies, and so much more to benefit the clients of the organization.

When she pauses, I notice her eyes are teary.

"Oh, Diana." I grab her hands in mine, my own eyes burning with tears at just how overcome with joy she is.

"I just… I can't believe it. We needed this so bad. And it actually happened."

"Sometimes stuff works out when you need it to." I fight a wince at how ridiculously cheesy and generic that sounds.

"I wish I knew who the donor was so I could thank them," she says. "They're helping us so much."

I give her hands a gentle squeeze. "I'm sure they have their reasons for wanting to stay private."

Part of me is curious too, though. I know Lewis is intensely private, so it makes sense that he didn't publicize his donation, but if he had, that would have gone a long way to restoring his Hollywood image. It probably wouldn't fix everything that's gone wrong for him, but the public goes wild when a celebrity does something kind and giving. A lot of people would think highly of him if they knew he gave such a large sum of money to a relatively unknown charity that's doing incredibly important work.

Diana smiles and says she's going to call Frank, the other founder of the charity, to tell him the good news so they can start planning what to do with the money.

When I head back to finish my meeting, I'm smiling to myself. Turns out that badass "I don't give a fuck" Lewis has a heart of gold, after all.

When I walk into the house, I don't see Lewis in the kitchen or the living room. He must be resting in his room.

I open one of the cabinets to grab a glass for wine and still my hand. The door easily swings back and forth. It's not wobbly, and it doesn't creak. I open and close all the cabinets, smiling when I hear silence. As I head to the refrigerator for the white wine, the French doors whoosh open.

"So? What do you think?" Lewis grins as he stands in the doorway and juts his chin at the cupboards.

"Amazing. You're a freaking magician, Lewis. Thank you so much for fixing these cabinets."

I open the fridge and am stunned at the sight of what appears to be three dozen bottles of organic pressed juices taking up the entire middle shelf.

"Wow. So you're really into juice, then?" I twist around to look at him.

He aims a flustered smile at the floor as he leans against the door frame. "Kind of. Gotta stay healthy even while I'm away from LA."

"Ah. Makes sense." I should have known. Even though he's hiding out, he's still a celebrity, and downing celery and wheatgrass juice on the daily seems like a very celebrity thing to do.

"Sorry to take up so much fridge space."

"Not at all. You live here now too. Stock it with whatever you want, but you don't have to worry too much about me stealing one of your surely delicious concoctions."

He nods at the glass of wine in my hand. "Rough day?"

"Not at all. Amazing day, actually."

"Wanna toast to it on the veranda with me? Hope you don't mind, but I cracked open a beer after I finished the cabinets and wanted to enjoy it with a view."

"That sounds perfect."

I follow him out to the veranda, glass of wine in hand. He shuts the doors, then gestures to the two lounge chairs at the far end. When we sit down, he raises his glass, but I stop him.

"This toast is to you. Thank you for the donation you made to Glad You're Here." I try to say more, but all I can do is stammer, I'm still so blown away.

Lewis's eyes fall to his lap, the shiest smile tugging at his lips. "It was nothing."

"Nothing? Lewis, it was everything. I've volunteered at Glad You're Here off and on ever since college, and I know just how much every single dollar they get means to them. They're going to be able to help so many more people because of you. You should have seen Diana's face when your donation came through. She was crying tears of joy."

"Who's Diana?"

"One of the cofounders. She was inspired to start the organization after seeing all the struggles her dad went through after he immigrated to the US. Stuff like learning English, applying for jobs and apartments, buying a car and a house, enrolling kids in schools. Her and her cofounder's mission is to offer as much support as possible to every person who requests their services. That's why I started volunteering there. My grandparents were immigrants too, and I know they struggled a lot when they first moved to this country."

I stop myself when I realize I'm rambling.

"Sorry, I got way off track there. We're supposed to be toasting to you."

"No way. I can see how passionate you are about this. It's incredible."

I go quiet when I notice the warmth shining through Lewis's hazel eyes as he gazes at me.

"Back to your toast." I raise my glass. "To you, Lewis. You are making a difference."

I clink my glass against his, which makes him laugh. We sip our drinks, then gaze ahead at the rocky hillside that juts up against the sky, which is bathed in a periwinkle hue. For a few quiet moments, we stare at the scenery and sip our drinks. Because the house is situated at the end of a quiet road, the sound of the waves crashing along the coastline just a handful of miles away overrides the faint echo of traffic in the distance.

I close my eyes and savor it. It's never this quiet in Nob Hill—or any part of San Francisco. As much as I love that city, and spending my twenties and the first few years of my thirties there, I adore being somewhere new, somewhere quiet, surrounded by the ocean. It's the perfect way to recharge after living so many years as a workaholic in the city.

"Absolutely." He hops up and slips back inside, returning with two fresh glasses in one of his massive hands and a frosty bottle of vodka in the other.

"*Apong* Bernie—my grandpa—always told me that the most important thing you could ever be in life is honest and true," I say as Lewis pours me a glass. "That's always stuck with me. And I guess I just try to do my best to live that way."

"Sounds like your grandpa was a stand-up guy."

"Oh, he was. Pretty old-fashioned, but in a good way."

"Old-fashioned how?"

"Like, he always opened doors for my grandma. If they were out walking, he insisted on taking the side closest to the road. If it rained, he'd hold an umbrella for her. He refused to curse around her too."

Lewis grins wide. "Damn. He sounds like a class act."

"In every sense of the word." I glance around at the veranda and tap my sneakers against the sturdy wooden planks. "I miss him. He'd love how this place is shaping up."

Just the thought of him sitting here next to me makes my throat go tight for a long second, but I quickly swallow it back.

"I think he'd be damn proud to see what his brilliant architect granddaughter did to his house."

Lewis's words send a wave of comfort through me. I smile a thanks.

"Are you close with your grandparents?" I ask.

"I was close to my grandpa before he passed away a handful of years ago. He's the one who taught me everything I know about home renovation and repair. He was a contractor and handyman in the LA area, and as a kid

I'd tag along with him to jobs. I started working for him when I was in high school."

"That's so cool."

I try to picture kid Lewis wielding a hammer on a work site and smile to myself. "Did you wear a little tool belt?"

His right cheek scrunches as he smiles, and that dimple I adore appears. I swallow more vodka.

"Yup. When I was little, my grandpa took one of his old tool belts and fitted it down to my size so I could feel like a proper handyman, just like him."

"That is adorable."

I finish the rest of my drink and set the empty glass down by my feet. Lewis reaches up to turn on the tea lights I strung up along the top of the veranda.

"It's been a while since I've done this," Lewis says.

"What? Drink vodka on a veranda?"

"That too." He rubs the back of his neck before pivoting to face me. "But it's also been a while since I've sat around and talked about my grandpa. Thanks for giving me the opportunity."

Something about the way he says that lands deep inside me. I can tell he's sad and grateful at once.

"You don't get to talk about him much with your family? Or friends?"

He shakes his head, his expression shifting from wistful to regretful.

I stop myself from asking him why. It feels like I've asked enough prying questions for one conversation.

"Well, you can talk to me about him whenever you feel like it. I'm happy to listen."

And suddenly, right now as I gaze at Lewis, I don't see a celebrity. I see a regular guy who's harboring a good bit of pain behind those expressive hazel eyes. I'm not sure what's causing it, and I know it's too soon to ask him about it—we've only known each other for a few days, after all. But I'm certain in this moment that I want to get to know Lewis even more, more than just a pleasant chat while sharing a few drinks at the end of the day. I want him to someday feel comfortable enough to tell me exactly what's on his mind—the good, the bad, and everything in between.

I go the slightest bit dizzy, thrown off by this realization. This is our first full day of sharing this house, but already I feel a pull toward him that I'm not sure I've felt for anyone before. Maybe it's the random way we met or this strange-as-hell setup we're in that's making the situation feel more intense.

Or maybe it's simpler than that. Maybe it's because I'm realizing just how much I genuinely like him.

I stand up too fast and wobble slightly, but Lewis's muscled arm shoots up, gently grabbing me at the elbow and steadying me.

"You okay?" he asks as he stands up.

I nod. "I think so."

"Too much vodka?"

The feel of his hand on my skin turns hot.

Nope. Definitely not the vodka.

"Something like that," I mumble.

When his arm falls away, my skin tingles at the memory of his brief touch. I twist my head to glance up at him. "Thanks for…" I trail off when I see our faces are a mere two inches apart, because he's leaning down to support me. "…saving me."

All I can do is look between his cloudy stare and those perfectly plump lips of his.

"Um, any—any, uh, anytime."

*

He clears his throat a half dozen times in that reply, his gaze on my lips. It all happens in a span of just seconds, but it feels like slow motion at the same time.

And that's when it hits me. We're going to kiss.

I lick my lips in anticipation, my breath hot and wet as it glides out of my mouth, my skin tingling, my body aching in anticipation of what Lewis Prescott's lips and tongue are going to taste like.

When his mouth parts open, my mouth waters and my heartbeat kicks into a frenzied gear. And then he blinks. That dazed look fades, like he's coming to his senses.

He shakes his head, and I feel his body loosen around me. A beat later he pulls his arms away and takes two steps back.

"Sorry, um, I gotta go check on something."

Lewis jogs back into the house, and I'm left standing on the veranda, speechless and shocked at what almost happened.

Chapter Seven

Lewis

Christ.

That word rings in my head over and over like a siren as I jog back into the house, down the hall, and into my bedroom. I shut the door and pace the small space like a confused tiger prowling back and forth in a cage, my breath ragged, heart thundering.

I was a split second away from kissing Harper.

Seriously, Prescott. What the hell has gotten into you?

"Wish I knew," I mutter to myself.

I'm one full day into this setup with Harper and I've already nearly blown it. This arrangement is strictly business. We both agreed to that. Harper is essentially my housemate for the next ninety days, and if we were to blur the lines by kissing—or doing anything physical—it would no doubt ruin things. Because hooking up with your housemate is rule number one on the list of things you're never, ever supposed to do. It always, always, always complicates things.

Our arrangement is akin to a contract, an exchange of goods, like any other agreement two human beings could make. Getting physical would be a one-way ticket to fuck this all up.

You got pretty damn physical this morning.

I grit my teeth, wishing I could turn off that smart-ass part of my brain. I halt in the center of the room, drop my hands to my hips, and force myself to take a deep breath. This morning was different. Way, way different. It wasn't intentional. It was an honest mistake caused by clumsiness and lack of sleep.

Is that why you jerked off too? Because you were clumsy and sleepy?

I grit my teeth and quietly admit defeat to myself. Okay, yeah, the decision to crank one out this morning was an undeniable physical and sexual moment. But that only involved me.

The almost kiss that happened seconds ago, though? That definitely didn't involve just me.

Sure, it kicked off because Harper lost her balance… but I could have stopped gawking at her luscious-as-fuck lips and those mesmerizing eyes… I could have let go of her sexy little body…but I didn't. Because I wanted to hold her. I wanted to touch her.

I wanted to kiss her…and I'm pretty sure she wanted to kiss me too.

Pressing my eyes shut, I shake my head. Maybe the sudden jerky movement will dislodge that thought straight out of my head. It doesn't.

"You can't do this. You can't be attracted to her."

My muttered scolding does little to quell the fire burning inside me—the fire I feel for Harper.

I plop onto the edge of the bed and let out a sigh. There's no use denying it. I'm attracted to her. And if I'm being truthful, I was attracted to her the moment I met her. Meeting a cute and sexy woman who had no idea who the hell I was, who had no agenda to push onto me, who didn't want a selfie or my autograph— who joked with me at the coffee shop, who charmed me with her sense of humor and how easy she was to chat with—hooked me instantly. She was a goddamn breath of fresh air compared to the near-constant superficiality I'm bombarded with.

The more I've gotten to know Harper, the more I like her. Having all this unintentional physical contact with her is sure as hell amping things up too.

But we can't take things any further—*I* can't take things any further. Not if I'm serious about making this setup work. Not if I'm serious about getting my career back on track.

I rest my elbows against my knees and cradle my head. What happened tonight on the veranda was a mistake. It can't ever happen again. I've got to draw clear boundaries and keep them.

And starting tomorrow, that's exactly what I'm going to do.

In the morning, I peek my head out of my bedroom doorway and make sure the coast is clear before I step to the bathroom. I do the same after I shower, walking out fully clothed this time, before padding into the kitchen for a cup of coffee and breakfast. Then we're kicking off today's project: ripping up the floorboards in the open-concept living room and dining area.

I'm downing my second mug when Harper strolls into the kitchen, decked out in plaid shorts that hug her beautifully plump ass and hips. My eyes bulge over the rim of my cup, and I choke on a sip.

I slam the mug on the counter while I cough and wheeze. Her eyes go wide before she rushes over to me.

"Are you okay?"

She moves to thump me on the back, but I step out of her reach and pivot. I look like a running back dodging a defensive lineman. She takes in the odd movement with a confused frown.

I hack for a few more seconds before holding up my hand. "I'm fine. Just fine," I choke out.

She narrows her gaze at me. "If you say so."

She tiptoes up to grab a mug from the cupboard, and I catch a glimpse of her tank top riding up her back, revealing a delicious strip of tanned skin. And then I see them: the most perfect pair of lower-back dimples, right above the swell of her ass.

"Oh, for fuck's sake," I mutter.

She spins around. "What was that?"

I frown and shake my head while mumbling, "Nothing."

"So we're prying up the hardwood floorboards today, right?"

I tell her yes while I swipe randomly at my phone screen—just to have something to look at other than her dynamite body.

"You should put on some work clothes." Jesus, I sound severe. But that's the only way I know how to play this. I'm not ballsy enough to initiate an uncomfortable-as-fuck conversation about how ridiculously hot she is and how it's taking everything in me not to pull her into my arms and finish what we almost started last night.

So I ignore what's bothering me and attempt to move on with a no-BS attitude.

"Okay. Um, I will." Harper gulps her coffee before

setting the mug on the counter. "You're acting weird," she says. "Is this about last night? How we almost kissed?"

Again I'm choking on my coffee. Damn. She went straight for it.

I mutter a "goddamn it" between coughs, jolted by the way she chuckles. The sound is so light and warm—like she's completely unbothered by what happened. By the sound of it, I bet she didn't spend half as much time obsessing over the moment last night as I did.

"Uh, yeah," I finally say after wiping my mouth on a cloth napkin.

She crosses her arms and tilts her head at me. The gesture comes off like she's amused. "We don't have to make it into a bigger deal than it is," she says. "It was probably just the vodka. And the pleasant conversation. And the full moon too."

"Yeah. Definitely the full moon."

She shrugs, her smile slight and easy. She is the picture of unfazed. "We can just forget about it. It wouldn't be the smartest thing in the world for us to have kissed given our setup. We're living together, after all."

The pressure in my chest dissipates. "That's exactly what I think."

"Cool. Then we can just go back to being housemates. And friends."

"I'd like that."

She nods once before spinning around and padding to her bedroom. I try not to look at her ass as it sways with the movement. Because like we just agreed, we're friends—and friends don't check out each other's asses.

I head out to the garage to grab a couple of hammers, a pry bar, and my recip saw and get ready for the day.

Chapter Eight

Harper

Well, damn. That went…differently than I expected.

As I brush my teeth in the master bathroom, I take a good look at myself in the mirror. Just a slight flush on my cheeks. My eyes are clear and bright. My posture's not one bit hunched.

I'm weirdly proud of myself for keeping my composure during that awkward-as-hell discussion about our almost kiss last night. Not gonna lie, it did sting a bit to receive Lewis's frosty reception this morning. But I can't be all that surprised. After all, *he's* the one who backed out and ran off, disappearing into his bedroom for the second time in one day.

I was pretty stunned as I stood there on the veranda, processing what happened. But once it all soaked in, it was clear: he didn't want to kiss me. And realizing that kind of sucked, because it always sucks to be rejected. But he's right—it wouldn't be the smartest thing in the world for us to kiss.

As I splash water over my face and lather my cleanser over my skin, I feel my cheeks go hot. I can't believe I nearly jeopardized everything for a single kiss. Granted, it probably would have been one hell of a kiss, but still. It wouldn't have been worth losing this golden opportunity to finish this remodel for free. Nothing is worth losing the chance to fix up *Apong* Bernie and *Apong* Vivian's house in the most beautiful way.

I towel off, and when I pat moisturizer all over my face, my skin is cool to the touch. My head is clear, and my thoughts feel more focused. Last night was a fleeting moment. Today is a new day. We're back to what we are: two people who are engaging in a mutually beneficial arrangement. Nothing more, nothing less.

When I'm dressed for the day, I walk out of my bedroom and back into the living room newly energized, ready to forget the awkward moment. I stop a few feet from where Lewis is standing, surveying the pile of tools next to his work boot–clad feet.

I clap my hands once. His eyebrows jump slightly when he looks up at me, then his expression turns amused.

I nod at him. "Let's do this."

"I honestly can't tell the difference between gray-green and green-gray," Lewis says, quirking his brow at the two color swatches I've painted on the living room wall.

"Seriously?" I huff out a breath and twist my neck to look at him as we stand side by side. "The gray-green one is slightly grayer. The green-gray one is slightly greener."

"I guess I'll take your word for it." A deep sigh signals just how tired he is of me fixating on paint colors for the past week.

I ramble about how the sunlight can affect how bright certain paint colors appear.

Lewis nods along, slowly blinking, clearly still no

more invested in one color than the other. "Choose whatever color you want, and I'll order more paint so we can finish the living room and dining room walls," he says.

I dart my gaze back and forth between the two squares. "It's just so hard to decide. Green was my grandma's favorite color, and gray was my grandpa's favorite color. I want whatever color I choose to represent them both equally."

Lewis's tired expression eases slightly.

For the past week, we've been working on carefully ripping up the hardwood flooring in the living room and dining room. Our knees and backs are trashed from hunching and kneeling several hours in a row every day, so we're taking a break and selecting the shade to paint over the horrible puke green Vlad's crew painted the walls. For the past couple of hours, I've been working my way through paint samples I picked up from the hardware store, still nowhere closer to deciding on a color while poor Lewis patiently waits for me to decide.

One upside to all this tedious and backbreaking work? It's distracted us from the awkwardness. We don't have the energy to be nervous around each other while performing intense physical labor for hours every day. Now it feels like we're just two workers on a reno crew busting our asses, ending each day completely exhausted.

"Didn't you go through this when you renovated your house?" I ask, still glancing back and forth between the swatches.

He shrugs. "I hired a designer for that part."

"Oh. Right." I force a chuckle, feeling the slightest bit sheepish. Of course Lewis Prescott doesn't obsess over paint colors. He's a rich and famous celebrity who can afford to hire an entire staff of people to choose the most beautiful paint-color scheme, furniture, fixtures, decor, and literally anything else for his home. Listening to me go on and on must be boring him to tears.

"I'm sorry I'm being so tedious about this. You must think it's silly."

"I don't think it's silly." He smiles. "I think it's really sweet how thoughtful you're being."

"Thanks."

"How about we get back to the flooring for a bit? Maybe that'll help clear your mind and you can come back and look at the colors from a fresher perspective."

"That's a great idea."

For the next hour, we're back on the floor. I wring out my achy hands before gripping my pry bar once more. Just like every other day I've worked on this, I recall Lewis's instructions on how to remove floorboards so that they stay intact. I slide the pry bar between the hardwood plank and the floor and gently wiggle until I feel the plank come loose. Then I grab the recip saw, reposition myself so I'm kneeling on the bare flooring, fire up the saw, and carefully glide the blade under each staple that pins the deep walnut–finished hardwood plank to the floor. In seconds, the floorboard is loose, and I carefully place it on top of the massive pile of wooden planks against the wall.

When I stand up and stretch, everything from my knees to my core to my arms to my wrists throbs. I wipe the sweat from my brow with the back of my hand and guzzle water from my bottle while glancing at Lewis as he works. Brow furrowed, he purses his lips in concentration as he loosens floorboard after floorboard at a dizzying pace.

He groans. "I'm getting too old for this."

I roll my eyes. "You're thirty-two—one whole year younger than me. You can shut up about how old you feel."

He laughs before doing a slow scan of the space, his gaze landing on the last remaining stretch of hardwood floorboards near the fireplace that still needs to be removed.

"We've got the floorboards along the edge of the living room left to pull up," he says. "Then we're done."

I mock groan. "Done with this part. We still have to relay the wood onto the flooring, remember?"

He holds his palms up at me. "Ha. Okay, okay. We're almost done with this part. That's cause for celebration."

I head over to the fireplace and get to work on removing the floorboards with my pry bar and recip saw.

"You sounded like my grandpa there for a sec," Lewis says as he sets up beside me. "He didn't like it when I glossed over the details while working either."

"I'm a detail fiend. I had to be for my old job."

"What was that like? Working as an architect?"

"Stressful. Long hours. Frustrating at times, depending on the personalities of the people on my team."

"How so?"

I grunt as I tug loose a particularly stubborn hardwood plank. "All too often, I'd have an older guy working for me who assumed that because I was young and female, I didn't know what I was doing. They'd second-guess me or talk down to me. It was par for the course."

"Shit, really?"

I nod.

"I'm sorry." From the corner of my eye I catch Lewis staring at me.

"You don't need to be sorry. There's nothing in the

world I love more than being underestimated and then nailing the underestimater's ass to the wall."

When Lewis doesn't respond right away, I glance over at him.

"That's hard-core. I dig it."

I chuckle.

"So how did you go about nailing asses to the wall?" he asks.

"I just confronted them head-on, usually in front of the rest of the staff. I remember this one time a few years ago when I was heading an expansion on a museum near the Civic Center in San Francisco. I was holding a meeting right before the project kicked off to explain the construction of the entryway that I had planned, and one of the other architects interrupted me and said, 'Are you sure that's the best way to go about it?'"

Lewis winces.

"That's the exact reaction my team had."

"What'd you do?"

"I stood up from the head of the conference table, rested my hands on the edge, looked him square in the eye and said, 'Are you asking me, the head of this project, if the design I've spent months perfecting is the right way to go?' And then I just stared. And stared. And after a few seconds of stammering, he muttered, 'Sorry,' and then I moved on with the rest of the meeting."

"I like your style. To the point. In-your-face."

"I've learned that the best way to tell someone off is to just repeat their words back to them. They realize real quick just how ridiculous they sound when they're promptly called out. It's my go-to method."

I run the blade of the recip saw along the bottom of another loosened floorboard, then set it aside with the rest.

"Did that happen to you a lot? People questioning your authority?" he asks.

I set down the pry bar, taking a second to rest. "It happened more frequently in my first couple of years at the firm. By the end of my time there, the people I worked with knew me and my work well, so they didn't doubt me. But it was something I've always dealt with. I suspect I will again whenever I decide to go back to work."

"Is that your plan after the renovation? To work at an architecture firm again?"

"Yeah, probably."

When I look up, I catch Lewis studying me.

"What?"

"You don't sound excited about it," he says.

I shrug. "I love being an architect. I just want to do something meaningful too. That's why I'm volunteering a lot more now that I'm not working, since it was hard for me to do it much while I was putting in long hours. But corporate gigs pay the best and the Bay Area is expensive to live in, so I always feel like those are the jobs I need to take. When I do eventually go back to work, I'll be sad to have to cut down on my volunteering."

"What's your dream job?"

His question jolts me. No one's ever asked me that before.

"Honestly? I don't know. As much as I love being an architect, I think I love volunteering for Glad You're Here more. It's so gratifying to help people."

"Then why don't you just make that your job? Do what you love."

I laugh. "Yeah, right. As if it's that simple."

"Isn't it?"

I tilt my head at him. "No, it's not. I've looked into

nonprofit jobs before, and the pay is a lot lower than what I made as an architect. As much as I wish money didn't matter, it does. This is an expensive area, and I want to stay here. And be able to help out my family whenever they need it."

"Right." His cheeks flush pink as he glances down. "Sorry, I guess I sounded pretty out of touch there. Easy for someone like me, an actor, to say do what you love. Kinda obnoxious, now that I think about it."

I tell him it's okay while quietly acknowledging the glaring differences in our lifestyles. I wonder what it's like to be working your dream job that pays millions and you never have to worry about finances.

"For what it's worth, I'm sorry you had to deal with people doubting you in your old job. I hope that doesn't happen when you start working again."

I shrug. "I'm not what some people picture when they think of a corporate architect. I know I look young for my age. My thick-rimmed glasses don't help, but I hate wearing contacts. I'm sure there are a lot of things I could have done appearance-wise to present as more professional. But I'm not the kind of person who's interested in fitting into other people's expectations. As long as I do my job well, I should be able to look however I want."

When Lewis stretches his fist to me, I laugh and return the bump.

"Spoken like a true badass," he says. "You're a talented and qualified architect, Harper. The work you did on the additions to your house is some of the best that I've seen." He ruffles his hair with a hand as his gaze drops to the floor. "Maybe that's not saying much since it's been years since I've worked full-time on a jobsite, but I recognize quality when I see it."

Was I imagining it, or did his eyes linger on me a little longer after that statement?

"No. It means a lot. Thank you."

The few seconds we spend smiling and looking at each other makes me go warm and gooey on the inside. I've always been confident in my abilities as a professional, but it's always nice to hear a genuine compliment from someone.

"Did you ever feel the urge to tell any of those guys who doubted you to fuck off?" Lewis asks after a few minutes of us quietly working.

I burst out laughing. "Of course I did, but I didn't want to get disciplined or fired for unprofessional conduct."

My mind flashes back to the footage I saw of Lewis telling the paparazzi to fuck off when they refused to leave him alone at Chateau Marmont. And that was after a string of *fuck you*s doled out to interviewers who crossed a line with him.

"Good for you for having the composure I'm lacking to tactfully tell people off instead of just yelling profanity at them like I do." He grunts as he loosens another floorboard.

"I wish I were as ballsy as you to cuss people out."

"Well, I wish people took me as seriously as they take you."

"People don't take you seriously?" I ask.

"I get cast as the pretty boy or the bad boy. A lot. It gets tiring after a while."

This time when he grunts, I think it has less to do with the physical labor he's performing and more to do with the frustration in what he's told me.

"Have you tried to branch out into different roles?" I

ask, feeling foolish for assuming that he enjoyed always playing the hot guy or the bad boy.

"Yeah. For a long time, actually. But the pretty boy/bad boy work is what pays the bills. It has for a while now, and I think casting agents, producers, and directors are hesitant to let me do something meatier, even though I've been dying to."

"What does your agent say when you bring it up?"

"He's not much of a risk taker when it comes to my career. Trent tells me it's best to stick with a sure thing. That it'll help me build a solid name for myself, then maybe in a few years I can think about branching out."

I scoff. "That's such bullshit."

He starts to laugh, but I reach over and touch his arm. He goes quiet instantly.

"I'm serious, Lewis. Your agent works for you, right? I mean, he may help get you parts, but you're the one who does the actual work. Without you, he'd be nothing. And for him to dismiss your goals and dreams for his own 'sure thing' is pretty upsetting."

When I feel the muscle in his forearm flex, it suddenly registers that I'm still touching him. I let go and place my hand in my lap.

"Sorry, I don't mean to tell you what to do," I mumble. "I don't have the faintest clue what it's like to work in the entertainment industry. I'm sure it's a lot more complicated than I'll ever know. But you're a talented actor. You're so invested in every role I've seen you in. It's like you're embodying the character, not just reciting the lines. And I have zero doubt that you're going to knock your first serious role out of the park."

His eyes widen the slightest bit, like he can't believe what I've just said. "That means a lot. Thank you."

"What's your dream role?"

He leans up on his knees, resting his hands on his denim-clad thighs. "There's this script I read last year. A friend's friend wrote it, and it's so incredible, I read it in one sitting. It's a coming-of-age teen romance with a nonbinary main character. There's a supporting role in that—the main character's older brother. He's been in and out of jail and comes off as a questionable character at first, but he's the main character's biggest supporter. And as the movie progresses you learn that deep down, he's a truly good person. His support for his sibling never wavers. He openly calls out people who bully them. And he's the one person the main character knows they can count on to accept them, no matter what. Yeah, he's been to jail, but for petty stuff here and there. When it comes to what matters—standing up for what's right—the older brother always delivers. I'd love to play that part, to show that people can be flawed and still be good."

There's a fire that lights behind Lewis's eyes when he talks about this role, this movie.

Passion.

I've never witnessed him talk about anything with as much passion as he showed just now.

"You'd be amazing in that role. I would watch the hell out of that. Loads of people would."

His shoulders hunch forward slightly, almost like he's deflating. "Yeah, well, my agent thought it would be a pretty risky move for me, taking on a gritty indie role, so I passed on it. Last I heard, a couple of smaller studios were thinking about developing it into a series. I'm sure they'll cast someone great as the older brother."

As I watch him work to remove plank after plank from the floor, it dawns on me just how insecure he is. It's a strange realization—how can someone so handsome and famous and successful harbor so much doubt about himself? It's not something I've ever noticed him display in any of his interviews that I've seen. Even when he's pissed off, there's this air of confidence about him. And I certainly haven't noticed it over the past week, as he moves with complete confidence and know-how through each physical task he approaches.

But then it dawns on me: maybe he's letting himself be vulnerable right now because he feels comfortable—because he doesn't feel like he has to be on like he does in his LA life.

It feels so special to see him so raw, so honest.

"Hey."

He glances up at me.

"I hope you reconsider, because you'd be perfect for that role."

He smiles slightly. "Maybe I will. Thanks, Harper."

My phone rings, and I crawl to the other side of the floor to see who's calling. When I see it's my mom FaceTiming me, I answer.

"Sweetheart! Hello! I know you're probably so busy working on your grandma and grandpa's house, but I wanted to see how things are going and make sure you're taking care of yourself."

Her crystal-blue eyes shine as she beams at me before leaning down to catch my great-uncle Pedro in the frame.

"Also, someone misses you and wanted to say hello," she says.

"Uncle Pedro! How are you?" I do a quick scan of his face as he says hi, relieved that he looks better rested than the last time I saw him just a few days ago. Even his deep brown eyes are clearer and brighter.

"Pretty good, *anak*. Still a little tired, but I'm walking around more. And my appetite's back too."

"He had two servings of my chicken and broccoli casserole," Mom announces proudly, her wavy silver-blond hair bouncing as she turns to look at Uncle Pedro. He affirms that it was delicious and much better than any of the hospital food he ate.

"He even ate more than your dad did!"

"Way to go, Uncle Pedro." I chuckle. "How's Dad?"

"Still working way too much." Mom tsks. "I tell him he needs to cut back on picking up all those extra shifts, but he swears they're what keep him young."

I roll my eyes. "Sounds like something he'd say."

He's worked as a technician for an electrical company ever since I was a toddler and hardly ever says no to an offer for overtime.

"It's in his blood to work hard," Uncle Pedro says to Mom in a good-natured tone. "That's what we do. Look at our Harper. So successful that she could take a break from her job to fix up her *apongs*' house. So brilliant, *anakko*. I brag to all my friends about you every week at the senior center."

"It's true," Mom says. "Every time I drop him off and pick him up from there, all of his friends tell me to bring you over someday so they can introduce you to their grandsons and nephews. They're very impressed by you, honey."

Mom winks at me, and I let out a groan-laugh. I hope Lewis doesn't notice the flush creeping its way up my cheeks at his overhearing my family as they offer to set me up for the millionth time. I glance over and catch him smiling to himself as he pries another floorboard loose.

"I appreciate the offer, but I'm good."

"How's the house?" Uncle Pedro asks.

"It's coming along well so far." I opted to keep my parents and Uncle Pedro out of the loop when it came to the disaster with Vlad. They're already dealing with enough on their plate now that Uncle Pedro is living with them while he fully recovers from his bout of pneumonia.

"I know we've said this a million times before, but we're so proud of you, taking on the renovation," Uncle Pedro says.

Uncle Pedro is my *apong* Vivian's younger brother, and I know just how much it would mean for him to see his sister's house updated after all these years.

"Thanks, Uncle Pedro. Oh hey, let me get your guys' opinion on something."

I hop up and walk toward the far wall in the living room, which boasts the two color squares I've been obsessing over all day.

"I painted these samples earlier this morning. Which one do you like best?" I ask, holding up the phone so they can see the swatches on the wall. I explain how I'm trying to capture both of *Apong* Vivian's and *Apong* Bernie's favorite colors.

"Oh, honey. How thoughtful. That would make them so happy," Mom says.

She and Uncle Pedro chat about the merits of a neutral like the light gray-green hue in the middle versus the slightly more pronounced color of the green-gray one. These are obviously my people.

"You know, *Apong* Bernie never much cared for decorating, not like your *apong* Vivian." Uncle Pedro chuckles. "He'd always let her take charge, so I say go with the one she'd like. That's what Bernie would have done."

"You're right." I turn the phone around and beam at the screen. "I remember that about them. Green-gray it is."

I run to the kitchen to show them the cabinets, then give them a quick view of the finished part of the hardwood flooring, careful to keep Lewis out of frame. Mom and Uncle Pedro don't pay attention to celebrity gossip, so I'm certain they wouldn't recognize him even if they were to see him, but the whole reason why he's here is because he's hiding out. I want to respect his privacy.

"Wow!"

"It looks so good already!"

I spot Lewis smiling to himself.

"The contractor you hired is doing a good job, then?" Mom asks.

"Yes. He's knocking it out of the park." I glance over at Lewis, who's still loosening floorboards. "I should get going, though. I'm helping him with a project right now."

"See? Always working so hard. What I did I tell you?" Uncle Pedro chuckles.

"It's cheaper if I help with some of the labor. Luckily the contractor I found was okay with that."

"So smart and practical. Good on you, *anak*."

"That's our girl!" Mom cheers.

I chuckle at how ridiculously supportive my family is.

We exchange *I love you*s and I promise to come down for dinner sometime in the next couple of weeks. When we hang up, I glance up at Lewis, who's still kneeling on the floor.

"Sorry about that."

"About what? Your family sounds really great. And really proud of you."

I wave a hand. "They'd be proud of me for opening

a lemonade stand. It's amazing, but also kind of over-the-top."

Lewis goes quiet instantly, and I notice the expression on his face, a mix of wistful and sad.

"Sounds like the best kind of family," he says before firing up the recip saw and running it along the bottom of the hardwood floorboards.

As I get back to work helping him, I quietly wonder what prompted that look and those words. But as much as I want to ask, I remember our agreement. Total privacy is what I promised him, and so that's what he'll get.

Chapter Nine

Harper

"We're still on for wedding dress shopping on Friday, right?" I ask Naomi over the phone.

"Absolutely. I honestly can't wait! I know I haven't been the typical bride in a lot of ways, but something about picking out a dress has me all giddy."

"Maybe it's because you know you're gonna look freaking gorgeous in whatever you try on and Simon is gonna pass out at the altar at the sight of you."

Naomi chuckles. I pace slowly around the bedroom of an apartment I'm touring with one of the clients at Glad You're Here. I peer into the kitchen, where the client, Mina, is being shown all the amenities by the leasing agent. She turns and flashes a thumbs-up at me.

"I'm still sad that Maren can't come," Naomi says.

"Me too. You know how those hospital shifts are, though. It's almost impossible to swap a busy day shift at a trauma hospital in San Francisco."

"I know. It's just been so long since the three of us hung out."

Last month was the last time we saw Maren, our friend from college. The three of us have been friends since freshman year, when Maren was my roommate. She worked as a travel nurse for the majority of her career before getting an ER position at a hospital in San Francisco a handful of months ago to be closer to her family.

"At the very least we'll all get to hang out at your bachelorette party," I remind her.

"So how's the cohabitation going with the hunky TV star–turned–contractor?"

"Fine."

"Fine? That's all you're giving me?"

"Yes, because it's true."

The longer I stay quiet, the more I could swear I hear the gears in Naomi's mind cranking away.

"What happened?" she finally prods.

I roll my eyes and walk to the far corner of the room so that Mina and the leasing agent don't hear.

"Okay, so a few weeks ago...we almost kissed."

Naomi squeaks "what?!" so loudly, I have to hold the phone away from my ear.

"It was the evening of the day I accidentally grabbed his...you know."

"Wow. You two don't waste any time, do you?"

"Very funny. In all seriousness, it was another accident. Total mistake."

"Harper, the kind of accidents you have are very interesting. They seem to frequently involve you getting handsy with the intimate areas of your famous housemate's rockin' body."

I bite down to keep from groaning too loudly. "You're hilarious, Naomi. That evening, we were sharing a drink on the veranda, I tripped and lost my balance, and he caught me, pulled me to his chest, and that's when it almost happened." I'm careful to keep my voice low. "But then we came to our senses. Lewis was the first one to break the embrace. He ran off to bed, and I did too. The next morning we decided that it was just a weird moment. We're all good now. It's water under the bridge."

Naomi makes a "hmm" noise, signaling that she's thinking hard about what I said.

"Well, I definitely have to applaud you for handling this so maturely. But you gotta tell me…if he hadn't pulled away, would you have kissed him?"

I let out a breath. "Yeah."

"It's only a matter of time before you two jump each other's bones. I'm calling it right now."

I roll my eyes. That stubborn streak inside me rears its head at my cousin's smug tone. "You couldn't be more wrong. Lewis and I have an arrangement. We're both committed to maintaining our boundaries for the rest of the time we're staying together."

"Uh-huh."

Damn Naomi. She's always pulled off indifference so well. Ever since we were kids, she knew that was the quickest way to rile me up—by acting like she doesn't believe a word I'm saying.

"We've spent the past two weeks doing physical labor side by side at the house. We ripped up all the floorboards in the kitchen and living room and installed a whole new floor. I'm talking shoulder to shoulder, Naomi. Sweating and grunting and…"

Just the image of Lewis in his unofficial contractor uniform of a ratty T-shirt and ripped jeans slingshots to the front of my mind. I can't deny just how hot he is.

"Oh yeah, it sure sounds like you're completely unfazed by the man."

I push up my glasses and pinch the bridge of my nose. "I swear to God, no one gets me as worked up as you."

"Harper, you don't have to be all business all the time. You don't have to fight your own feelings—especially if he's vibing right along with you. If the stars align again and you have another flirty interaction—and it feels right—I say go for it."

For a moment, I contemplate my cousin's advice. Maybe it really can be that simple.

I glance through the doorway and see Mina waving me over.

"I gotta go," I tell Naomi. "Send me those dress pics you were talking about, okay?"

"Can't wait to see you next weekend!"

We exchange *I love you*s before I hang up and join Mina.

"I love it," she says. "It's the perfect amount of space for what I need and a great location."

The leasing agent beams. "I can take you back to the office and get you started on the application."

Mina says an excited yes, and the three of us make our way out of the apartment and to the office. She sits at the desk with the leasing agent while I pop to the bathroom just outside the office near the entrance of the building. When I walk out, I stop to get a drink at the nearby fountain. As I straighten up, I notice Mina rushing out of the office in tears.

I hurry to catch up with her. When I rest my hand on her arm, she stops right in front of the glass doors at the entrance.

"What happened? Are you okay?"

She shakes her head, tears streaming from her brown eyes. "It's just...one of the other leasing agents came in and said something pretty insensitive…about whether or not I'm able to speak English well enough…"

Every single muscle in my shoulders, back, and torso tenses.

"What did they say?"

Her lips quiver as she opens her mouth, but she shuts it quickly. After a few seconds she tries again. "Brittany and I were going over the application when he walked in. And then he interrupted us to ask if Brittany could come with him to his office. I overheard him telling her that he didn't want her renting out to 'people like me' anymore."

My jaw falls to the floor.

"Brittany started to argue with him, but then he went off about how it was impossible to understand me because of my accent and that I'll probably be late with rent all the time because I probably don't have a stable job. It was just awful. I didn't stick around for the rest. I was too upset and ran out."

A memory from decades ago dislodges from the back of my brain. I'm eight years old at the supermarket with *Apong* Bernie and *Apong* Vivian. While we were waiting in line to pay for our groceries, they were chattering to each other in Ilocano. *Apong* Bernie said I could pick out one piece of candy, so I giddily perused the selection next to the register as they chatted. And that's when I heard the words I'll never forget.

"Fucking foreigners."

My head whipped up to see an angry man glaring at my grandparents.

"Learn some English," the guy muttered.

I'll never forget the look on *Apong* Bernie's face as he straightened his posture and looked him square in the eye. "We do speak English, actually."

I didn't catch the muttered retort as the guy walked away to wait in line at a different register. All I remember is *Apong* Vivian pulling me close to her the rest of the time that we waited in line. I remember how quiet the car ride home was. I remember the short conversation they had while I stared at my unopened candy bar in the back seat.

"They don't even know us and they hate us," *Apong* Vivian said quietly.

"Forget them, ViVi," *Apong* Bernie said. "We have just as much right to live here as anyone else."

That's when his brown eyes appeared in the rearview mirror. The usual brightness I saw in them had dulled.

"Harper, *anak*." His voice was gentle yet firm, like it always was when he was about to tell me something important. "You don't ever let anyone tell you that you don't belong. You hear me? You belong here. Always."

The sound of Mina's sniffles yanks me back to the present, and I catch myself nodding, just like I did that day in the car with *Apong* Bernie.

Gently, I rest my hands on her shoulders. "Mina. There is nothing wrong with the way you speak. That guy is an ignorant prick. And he's not going to get away with saying that about you."

Acid swirls in my belly as I march back into the office. I hear raised voices from the back office, so I head straight there.

"Ken, do you even realize what you're saying? What is wrong—"

Both Brittany and Ken whip their heads at me when they notice me in the doorway.

Ken aims a glare at me. "Is there something we can help you with?"

"Yeah, actually. Ken, is it? I just wanted to pop in and say that you're a racist asshole."

His eyes bulge.

"What you said about my friend Mina is disgusting. She has a great job as a web developer and a solid rental history in the few years that she's lived in the US. She works hard every day to be a productive member of society and a good person, which is more than I can say for you. I hope you realize what a classless jerk you are and do some serious soul-searching so you don't die a bigoted jackass."

I pivot my gaze to Brittany. "You were wonderful. I'm sorry you work with such a prick." I shift to address Ken once more. "I'll be filing a complaint with the Better Business Bureau about you and this company."

My heart rams against my rib cage as I march back out to the entrance, where Mina's waiting. I take her hand and lead her back to my car. Before I can climb into the driver's seat, she stops us and pulls me into a hug.

"I heard what you said. Thank you."

My eyes well with tears at the sorrow in her voice, at how hard she's holding me.

I clear my throat and squeeze her tight. "You don't have to thank me, Mina. That guy deserved to be told off."

"I just wish more people spoke up like you did."

As we climb into my car and I drive back to Glad You're Here, I grip the steering wheel so hard that my knuckles ache.

"Me too."

Chapter Ten

Lewis

I finish tightening the last screw on the frame of the brass chandelier. When I make my way down the ladder and walk back a few feet to take in how it looks hanging in the foyer, I smile. Looks good.

I wasn't planning to tackle the chandelier today, but the idea of spending another full day peeling slabs of tile from the wall in the hallway bathroom sent phantom aches down my lower back. I figured installing the chandelier would be a good break from that while at the same time being a nice surprise for Harper.

Just imagining her reaction when she walks in has me pumped. I remember how excited she was when we went over the plans for its installation a few days ago. That urge to make her happy lands hard, right at the center of my chest. Like a punch. But nicer.

Harper's words from our conversation days ago echo in my mind.

You'd be perfect for that role.

Hearing her say that meant everything to me.

I've known her for just a few weeks, but she spoke with more conviction than most people I've known for years—like she had every confidence in my ability. And the impact of her belief in me hit like a freight train in the best way.

The industry I work in is full of fake people who blow smoke up my ass on an almost daily basis.

You're the most talented actor in the world... You light up the screen in a way like no one else does... You moved me to literal tears. LITERAL TEARS...

Even now I can't help but laugh. It's all bullshit. Don't get me wrong, I love performing, I love inhabiting a totally new character in every role I tackle, I love channeling my emotions through a creative outlet. But I'm not an idiot. I understand that what I do for a living isn't all that important in the grand scheme of things. There are people in the world saving lives, feeding the hungry, curing diseases—actual heroes. Nothing I do comes close to that. It makes my skin crawl when people fawn over me like I'm doing something life-changing when in reality I'm showing up to set and getting paid ridiculous amounts of money to play make-believe.

That's why what Harper said got under my skin. She's not the type of person who would say something she didn't mean. In the short time I've known her, I can tell that she's brutally honest—always in a respectful way.

And right now, as I attempt to crawl out of this professional black hole, her belief in me is helping to keep me going.

That's why I want to surprise her with the chandelier. I want to see Harper happy after she made me so happy.

I feel a squeeze in the middle of my chest right as my stomach dips. I go still right where I stand, soaking in the feeling…and struggling to remember the last time I felt that at the mere thought of someone…the last time someone else's happiness meant so much to me.

Never.

Just then I hear the click of the front door. I spin around right as she walks into the house. She kicks off her sneakers and looks up, freezing when she sees the chandelier.

Her mouth falls open slightly. All she can do for a handful of seconds is stare at it.

"Do you like it?" I finally ask when she stays quiet.

"Um… I…what about the crystals?"

Her stare turns dazed, and that's when I notice that her eyes are red and the skin on her cheeks and chin is splotchy. Like she's been crying.

"That box of crystals in the garage. I wanted to hang them on each of the tiers of the chandelier before you mounted it."

She speaks as she stares at the chandelier. Her voice sounds off. Weak. Detached.

"Oh. Well, um, even with the ceiling being reinforced, when I looked at the crystals, I realized they would have added too much weight. I figured it would be fine to hang it like it is."

Still nothing. Just more staring at the chandelier, a dazed look on her face.

"I still think it looks cool without the crystals, though," I say. "Like a bronze sculpture."

She finally pivots her gaze to me. Her eyes are swollen, and there's a slight wrinkle in her brow that makes her look confused and sad all at once.

"Sorry, I guess I should have told you before I hung it up. But I wanted it to be a surprise…"

I trail off as I notice her chin wobbling. Those full,

bee-stung lips start to tremble, and her face scrunches as tears stream down her cheeks.

"Lewis, I need…the crystals need to be on the chandelier. They're the whole point… My grandma…that box of crystals…she spent so many years collecting and storing them in that box… She was saving them for when she could remodel the house and find the perfect chandelier to hang them…"

Her voice, which has been straining the entire time she spoke, breaks completely. A sob squeaks out of her as she covers her face.

Instinctively I close the space between us, wrap my arms around her, and hug her to my chest. She tugs at the fabric of my T-shirt, like she's desperately trying to hold on.

"Hey. It's okay." I say it softly, hoping that I'm at least some bit of comfort.

My sweat-soaked T-shirt absorbs each tear as she shakes against me. I hug her tighter, heartened when she slides her arms around my waist. It feels a lot like permission, like her body is telling me it's okay that I'm holding her even though I didn't ask first…even though we've never touched each other like this.

By the time she calms down, I know what's bothering her is more than just the chandelier. Anxiety grabs hold of my heart, like a massive invisible bat thrashing through my chest. Just the thought of something or someone upsetting Harper this badly has me wild with worry…and some primal need to protect her.

"I'm sorry, Lewis. I'm so sorry. What you did was so thoughtful. I must look like a lunatic." She sniffles as she stays pressed against my chest.

"You're not. I don't think that at all." I tuck her head

under my chin and rest my palm on the back of her head. "What happened?"

Her breath heats against my shirt, my skin. And then her hands fall away from me, and she takes a step back. My body goes cold at the loss of contact.

She crosses her arms over her chest, like she's attempting to close herself off from me, but that's the last thing I want.

I gently grab her hand and lead her to the couch, which we finally put back into the living room when we finished relaying the flooring the other day.

She plops down on one end. I walk to the kitchen and grab her a glass of water. When I hand it to her, she says, "Thanks," and I sit down on the other end of the sectional.

"Do you want to talk about it?" I ask.

She murmurs "yes" after gulping some water.

"I was helping one of the clients at Glad You're Here apply for an apartment, and some asshole leasing agent made a racist comment in front of her."

I listen as patiently as I can, but when she tells me what the guy said, I bite down so hard, I fully expect my jaw to shatter.

"God, that's so fucked-up. Harper, I… I don't even know what to say. I'm sorry."

"I was so angry that I told the guy off and reported him to the Better Business Bureau. And I called the corporate leasing office for his company and complained about him. And I left a scathing public review of the leasing agency on Facebook specifically naming him. And when I got back to the Glad You're Here office, I told Diana what happened. That apartment complex is now on the 'do not contact ever' list. But the fact that there even has to be a list is a testament to how much work we still have to do in fighting for equality."

"You fought hard today, Harper. I'm proud of you."

When I see the corner of her mouth curve up, the pressure in my chest eases the slightest bit. She downs the rest of the water in her glass. I offer to fetch her another, but she says no thanks, and after a few quiet moments, she aims those doe-like brown eyes up at me. It feels like an arrow piercing straight through me. Seeing the redness in her normally focused and bright stare makes me physically ache.

"I'm sorry I freaked out about the chandelier," she says before glancing over at it once more. "Thank you for thinking to do that. It really does look nice. I just..."

When her lips start to tremble again, I reach over and take her hand in mine. "Hey. You don't have to apologize for anything, okay?"

She nods quickly, her eyes gleaming. When she squeezes my hand back, that pressure in my chest intensifies.

"It's just...hearing that guy say those horrible things about Mina triggered a memory when I was little of when I'd be out with my grandparents. Sometimes they'd speak Ilocano to each other, and someone would mutter horrible things to them, like how they should learn some English or how annoying foreigners are."

I hold back a growl.

"Anyway, my grandma, she always wanted to have a big, fancy chandelier displayed in the house with the pretty crystals she found."

A smile that's equal parts sad and wistful appears on her face. "But she never got around to it, obviously. When I planned this remodel, I wanted everything to be perfect—everything from the veranda to the chandelier to the direction of the hardwood floor planks to the color of the walls. My grandma and grandpa worked so hard for so many years and dealt with so much crap to establish themselves here in the US and start a life for their family. They always wanted to remodel their house, but they never had enough money. But I do. And I want everything in this house to be perfect. For them, for their memory. Even though they're not here anymore, they deserve that."

She bites her trembling bottom lip, then goes quiet and stares at our joined hands.

"Harper, first of all, I'm so sorry that racist prick said those things about Mina. That's horrible. And I'm sorry that your grandparents were treated that way. They deserved so much better."

She murmurs a thank-you.

"I know that I never knew your grandparents, but I remember your FaceTime conversation with your mom and great-uncle. It's obvious how proud they are of the work you're doing on this house. I promise you, your grandparents would be so proud and blown away at what you've done with their house."

Her shoulders rise and fall with the breath she takes. "Thank you. I needed to hear that."

"I'll tell you as many times as you'll let me. I've never seen such a thoughtful gesture as what you're doing with this house. This is one of the most selfless things I've ever seen anyone do."

Her full cheeks turn pink, and I lose my breath. Harper is gorgeous when she blushes. Right then and there, I make it my life's mission to make her do it again.

"My cousin tells me the same thing," she says. "But

I guess I kind of dismiss her because she's family, you know? Your family's job is to build you up, always, no matter what you're doing."

I clear my throat as I process what she's said.

"I guess that's true," I manage. "But your cousin isn't building you up. She's just telling the truth. And hey, I'm so sorry for messing up the chandelier."

"It's okay. It still looks really nice."

When she starts to smile, it feels like a victory. In the short time I've known Harper, I've become so drawn to her, so invested in making sure this renovation goes exactly how she wants it. Seeing her sad and hurt makes me want to rage. Seeing her happy is the highlight of my day…and I want make her happy every single day that I'm here in this house with her.

I focus on Harper's gaze, how there's an intensity that wasn't there seconds ago. I get lost in those pools of rich hickory. All I can do is focus on her eyes, the touch of her hand.

And that's when I realize… I really, *really* like Harper.

"Thank you, Lewis. For everything." Her soft tone is laced with the most delicious rasp.

"It's my pleasure."

Part of me wants to stay on this couch, holding her hand, drowning in her beautiful eyes for the rest of the evening. But then my brain catches up. I'm here to do a job: fix her house while I repair my professional reputation. Giving in to this crush I have on her isn't serving either of those goals. Besides, I shouldn't be thinking of her in that way right now. She was upset and crying just minutes ago. She's vulnerable. What kind of creep am I to be fixated on how attractive she is in this moment?

I slip my hand out of hers and scoot away from her on the couch. "I'm gonna get back to work."

When I stand up, Harper hops up and throws her arms around me, hugging me tight. I hug her back, wondering if she can feel my heart as it thrashes in my chest—if she can feel just how much I like her.

Chapter Eleven

Harper

Wow. This hug…it's…just wow.

I close my eyes and relish the scent, the feel, the warmth of Lewis. He is absolutely perfect.

And not just physically, but the way he supported me just now blew me away. No boyfriend I've ever had has doted on me like that. Sure, I've cried in front of the guys I've been with when I've been stressed or sad. But they've always had the same reaction: visible discomfort. There must be something about the sight of female tears that sends them running for the hills.

But not Lewis. He comforted me. He held me. He gave me the space to talk about what was upsetting me when I was ready. And when I did, he listened intently.

You really, really like him.

I let the realization echo in the privacy of my mind, knowing full well that I'm not going to do a damn thing about it. Because this setup between us is purely professional, and I don't want to ruin it or make things awkward by admitting out loud that I've got a serious crush on him. I'm certain that most of the people he's ever come into contact with have a crush on him. He's talented, hot, and so freaking sweet. Who wouldn't fall for a guy like that?

I finally start to release my hold on him. I need to get it together. I can't be acting like some smitten fangirl just because he demonstrated empathy in my moment of need.

I back away just as Lewis's phone vibrates.

The hint of a scowl flashes across his face as he looks at the screen. "It's my agent."

"I'll give you some privacy," I say as I walk off to the kitchen while Lewis answers the call.

"Hey, Trent. What's up?"

"Lewis, my man! How're you holding up?"

I wince as I peer inside the fridge for a snack. Man, Lewis's agent is boisterous as hell.

"Doing good, I hope? I just wanted to update you on how things are looking for you, superstar."

Even as I warm up leftover *pansit* in the microwave, I can hear almost every word his agent says, about how Lewis is getting loads of inquiries around his availability and whereabouts.

"You've been getting offers left and right, my man. Interviews with every major entertainment news outlet and gossip site. You've even got an offer to be the featured centerfold in the bad boy issue of *Hotties* magazine. *Hotties!* You know what that means, right? You're hot! H-O-T hot!"

I almost choke on a bite of *pansit.* I really shouldn't be eavesdropping. But is it really eavesdropping if his agent's voice is as loud as a stereo speaker?

Lewis makes no attempt to turn away or make it seem like this is a private conversation. He stays standing in the living room just a handful of feet away from me, his expression a mix between unamused and annoyed.

"That's all quite riveting," Lewis mutters. "I'm not really interested in doing any of that, though." He scrubs a hand over his face, and his gaze turns focused. "But I mean, engaging a bit maybe wouldn't be the worst thing in the world at this point. Maybe a post on social media to connect with fans. I haven't been able to interact with them like I normally do—"

"Oh no way, my man! It's still too early. You're in hiding for the next two months—that means two more months of people going out of their minds, wondering where the hell you are, reaching out to me with offers up the ying-yang, all the while building up all this anticipation for your big comeback. We've got everyone right where we want them—dying of anticipation."

The cackle of his agent's laugh reminds me of an evil Bond villain.

"Just wanted to make sure you know what a hot commodity you are. H-O-T, my man. People are well on their way to forgetting your little meltdown and welcoming you back to Tinseltown with open arms."

Lewis stares blankly ahead, as if he couldn't be more bored with this conversation. He mutters a thanks before his agent promises to update him again next week.

"Sorry about that," he mumbles after ending the call. He walks over to the kitchen and grabs a bottle of vodka from the freezer.

"Your agent is very…loud," I say as I stand at the kitchen island and eat.

"That's probably one of the nicest things anyone's ever said about Trent."

"Of course that's his name."

Lewis makes a noise that sounds like a scoff-chuckle.

"You don't like him?" I ask.

"It's not that." He pours a few splashes of vodka into a clear glass and sips. "He's just really over-the-top. But he's a killer agent. He got me the leading role on *The Best of It* and a bunch of supporting movie roles before then. He's worth sticking with even if he's obnoxious."

I quietly take note of the strained look on his face and how rehearsed he sounds. I wonder if that's actually how he feels.

"So no *Hotties* spread for you, then?" I tease, hoping that eases the tension he's clearly feeling.

When he laughs, I cheer on the inside.

"Honestly? I actually think it would be fun to pose nude someday." He eyes me from above the rim of his glass as he sips, which causes my stomach to do a back-flip.

"But I don't really want to do it for some random spread about Hollywood hotties. I think I'm past doing stuff like that." He glances down at the glass as he swirls it in his hand.

"You'd rather do it on your terms?" I ask, trying to sound composed and not at all like how I feel: hot and flustered to the max as my filthy brain imagines what Lewis would look like nude.

"Yeah. I always thought it would be cool to do a nude photo shoot for charity. Like, people could purchase the photos and the money would go to a worthy cause."

When his eyebrow quirks up, it sets off an idea. An outlandish and filthy idea…but a brilliant one too.

"Then do it."

"Do what?"

"A nude photo shoot. For charity. And your fans."

It's clear this is something Lewis really wants to do. And even though he didn't go in-depth when explaining his relationship with his agent, it's obvious that because of Trent, Lewis doesn't often get to do what he wants. But Trent isn't here right now. I am. Maybe I can convince him to defy his agent and actually do this.

"Trent's not the boss of you," I say. "If you want to do a nude photo shoot for a cause you believe in, do it."

A chuckle falls from that scrumptious half smile. "Who would take the photos?"

"Me. I could do it on your phone." I straighten up, wondering if Lewis will take the plunge or back out.

He half smiles before quirking up an eyebrow. "A nude photo shoot? Seems a bit intimate for two people who are supposed to just be friends and housemates. You sure this isn't just an excuse for you to see me naked?"

He's right. This flies in the face of the "let's just be housemates and friends, nothing more" rule we set for ourselves when we started living together. Because orchestrating a naked photo shoot with your superhot housemate that you're crushing on is guaranteed to test that boundary.

But I'm one thousand percent okay with that. And there's a flash behind Lewis's eyes that makes me think that he's keen on the idea too—maybe he just needs some teasing words of encouragement.

And that spurs me on. This feels a lot like a naughty game of one-upmanship we're playing—let's see who's the first to admit that this photo shoot is as much an excuse for us to engage in some naughty activities as it is for charity.

"I'll admit, there are worse things in the world than seeing you naked." I keep eye contact with him as I speak, which he seems completely into, judging by the way his smile widens. "But it also sounds like you're interested in dropping a line to your fans on social media and staging your reentry to the business on your own terms. This could be a fun way to do that. You could post a few tasteful nudes on your accounts as a way to let your fan base know that you're doing okay. You wouldn't have to reveal your location, so you'd still be able to maintain your privacy, but it would be something you could give to your fans to show them that you're still thinking about them."

The gears in my brain crank at full speed as this idea takes hold.

"You could make a digital calendar out of the rest of the photos taken, and people can buy and print them. And you can give a portion of the profits to charity. This would be a great way to sort of test the waters of your comeback while you still remain on hiatus. You'll get an idea of how people will receive you when you're ready to step back fully into the limelight. And you'll be doing something sexy *and* charitable."

He makes a "not bad" face just before that half smile makes a reappearance. I bite my lip. He's completely into this, just like I am.

"We're adults," I say. "We can keep things professional during this naked photo shoot, I'm sure."

There's a flash behind his hazel eyes, like he doesn't quite believe what I've said and is just as eager as I am to see it all play out.

"So? What do you think?" I ask.

"I think that I'm on board. Let's do it."

"And you're sure that's not the vodka talking," I ask to confirm he's of sound mind and body before I take in all of his body…for the sake of the arts, of course.

"That might have loosened me up, but I'm ready to do this. And I trust you," he says.

Wow. I clear my throat to keep my triumphant squeal at bay. This is hands down the ballsiest thing I've ever done: proposing a naked photo shoot starring the celebrity I'm crushing on with me as the photographer.

But Lewis is completely into it. And it's for a good cause—not just an excuse to see him naked.

That's what I tell myself as I watch him down the last of his drink, mesmerized by the pulse of his throat as he swallows.

We chat and hammer out the details for the photo shoot. He mentions donating the money he receives from selling the pics to an LGBTQIA+ charity that his friend volunteers with.

"Seeing the work that you do with Glad You're Here makes me realize that I need to do more to support charities."

"That would be amazing, Lewis."

When everything's finalized, he sets the empty glass down on the counter and wags his eyebrow at me. "Time to get naked." He walks off toward the hallway, then spins around and winks at me. "For charity."

When he disappears, I take a second to think about what's about to go down. A nude photo shoot of Lewis with me as the photographer. Holy shit.

"Are you ready?"

Lewis flashes a crooked smile at my question, his eye contact steady, completely unfazed by the fact that in a matter of seconds, he'll be totally naked in front of me.

"I'm ready. Let's do this."

His hand falls to the belt of his robe, and like a reflex my gaze follows. He moves like he's about to loosen it, and my eyes widen. He tightens it instead, and I quietly clear my throat.

"Hey now. Eyes up here."

My cheeks catch fire at his teasing. When I look up at him, he winks, which makes me flash what I'm certain is the goofiest grin ever.

I quickly reel it in. "Just doing a quick wardrobe check."

"Wardrobe check? On a nude photo shoot?" He chuckles. "How very thorough of you. And professional."

"That's me. One hundred percent professional all the time." I turn toward the veranda, twisting my head away so that he can't see the giddy smile I fail to hold back.

He follows me out onto the veranda and I point to the chaise lounge. "Wanna start there?"

"Sure."

Sweat beads at my brow. And the back of my neck. And between my boobs. I'm about to photograph one of the hottest TV stars in the world. In my house. Butt-ass naked.

I swallow all the saliva in my mouth and hold up his phone. "Whenever you're ready. Whatever pose you'd like to start with."

"I was actually wondering if you had any ideas on where you'd like me to start. I know this is pretty casual, but you're the photographer—the one in charge. You get to tell me what to do."

My gaze lands on his hand while he plays with the knot of his robe.

"Where do you want me?"

My throat goes dry at his perfectly reasonable question.

What are you, thirteen? Get it together.

I start to answer, but then he pulls the belt completely

loose and in one swift move shrugs off his robe. A millisecond later I'm staring at Lewis in his birthday suit.

I tell my eyes to behave themselves. I remind myself of the manners my parents ingrained in me since I was a little kid, of how it's impolite to stare. But if my parents were standing here looking at Lewis in all his nude glory, they'd be staring wide-eyed too. Anyone would be.

Any semblance of the half-hearted professionalism I've been maintaining ever since we kicked off this shoot goes flying out the window. Because all I can process in this moment is how incredible Lewis looks.

I scan his body from head to toe in a millisecond, but I capture a lot in that small amount of time. His six-foot-three frame is a beautiful blend of lean muscle, tan skin, and golden body hair. And lines. So many hard lines. Like the ones running along his abs. And his chest. And separating his impressive quads from his hamstrings. And those deep V lines running along his obliques that lead straight to his…

The breath I let out while I fixate on his impressive length is so hot, I fog up my own glasses.

Dear god. You are such a cliché.

"I look okay, then?"

I divert my bulging eyes back up to his face, which is sporting a cheeky grin.

I clear my throat. "I think you're well aware of how you look." I'm proud of just how steady my voice sounds when I'm a raging five-alarm fire on the inside.

His smile widens, and that dimple I love so much appears in his right cheek.

"I am aware. But it's always nice to hear from the photographer on a shoot if they think I look good. Helps build up the confidence to get a professional's opinion, you know?"

I chuckle at how playful he's being.

"In my professional opinion, you look hot as hell, Lewis." I manage a steady tone even as my cheeks tingle.

"Thanks."

He lowers himself onto the chaise and lies down, keeping one leg flat while bending the other to shield his goods. He drapes one arm over his chest and lolls his head slightly to the side. I snap a few shots before he sits up and poses with his legs bent, elbows resting on his knees. I move over to get a profile shot of his pose.

"Thank god no one has built up that hillside directly opposite your house, huh? They'd be in for one hell of a shocking view if they looked out their window right about now."

I laugh and suggest he stand up and lean his elbows on the wooden railing of the veranda while looking out into the distance. "And try for a more thoughtful facial expression, a side of you people aren't used to seeing," I suggest, managing to get into the actual aesthetic of the shoot.

Lewis takes direction like the pro he is. He knows when to vary his movements only slightly to refine a pose and when it's better to try something different.

"You're really good at this," I say as I move around to follow the sunlight to better illuminate the shot.

"You're a good photographer," he says, and he holds that pensive look on his face as I snap a pic.

"It's only because I have a good model to work with. I honestly have no idea what I'm doing."

"Well, you're doing a better job than a chunk of the photographers I've worked with. You're not screaming unintelligible directions at me or making me hold uncomfortable positions. That slingshots you all the way to the top in my book."

I chuckle a "thanks" before pausing for a moment. "I know we talked about not having any full-frontal nudity, but how would you feel about a backside shot? You leaning on the railing, flexing a bit to really show off your back and leg muscles? With the sun lighting you from behind and the rocky hillside in the background, you'd look like a warrior. I think your fans would go wild for that."

He beams. "I'm into it."

I take a few snaps. When I walk over and show them to him, his face lights up. "Damn, you're right. Something about that image looks so raw."

"And powerful."

I reach up to smooth down his hair.

"Did I get a bit messy?" He grins.

"A little."

Our stares connect for a few seconds. I'm standing just inches from his naked body. I can feel the warmth from his skin skimming along my body.

As much as I love it, I take a step back so I don't come off like a total creep. "Should we take some interior shots?"

He nods, and I notice the look on his face is slightly dazed. For the next hour, I take photos of Lewis lying down on the hardwood floor, in the doorways of the house, even next to a pile of raw construction materials in the garage.

By the end of it, we're laughing and chatting, like we've done this a million times before.

"These photos are incredible, Harper," he says as he

secures the belt of his robe around his waist. "Your eye is really sharp."

"Maybe my architect's eye for design and aesthetic came into play. But it was mostly due to you. It's amazing how comfortable you are in front of the camera with no clothes on."

"It's always better to be naked," he says before filling a glass with water.

I ignore the flash of heat his teasing words unleash inside me. He's clearly joking, so I offer my own joke in return.

"Except when you're in public," I say.

When I look up, I notice he's still got that easy smile on his face, but his expression has turned determined.

"Is that a dare?" he asks.

I bite my lip, knowing full well where this line of teasing is headed. "If you want it to be."

He steps toward me, takes a swig from the glass, then roughly wipes his mouth with the back of his hand. "I don't ever back down from a dare."

His voice is a low growl that has me aching to push this playful moment even further. It's clear he's game for it.

"Okay. I dare you to pose nude in public."

He's full-on beaming, like he's been waiting for me to say those words all day.

Eyes still on me, he takes another step toward me before taking a long pull from his glass. "Just name the time and place. I'm there."

My throat's gone dry and my skin is tingling at this ridiculous yet totally hot back-and-forth. I grab the glass from his hand and drain the rest of the water.

My chest heaves as I catch my breath. "Tonight. Ten

o'clock. Wear something loose fitting that you can take off and throw back on quickly."

Lewis licks his lips as he smirks. My entire body catches fire.

"Yes, ma'am."

Chapter Twelve

Harper

It's past eleven when I pull into the Marina District of San Francisco. I'm pumped when I see a free spot along Baker Street, right next to the park that houses the Palace of Fine Arts. I turn off the headlights before I even shift into Park. Gripping the steering wheel with both hands, I peer around the darkened grassy area. No sign of people loitering around, just like I hoped.

"You going into spy mode?" Lewis chuckles from the passenger seat.

"Just trying to make sure the coast is clear."

I glance over at him. He's dressed in gray sweats, flip-flops, and a long-sleeve T-shirt—all items that are easy to throw on and off quickly, which is crucial for this stealthy photo shoot to work out.

I twist in my seat to face him. "You sure you're okay with this? It's fine if you want to back out."

"Nope. Like I said before, I never back down from a dare. I'm pumped for this."

Nerves and excitement have overridden our flirty vibe from earlier today. Now my main concern is getting some killer shots of Lewis without getting arrested for trespassing. Even though the park is technically closed at night and there's no one around, we need to work quickly while also being as quiet as possible so that we're not spotted.

"Okay, so, I was thinking we could do some shots of you in the middle of the actual palace structure. Somewhere you're standing and then a couple where you're sitting or leaning against the structure and mimicking the pose of *The Thinker.*"

"I like that."

"I think we'll be able to get some epic shots of you that would look amazing in the calendar. And since the Palace of Fine Arts is such an iconic San Francisco landmark, any fans and paparazzi who happen to see the photos will flock there, thinking that's where you are, when you'll actually be in Half Moon Bay."

"Genius."

I take a deep breath and grip my phone tight in my hand. "You ready?"

Lewis's eyes sparkle. "I'm ready."

Together we climb out of the car and shut our doors as quietly as we can. We walk side by side in total silence through the grass leading up to the Greco-Roman-style rotunda of the palace, which is the architectural focal point of the entire park.

When we reach the structure, I scan the surrounding area once more. A few cars drive along the street nearby, but they don't seem to notice us in the dark.

My heart assumes a frenzied beat as I turn to Lewis, who's already shed his clothes and is standing in the center of the rotunda. I quickly snap a dozen photos of him as he stands tall. Thankfully the nearby streetlights and the full moon above provide just the right amount of light to illuminate his form in the darkness.

"How's this?" he whispers as he turns to give me an exquisite shot of his backside.

"Perfection."

He leans against the gold-brown-hued structure and mimics the *Thinker* pose. I hold back a squeal. "This is dynamite, Lewis. People are gonna flip when they see—"

"Hey! What are you doing here? The park's closed!"

I whip my head around and spot a dark figure about a hundred feet away jogging toward us, flashlight in hand.

"Shit," we blurt in unison.

"Run?"

"Run!"

Lewis doesn't even bother to throw on his clothes before he takes off, his sweatpants and shirt in hand. I sprint as fast as my short legs will take me, but I can't keep up with his monster stride.

"You stop right now!" the guy, who I assume is either a security guard or cop, yells behind us.

My lungs are on fire as I pump harder and harder in an attempt to catch up to Lewis. Just then, he spins around, scoops me off my feet, and chucks me over his shoulder.

I yelp at just how swift and strong he is. Even my added weight doesn't seem to slow him down. He speeds ahead toward our car, barely even panting.

"Almost to the car," he huffs.

And that's when I realize I'm facing his ass. His beautiful, bare, solid, upside-down ass. My eyes go wide at the sight. Even in the nighttime, it's crystal clear just what a flawless backside Lewis has.

Before I can dwell too much on it, he sets me down, opens the passenger door, and I jump inside. He hops into the driver's seat, starts the car, and speeds away. As he peels down the street, I twist in my seat to catch a glimpse of the person chasing us, who's now a tiny dot in the distance. I let out a shaky breath. That means he didn't get a good look at us or my car.

Lewis weaves through the hilly streets of San Francisco for the next minute before easing to a stop at a traffic light. When we turn to look at each other, we don't speak a word—I'm too busy processing the chaos of the last minute, and I bet he is too. His face is red from running, and our chests heave in tandem as we catch our breath. Then I glance down at Lewis's torso…and promptly direct my eyes back to his face. Because he's still totally naked.

We burst out laughing at the same moment.

"Apologies for riding bare-ass in the driver's seat of your car," he says. "There was no time to get dressed."

I spot the pile of his clothes bunched up near my feet. I clutch my stomach as I nearly pass out, I'm laughing so hard. When I catch my breath, I wipe my eyes. "No apologies necessary. Especially after you scooped me up like a superhero and sprinted us to safety. I was definitely deadweight, and we would have gotten caught if you hadn't done that."

The light turns green, and he pulls ahead. "It was no problem. You mind if I find a place to park so I can get dressed?"

"Go right ahead."

I put my hand over my mouth, in awe of this moment. We went from the adrenaline rush of almost getting arrested for trespassing to laughing our asses off in less than a minute. And now, as Lewis drives my car stark naked, it somehow feels so natural and comfortable. I can't remember the last time I did something so ridiculous or had so much fun.

Lewis pulls into an open parking spot in front of a late-night diner. I hand him his clothes and pivot slightly to my right and look out the window, giving him as much privacy as I can in my cramped hatchback while he gets dressed.

"Decent," he says after a minute.

"You want some food?" I point to the diner, which boasts a sign on the window touting the best milkshakes and fries in all of the Bay Area. "My treat."

He grins. "Sure."

We order two milkshakes and a large basket of fries to go, then sit on the hood of my car and chow down. I glance over at Lewis, about to tell him that we can sit in the car if he wants to avoid being spotted, but he looks completely relaxed. If he were uncomfortable, I'm sure he would have said something.

"Sorry I almost got us arrested. Or ticketed. Or whatever the penalty is for loitering at a public park after dark to take nude photos," I say after sipping my strawberry malt.

Lewis frowns at me. "Why are you sorry? That was a blast. I haven't had that much fun in a long, long time."

"Really?" I quirk an eyebrow at him. "You go to award shows and galas and premieres. Running buck naked from a security guard on a random night while carrying me over your shoulder is your idea of a good time?" I tease.

Something flickers behind his eyes as he stares at me. "Yeah. It is."

My instinct is to assume he's just being polite. He's a celebrity—a bona fide TV star. He's accustomed to doing exciting and glamorous things every day—things that regular people like me could never imagine doing.

Or maybe he's telling the truth and really did have fun. But that's probably just the novelty of doing something completely different. If Lewis had to live the regular life I lived in Half Moon Bay day after day, long-term, I'm sure he'd grow bored of it. A guy who is used to working on TV and movie sets all over the world wouldn't be happy living my normal-person life.

"Do you miss the city at all?" he asks, pulling me out of my thoughts.

I take in the bustle of San Francisco at night, something I haven't seen in the last month that I've been gone. Even though it's the middle of the night, it's still busy. Vehicles dart in and out of traffic, honking their horns every few seconds. People make their way up and down the street, filtering in and out of the nearby businesses, not paying one of bit of attention to us. I chuckle.

"Yeah, I do miss it."

"Is it hard being away?"

I shake my head. "I love Half Moon Bay. And as much as I enjoy the vibe of San Francisco, the food, how gorgeous it is, it's nice to take a break and reset for a while. I'll live here again someday. I still own an apartment in Nob Hill that I love, despite how tiny it is compared to my grandparents' house. And it's easy for me to make it out here when I start to miss it. Like tomorrow, I'll be here with my cousin to help her shop for wedding dresses. We'll spend most of the day hitting up some of my favorite places. I'll get a taste of what I love before heading back to Half Moon Bay."

Lewis looks down at his feet and shoves his hands in his pockets. "I get that. Sometimes you have to go away for a while and miss where you come from to really appreciate it."

"Do you feel that way about LA?"

"Not really. LA is fine, I grew up in the area, but after my grandparents died, it's never really felt like home, honestly. I just live there because it's more convenient to be closer to most of the major studios and lots. I like San Francisco a lot more. And Half Moon Bay too. The vibe is more on par with what I need right now. Half Moon Bay is more relaxed and laid-back instead of hustling all the time." He pivots his gaze back to me. "I never thought I'd like hiding out at some coastal town. But I do. And it's because of you."

"Because of me?"

The muscle in his jaw bulges slightly while he nods at me. "Yeah. I thought hiding out for three months was gonna suck. But then I met you, and you turned my world upside down in the best way. Living with you, seeing you every day... I've never had a better time with anyone, Harper. You're incredible."

He runs his tongue along his bottom lip while keeping those hazel eyes on me. I swear something inside me breaks. A second later I realize what it is: my resolve. Because I think I'm on the verge of setting fire to that "let's just be friends and housemates, nothing more" boundary after what Lewis just admitted—and I think he is too.

"You wanna head back?" My voice is raspy even after I clear my throat. "It's late and we've got a bit of a drive ahead of—"

"Yeah," he growls.

We hop into the car, and Lewis speeds us out of the city toward Half Moon Bay. We stay quiet for the first part of the drive, almost like we know that attempting small talk is no use given the palpable tension between us.

"I like you, Lewis," I blurt when we make it onto the interstate.

"I like you too," he says, his gaze focused on the darkened road ahead.

"I'm, like, insanely attracted to you. Like, off the charts attracted to you." My heart thunders as I admit this out loud. Yeah, it's wild that I'm being so up front about this. But I've never been someone to beat around the bush when it comes to romantic feelings. In the past, when I liked a guy, I told them. Sometimes it worked out, sometimes it didn't. My personality is to be as direct as possible when I feel like it's the right thing to do. I don't want to waste anyone's time, including mine.

"Well, that works out pretty well, because I'm insanely attracted to you too," Lewis says.

I swallow back a moan. "Good. That's really, really good."

We both clear our throats and shift in our seats at the exact same moment.

"I'm gonna pounce on you," I say, mimicking his straight-ahead stare. "The minute we get into the house, I'm gonna tackle you. I'm gonna tear your clothes off your body. I'm not even kidding. I'll probably shred the fabric."

A throaty chuckle rips from his throat. "Good. I like it when a woman gets rough with me."

My mouth falls open, and I inhale as pressure builds between my legs. I lick my lips while Lewis presses harder on the gas pedal. We're only halfway to the house, and my thighs are quivering with the urge to feel him everywhere. I close my eyes, my chest rising and falling with each breath while I pull up the memory of Lewis going hard in my hand all those weeks ago. Then I pull up the image in my brain of his dick from earlier today: unclothed, out in the open, in all its glory.

The ache between my legs throbs harder and harder. Shit. I'm not gonna make it.

I slip my hand underneath the waistband of my yoga pants and let out a slow hiss.

"Holy shit."

I glance over at Lewis, whose eyes are bulging as he gawks at me. He swerves slightly, then quickly straightens out the car. There's a flash of lightning in the distance followed by a crack of thunder. Fitting that the weather is about to go wild right along with us.

"Eyes on the road, Lewis," I pant as I swirl the pads of my fingertips slowly around my soaking-wet epicenter.

He nods quickly before frowning down at his lap, then looking up again.

"I just need to get this first orgasm out of my system. And then..." My jaw drops as the pressure builds and I work my fingers faster. I inhale sharply. "You can have the next one."

"And the one after that?"

My head lolls against the headrest as I look at him. "That's ambitious."

His jaw tenses before he grins at me. "I guess we'll find out."

I can tell by the way he's white-knuckling the steering wheel, by the bulge in his sweatpants, that he's turned on seeing me touch myself, and it's giving me the biggest ego boost. Here's this sexy TV star that millions of people are in love with...and he's into me.

He pulls the car to the side of the road and turns off the engine.

"What are you…"

He unbuckles his seat belt and twists to face me, moving so he's just inches from me. "Show me," he growls. "Show me how you like it, Harper. I wanna see." Even in the darkness I can make out the generous angle at the front of his sweatpants. Seeing how turned on he is makes me even hotter. I lift my hips and yank my yoga pants down to my knees, then I slide my greedy hand back inside my underwear. I swirl my fingers as fast I as I can, limbs shaking, body aching. I've never done this before, touched myself in front of another person, and I'm blown away at how hot it gets me.

It's not long before I'm thrashing against the seat, yelping and screaming as pleasure pulses through me.

"Fuck yeah. Just like that, baby," he groans, his face next to mine, close enough to kiss me.

The gritty rasp of his voice has me shuddering while I ride the final wave of my orgasm. He shoves his seat back as far as it will go, lowers it down, then reaches over and pulls me onto his lap as I come down. I brace my hands on his chest.

He huffs out a hot breath, looking dazed. "Is this okay? Sorry, I guess I should have…"

I yank at his shirt and tug it off, tossing it aside. "More than okay. It's fucking hot. I've wanted to be on top of you since…since…"

"Since we bumped into each other in the hallway and you grabbed my dick." His chest rises with the ragged breath he takes.

I beam at him before leaning down and grabbing his face in my hands, and finally, *finally* I kiss him.

I try to go the slow and teasing route, to draw this out as much as I can, but I break seconds into it. Just the soft, warm, wet feel of Lewis's tongue drives me so wild that I turn sloppy. Soon I'm nipping at his divinely plump bottom lip.

"I've wanted to do this for so long too," he mumbles between kisses.

His hands glide up my back and under my top. I shiver. He drags his mouth along the hinge of my jaw and leaves a soft bite on my skin.

"Oh my god. Lewis."

"Fuck, I love hearing you moan my name. I wanna hear you scream it, though."

My head falls and I moan, savoring the feel of his mouth on the side of my neck. His hot breath ghosts across my skin, and I'm shaking. I need Lewis inside me right now. The prudent thing to do would be to get back on the road and drive to the house so we can ravage each other properly in bed, but I don't have the patience for that. We've been skirting around our feelings for each other for weeks, and I can't put it off a millisecond longer. And as I feel Lewis's cock turn to steel underneath me, it's clear he wants this just as bad as me.

"I have to have you, Lewis. I can't wait."

"Yes, baby. Take what you want from me. Right here, right now."

I lean up, propping my knees against the center console and the driver's side door so that I can yank his sweatpants down to his knees. My mouth waters at the sight of him, huge and hard, just for me. I'm stuttering as he pulls my panties down my legs with impressive smoothness and speed before ripping off my top.

"Wait."

"Condom."

I chuckle at how even in our massively turned-on states, we've both got safety on the mind. Lewis grabs his wallet from the center console, pulls out a condom, tears it open, and sheaths himself. With his hands on my hips, he gently lowers me down.

My jaw plummets to the floor, and my head falls back. "Holy…fucking…shit…"

He groans underneath me. "Fuck, you feel incredible."

"You're so big. Oh my god, you feel so good."

"Careful, you're gonna give me a big head—FUCK!"

His shout rattles the car as I start to bounce up and down on him. Maybe I should have given him a warning, but I can't help it. I'm consumed with the need to ride him.

As I work myself on top of him, the pleasure is almost too much. How can he make me feel this good, this quickly?

He digs his hands into my hips, and I take in the look of concentration on his face, like he's trying to hold on for dear life.

"I know… I know this isn't the most romantic thing in the world, to ride you in my car." I start to circle my clit with my hand, and I feel that telltale pressure and heat build inside me.

"What are you talking about?" A breathy chuckle falls from Lewis's lips. "You riding me is romantic as fuck in my book."

I let out a laugh that quickly turns into a moan. As my fingers work my clit faster and faster, I notice Lewis's gaze falls there.

"I'm dying to taste you, Harper. The second we get

back to the house, I'm taking you to bed and I'm going to lick your clit till you're screaming."

It's his growled words that send me over the edge. The second I explode, I'm thrashing and shouting his name. Underneath me I feel his body harden. A stream of profanity and grunts mixes with my yells. I collapse on top of his chest. For a minute I just lie there and catch my breath as raindrops pound the exterior of the car. Thunder cracks in the distance.

I glance up at him, heartened that he's already gazing down at me.

"Ready for round two?" he asks.

I nod and giggle before scrambling back to my seat. We quickly throw on our clothes, and Lewis speeds to the house in record time despite the rainstorm that's picked up. He hops out and jogs to my side, rips open my door, pulls me out, and tosses me over his shoulder again. I giggle, feeling high and dizzy from my orgasms and seeing Lewis pull such a carnal move.

He runs us so quickly to the front door we barely get a drop of rain on us, even though it's pouring. The second we step inside, he kicks the door shut and grabs me by the waist, pulling me against him. I reach up and lead him into a filthy kiss. It's slower than when we were kissing in the car. He runs his hands along my arm, my waist, my hips. It's like he's taking his time so that he can savor how I taste, how every part of my body feels.

It's exactly what I hoped he'd do. As glorious as it was to have the frenzied, desperate fuck in the car, it felt a lot like blowing off steam—in the hottest way. That was the culmination of weeks of tension and flirting, and it was incredible. But I want this time to be slower and longer.

He hoists me up, and I wrap my legs around his waist. Just like earlier this evening, he carries me with ease, only this time he's kissing me breathless.

"Where do you want this? My room or yours?" he asks between kisses.

I tug at his hair. "Whichever is closer."

He smiles against my mouth, then walks us down the hall and turns right into the guest bedroom where he's staying. When he lowers me onto the bed, he pulls away from me and tugs off his shirt.

"I really, really like it when you do that."

The corner of his mouth quirks up. "Do what? Take my clothes off?"

I nod excitedly, which earns me a throaty chuckle.

"I think we've seen enough of me naked. How about you now?"

He leans down and skims the hem of my shirt with his fingertips. Even though it's such a light amount of contact, it still sends goose bumps flying across my skin. Right as I move to pull off my shirt, there's a deafening clap of thunder that shakes the entire house.

Lewis leans back and stands, gazing up. "Holy shit, that was loud."

"I bet we can be louder."

I tug him by the waistband and he turns back to me, smug grin on his face. "I like the way you think."

He leans down and slides his hands up under my shirt, palming my boobs. I moan against his mouth at the feel of his broad, firm palms cupping my soft flesh.

Outside the wind and rain pick up, pounding harder and harder against the windows and the roof. Another crack of thunder causes us to jump, and we chuckle as we kiss. A massive gust of wind howls outside, causing the lights to flicker for a half second.

Just then a loud crashing noise blasts through the house, shaking the floor.

I yelp right as Lewis jumps off me.

"Shit!"

I clasp my hands to my chest and breathe. Lewis grabs his pants from the floor before walking out of the room. I run after him, and together we look all over the living room and kitchen but find nothing out of place.

"It sounded like it came from inside the house. This makes no sense," I say.

"Maybe it was the garage."

Lewis opens the door to the garage, and we step outside to investigate, but we find nothing. He hits the garage door opener on the wall, and as it slowly rises, our jaws drop.

"Oh no," we mutter in unison.

The elm tree that used to stand near the front of the yard lies across the driveway, just a foot behind where our cars are parked. As if on cue, the rain lightens to a sprinkle and the winds die down. It's like someone flipped a switch.

"At least it missed our cars," I mumble.

"Yeah. That's lucky." Lewis lets out a sad laugh. "We should probably start cutting it up to remove it."

"What—now?"

He nods. "You're going back into the city to meet up with your cousin tomorrow, right?"

I deflate. He's right. I'm due for a ten o'clock appointment at a bridal boutique in San Francisco to help Naomi try on wedding dresses.

I tug at my hair and groan before stepping up to him.

"I was so ready to say screw the tree, we'll take care of it later, and drag you back to your bedroom for round two."

He pulls me into him and wraps his arms around my waist. "Believe me, I want to do that more than anything." He presses his hips forward and I feel the unmistakable evidence of just how badly he wants that. "But you can't miss seeing your cousin. And now that the storm's passed and it's just raining, it's best to get started on chopping that tree up now. It's likely to take a few hours." He pulls his phone out of his pocket and squints at the screen. It's already almost three in the morning.

"But what about…" I nod at the massive bulge at the front of his pants.

He swallows and flashes a strained smile. "The minute I start working on that tree, it'll go away."

When he leans over and kisses my forehead, I instantly melt.

"We'll start things up after you get home from going out with your cousin," he says before leaning down to kiss me on the mouth. "Or the day after. Whenever you want me and you're ready, I'm here for you."

Just when I didn't think I could melt any more, I do. Right here, standing in the garage, into a puddle of pure goo. Because Lewis's sweetness is off the charts, and I absolutely adore it.

I squeeze my arms tighter around him, relishing how good it feels to cuddle against him. "You're the best, you know that?"

"So I've been told."

We pull apart, and Lewis throws on his work boots, then grabs the chain saw from the corner of the garage. I opt for the small axe covered in dust that *Apong* Bernie would use to chop firewood when I was a kid. I've gotta expend this pent-up sexual energy somehow. May as well take it out on the fallen tree.

Lewis steps out into the light rain, then twists back to look at me. "Ready to get to work?"

I sigh. "I'm ready."

Chapter Thirteen

Lewis

I reach into the shower and turn the water on hot. Steam fills the narrow bathroom as I shed my soaking-wet clothes onto the floor. All the muscles in my body are aching from spending the last few hours slicing up the fallen tree. But there's only one ache I'm focused on.

I glance down at my rock-hard dick. Just the memory of Harper getting herself off while sitting next to me in the car, then riding me until I burst, has me steely. I close my eyes and groan as I tug the base of my shaft.

I'd give anything to feel her dainty hands on me instead of my own. But that's not a possibility. She's got to meet her cousin in a couple of hours, and she needs to be rested for that. That's why I sent her inside after an hour of helping me chop the tree. As badly as I want her again—as much as I'm going out of my mind imagining her silky skin on my skin, her full, soft lips all over me—it wouldn't have been right. Because when our second time together happens, I'm gonna need to take my time. Right now we can't have the kind of long, slow, carnal fuck I'm aching to give her. So a quick jerk-off in the shower is what I'll have to do to tide myself over until we can finally be together the way that we deserve to be.

I reach my free hand into the stream of water, pleased at the steamy temp. Stepping in, I turn away from the spray and let the hot water pound my aching back and shoulders. When I close my eyes, I see a highlight reel of my favorite images from the drive back from San Francisco. Harper's hand sliding down the front of her yoga pants. Her teeth biting down on those beautifully bee-stung lips. The pink flush painting her cheeks. How her nipples turned to stiff peaks under the thin cotton of her top. How her tits bounced as she worked herself on top of me. How fucking good she felt. How her sweet sounds of ecstasy made my heart race and my dick throb.

I tighten my grip as I work myself in my own hand. God, this woman. I've never met anyone like her. Feisty and fierce, gorgeous and confident, brilliant and sweet, all in equal amounts.

Pleasure pulses through my body in the form of an ache, starting at the base of my spine and shooting all the way to my torso and my lower abdomen. I bite back a groan as the ache between my thighs gets hotter and harder. As loud as I wish I could be in this moment, I don't want to wake Harper.

Eyes still closed, I spin around to face the spray of hot water and press the palm of my free hand against the tile wall to brace myself. I pull up the memory of her coming on top of me in the car just hours ago. And then I pull up the memory of her grabbing my cock weeks ago. I still think it was hot. As fuck.

Already my knees are weak, but that's how wild she makes me. One accidental grip of her hand around my cock, one hot makeout session, one frenzied fuck in the car, one instance of me watching her touch herself has me ready to come quicker than I ever have.

I work my hand faster, the familiar crushing sensation hitting my chest. I know what a terrible idea this is, us hooking up. We're only halfway through our time together, and things are bound to get complicated from this moment on.

But I don't fucking care. She's worth all the risk.

I think of her perfect little body, that sexy-as-fuck smile, her sweetness, her kindness, her thoughtfulness, her moans, the way her voice goes soft when she's tired...

No one, not one single person I've ever met before has ever gotten me this turned on this quickly. There's a connection between us, something I can no longer fight—something that I don't want to spend one more second denying. Something I've never felt with anyone before.

I care about this woman. I care about what makes her happy. I care about her needs, what her goals and dreams are, how she takes her coffee in the morning, whether she likes it hard and fast or sweet and slow in bed...

My breath catches as the pressure inside me intensifies. My spine turns to liquid and my knees nearly give out as the pleasure climbs higher and higher...

Consequences be damned, I want Harper—I *need* Harper.

I explode with a caveman grunt that echoes against the bathroom walls. It's so powerful that my ears ring when I spill against the shower wall in front of me. I swear I go blind for a solid five seconds while my body shudders through my climax. Blinking furiously, I start to make out the slate gray tile and the stream of water in front of my face. I do a quick shampoo and soap up my body, then rinse before shutting off the water and drying off.

As I wrap the towel around my waist and wipe away the steam from the mirror, I catch a glimpse of my reflection. I'm smiling like a smug bastard. Because I know that I'm screwed. I'm so damn into Harper.

Shaking my head, I brush my teeth and get ready for bed, counting down the hours to when I get to see her again.

Chapter Fourteen

Harper

My jaw falls to the floor when Naomi strolls out of the dressing room and into the open area of the bridal boutique.

I straighten up in the plush armchair I'm sitting in. "Holy shit."

She flashes a hesitant smile. The store associate, Mari, offers her hand to help Naomi step on the round fitting platform that faces a semicircle of mirrors.

"You look stunning," I say. "You're the most beautiful bride I've ever seen."

She chuckles as she glances down at the delicate lace material of her dress, like she doesn't believe me. But when she looks up and sees her reflection in the mirror, her brown eyes bulge.

"Whoa…"

Mari lets out a laugh. "And you thought the long sleeves and lace would make you look old-fashioned."

"I was wrong," Naomi murmurs.

"The color scheme gives it such an updated touch too," Mari says. "The super-soft rose-gold hue under the white lace makes your tan skin glow."

I nod along with Mari. A beautiful smile spreads

across Naomi's face as she looks at herself in the mirror. She runs her hands along the bodice of the off-the-shoulder sheath gown that flares slightly at the hem. It fits her tall frame perfectly. Even the gentle sweetheart neckline hits at the perfect spot: it covers her chest completely while leaving a tiny peek of cleavage for a hint of sexiness. A moment later she starts to tear up.

"Oh my god." I fan my face when my eyes begin to well up too.

Naomi cups her hands over her mouth. "I think this is the one."

I nod quickly, thanking the associate when she hands me a tissue, then gives one to Naomi. I stand up and walk the few steps to my cousin and hold her hand.

"I've never seen you look so beautiful," I say with a shaky voice.

Naomi blubbers a thank-you before leaning down to hug me. "My mom's gonna be so mad that I found the dress without her."

I let out a snotty laugh, careful not to cry on the wedding gown.

"I really didn't think I'd find the one my first time shopping," she says as we break apart.

"Finding your dress the first time you shop happens more often than you think," Mari says before darting off to grab a tape measure to take her measurements.

"Your mom will forgive you when she sees you in it," I say.

While we're dabbing at our eyes, the door flies open and in walks Maren, our friend from college, dressed in a pair of light blue scrubs. Her mouth opens as she cups her hands over her face. When she stumbles over, I pull her into a hug.

"You made it!" Naomi squeals.

"I thought you had to work!" I squeeze Maren's tall and lanky frame in my arms.

She shifts her teary gaze from Naomi to me. "I managed to get someone to cover the second half of my shift at the hospital." When she lets go of me, she steps over to Naomi and pulls her into a hug.

"You are the most beautiful bride I've ever seen," Maren says, her lips trembling.

"That's what I said." I wipe at my eyes, and the three of us share watery laughs.

Naomi grabs my hands in both of hers. "Thank you for coming with me. I'm so happy I got to do this with you. And that we ended up falling in love with the same dress. I was scared for a while there."

I chuckle while thinking about the first three dresses she tried on. Either she hated one that I loved or the reverse happened. I fill Maren in on how contentious the first half of the appointment was.

Her head falls back as she laughs. She tugs loose her messy bun, and a cascade of wavy black tendrils falls nearly to her waist. "What do you think? Should I get it cut before your wedding or leave it long?"

"Long," Naomi and I say at the same time.

"You look like a mermaid," Naomi says. "So pretty."

Maren makes a scrunch-smile face. "You sound like my *apong*. She's says I shouldn't ever cut my hair because I look more attractive with it long."

"I feel attacked." I point to my messy bob that hits just under my chin.

Naomi and Maren burst into giggles. Mari returns and begins taking Naomi's measurements.

"Simon is gonna pass out when he sees you walk down the aisle," I say.

Naomi's expression turns wistful. She scrunches her mouth right as a cheesy grin appears. "I hope so."

"One thousand percent he will," Maren says. "How's the venue hunt going?"

Naomi beams. "Oh, I forgot to tell you! We're doing it at the San Francisco Mint."

Maren gasps. "That's so romantic!"

I nod my head, still impressed by how Simon pulled off one hell of a romantic gesture there. One of his clients held their vow renewal at the Mint over a year ago. That was when Naomi was filming Simon for an online series she was working on for her job...and they were harboring hard-core feelings for each other while engaging in a friends-with-benefits relationship. Naomi's commitmentphobic tendencies at the time after years of failed relationships were the reason why she was so hesitant to pursue anything serious with Simon. But after he gave an impromptu speech following the renewal ceremony, during which he confessed his love for Naomi, she realized just how badly she wanted to be with him. They confessed their feelings and exchanged *I love you*s. It was the official kickoff to their relationship.

While Mari takes Naomi's hip measurement, Maren's phone rings. When she steps away to answer it, Naomi pivots toward me. "So how are things going with your living situation?" she whispers.

The memory of what went down between Lewis and me just hours ago floats to the front of my mind, causing every inch of my skin to tingle.

"It's going fine," I mumble.

"Just fine?"

I fumble with my crumpled tissue, trying to memorize each crinkle. If I make eye contact with my cousin, she'll know right away that something's up. It's a miracle she didn't notice when I first arrived to meet her at the boutique. I've been sporting a permanent flush across my cheeks and chest in the aftermath of what Lewis and I did last night. I've never, ever acted so bold as when I touched myself in full view of Lewis, then rode him to climax immediately after. That thought on top of the vivid sex dream I had when I fell asleep is likely why I feel so dazed and flushed…but Naomi was so focused on trying on wedding dresses that she didn't notice. And for that I was grateful. As soon as we shifted into dress-hunting mode, I was fixated on helping her find the gown of her dreams.

But now that the focus is back on me, I know it's only a matter of time before I break.

"Why are you so red?"

And that's when I know I'm busted. I finally bring myself to look up at her.

"What's up with you?" she presses. "You've got that look on your face."

"What look?"

"The one where you did something major and you're trying to work out in your brain how to tell me."

"Is it that obvious?"

Naomi lifts an eyebrow. "Uh, yeah."

Mari excuses herself to put in the info for Naomi's dress order.

"What living situation?" Maren's smoky topaz eyes dart between me and Naomi after she steps back over to us.

I shoot Naomi a pointed look. Her face twists into a guilty expression. "Sorry," she says softly.

I sigh, wondering what I should say.

Maren holds up a hand. "Okay, I know I've been

slammed with work ever since I moved back to San Francisco, but I'm feeling a bit left out."

I hesitate for a second before realizing how shitty it would be to keep this from Maren. She's my other best friend next to Naomi. I've shared every important personal issue I've ever had with her because she's trustworthy and kind. She'll be able to keep this secret for me, just like Naomi has.

I give Maren a brief summary of the strange sequence of events that led Lewis to become my live-in contractor.

Her mouth is a perfect O when I finish. "Wait, let me get this straight. You're living with Lewis Prescott? *The* Lewis Prescott?"

I nod while glancing around to make sure no one in the salon heard. "You can't tell anyone, though. He's being stalked by the paparazzi and is using my house as a safe hideout. I don't want to betray his trust. He's doing me a huge favor by renovating the place for free."

She mimes zipping her lips. "Won't say a word. Promise."

I quickly tell them about the nude photo shoot and how that led to a flirty conversation, which led to the car shenanigans.

When I finish, Naomi's eyes are bulging, and Maren's mouth is wide-open.

"No way! Oh my freaking god, Harper! You're such a sex kitten!"

I shush Maren. "Would you keep your voice down?"

I glance around the boutique, grateful that we're the only ones in the open area right now.

She whispers, "Sorry."

"Holy crap... I just... Wow," Naomi says. "I didn't think you had it in you. You've always been so... boundary-driven."

"What does that even mean?"

"Just that you're not one to let your emotions get in the way of anything, especially not work, family, all that. I've seen you keep your cool in the most stressful situations. I've seen you shoot down the most suave guys when they try to approach you. The fact that you're letting loose around Lewis is a big deal."

Maren nods in agreement.

The truth of Naomi's observation jolts me. "I guess that's what happens when you have to share a living space with a hot TV star," I say. "My resolve isn't iron-clad. I was bound to break."

"You're only human, Harper. And honestly? You deserve this fun hookup."

Maren piggybacks on Naomi's comment. "You spent years putting your career first and your love life on the back burner. When was the last time you had this much fun with a guy?"

I rack my brain, unable to come up with a single guy I dated who compares to Lewis.

A satisfied smile tugs at Naomi's lips. "You should definitely make up for lost time."

"If you won't, I will." Maren wags an eyebrow. "Lewis is one of my hall passes."

Excitement courses through me at the thought of pouncing on Lewis when I arrive home in a few hours.

"Your face. You are so gonna go wild on him," Maren teases.

I roll my eyes in a pathetic attempt to play it cool. It's like we're in middle school and she's teasing me about a boy I'm crushing on.

"You gotta bang in every room of the house," Naomi says matter-of-factly. "To really break it in and make it feel like yours. I mean, I'll always think of it as *Apong* Bernie and *Apong* Vivian's house first and foremost, but the second thought that'll come to mind will be that it's the house where my cousin got it on with a hunky TV star."

I crumple up a tissue and toss it at Naomi, but she sways out of the way, giggling. "Way to taint the sentimental mood of dress shopping today with all this sex talk."

She tilts her head at me. "Have you forgotten just how inappropriate you were when Simon and I were in our 'will we or won't we' phase just before we hooked up? You were hiding vibrators in my work bag. This is payback."

I mumble a disgruntled sound and silently admit that she's right. I teased the hell out of her when she and Simon were trying to stay in the "strictly just coworkers who just so happen to be attracted to one another" zone. I deserve all the shit she's giving me.

"In all seriousness, Harper. You seem really happy lately." Naomi's expression turns tender. "Ever since Lewis started working on the house, you've sounded more excited when we chat on the phone and when you tell me about all the projects he's working on and how much fun you're having just hanging out together. You even use more emojis in your texts to me. Did you realize that?"

I shake my head.

"It's clear Lewis makes you happy in a way that I don't think anyone has before," she says, her soft tone knowing.

"You're right. He does." My chest and cheeks flush with my admission. Even though I've been well aware of my growing feelings for weeks, it still feels so weird to admit it out loud.

"What's with the freaked-out look on your face?" she asks.

"I'm not like this. I don't fall hard and fast for a guy."

She shrugs, like it's no big deal. "That's just it, though. Sometimes someone comes into your life when you're not expecting it. They blast through every expectation and leave one hell of an impression. That's how you know they're special."

My cousin's words hit me at the core. That's exactly what being with Lewis feels like. But I can't ignore the one glaring difference between us.

"He's a celebrity, Naomi. I'm a regular person. Even if this were to become more than just a temporary fling, how could it ever work out between us?"

"You have a connection. That's all that matters."

"It doesn't, though. He and I come from completely different worlds. I live the most normal life you could imagine. Meanwhile, people all over the world know who Lewis is. He can't even go to the grocery store without getting hounded by fans and photographers. Yeah, everything is great now, when we're holed up in the house, but what happens when…"

I don't let myself finish the rest of that thought, because that's when I realize that I'm envisioning a future with Lewis. And that's something I absolutely, positively should not be doing. I'm embarrassed for even letting myself think that far ahead.

"You don't have to analyze this like you do with everything else, Harper," Maren says. "Try to live in the moment. You're hooking up with a hot celebrity. Enjoy it for what it is."

I tell her that I will, but I can't ignore the doubt that

lingers in my mind about just how incompatible my normal-person life is with Lewis's superstar status, and how that could never work long-term.

Just then Naomi's eyes go wide as she clasps her hands together. "Oh, I have an idea!" Naomi says. "You should bring Lewis to the wedding!"

That giddy smile spreads across her face once more. Maren chimes in with her agreement.

My stomach seizes with nerves at just the thought. "No way."

"Why not?"

"Attending a wedding together is the exact opposite of living in the moment. No way that's happening."

Naomi and Maren let out dual sighs, clearly disappointed at my refusal to amuse them. Then, Mari returns with the info on the dress order, and Maren and I snap a million photos of Naomi looking stunning in her gown. Maren helps Naomi off the platform and offers to go with her back to the dressing room to change. While I wait for them so that the three of us can head off to lunch, I can't help but think about what it would be like to bring Lewis to her wedding...even though I just told her it was a no-go.

But the more I think about it—about sitting next to each other holding hands, whispering jokes, slow dancing—the more I feel my chest start to squeeze. Because if I'm being totally honest with myself, the thought of going to my cousin's wedding with Lewis makes me happier than I've felt in a long time.

Chapter Fifteen

Harper

When I walk through the front door, I'm greeted with the sight of Lewis's bare, broad, muscled back as he leans over the kitchen island, phone in hand.

He glances up at me, and my knees go weak. That smile. God, it slays me every. Single. Time.

"Hey."

"Hey."

My tummy flips at hearing him rasp that one-word greeting.

"What are you up to?" I ask as I walk over.

He grabs me by the waist and plants a kiss on me that leaves me shuddering.

"Just uploading some of those photos you took last night to my Instagram like you suggested."

"Can I see?"

He hands his phone to me, and I beam when I see the image he's chosen. It's the one where he's leaning his elbows against the railing of the veranda, and his back and ass and thighs are the focal point.

He opted for the short, simple, and cheeky caption I suggested, which makes me go warm all over in a way I didn't expect.

Not the post you deserve, but the post you need ;)
#timeout #getaway #seeyousoon #alliswell

"Love the caption."

He scratches the scruff along his jaw, a flustered smile pulling at his mouth.

My eyes go wide as I look at the screen. "Holy...one million likes?"

"Yup. And it's only been up for an hour."

He moves to stand next to me, wrapping his arm around my waist and pulling me snug against him. My heart flutters. That was such an affectionate move—a couple-y move.

I shove aside the thoughts of us being a couple. "I love the filter you paired with it. It makes it come off so artistic and moody."

"Nah, that's all you. Your brilliant eye captured that picture."

When he kisses my forehead, goose bumps flash across my skin.

"What's the response been?" I ask.

"Just like you predicted. Speculation on where I am and what I'm up to. Hardly any mentions of me cussing out the paparazzi at Chateau Marmont. It's working like you said it would—slowly pulling people's attention away from what I did and getting them to focus on what I might be up to now."

I do a quick skim of the top comments.

I definitely need me some of that perfect peach

DAT ASS

*Was dying for some content from you, this made
my day! Daaayuuuum!!*

*So good to see you pop up on here, Lewis! Hope
you'll be back on TV soon! We miss you!*

*Dude's really going buckwild after the #chateau-
marmontincident #yikes*

*Ooohhh this doesn't look like LA! Where are you??
Your adoring fans are dying to know!*

"Hopefully they'll be just as excited when I post about
the calendar in a few days," Lewis says.

"Have you read any of those comments? Their heads
will explode when you announce the calendar. You're
gonna break the internet."

He bursts out laughing, then reaches for his laptop.
"Wanna see what I threw together?"

"Um, hell yes."

He shows me the layout of the photos he worked on
while I was dress shopping with Naomi.

I gawk, my mouth open as I look over the spread.
"This is…wow. People are going to lose their minds."

"And hey, I promise I'll put in extra hours tomorrow
to make up for the hours I missed working on the house
today when I was putting the calendar together—"

I pull away and look at him. "You don't need to do
that. You're not on the clock. You can take time to do
whatever you want, Lewis."

A small smile pulls at his lips. "I just don't want you
to think that I'm going to let the remodel fall by the
wayside."

"I know you won't. Because I'll ruin you if you do."

He chuckles, then leans down to press a kiss to my lips.

"What's on the docket for tomorrow?" I ask.

"Painting the dining room walls. The paint delivery for the bedrooms arrived this morning while you were gone. Cans are in the garage."

"Yay."

"Excited to get dirty?"

With his arms wrapped around my waist, he pulls me tight against him right as he wags an eyebrow. For a second, I don't know if he's talking about the impending paint job or the fact that we're seconds away from pouncing on each other.

"I'm always down to get dirty with you," I say against his lips.

He makes a soft groaning noise. "Good. But first I gotta call my agent back. He's been blowing up my phone all day."

I tell him of course and make a beeline for the fridge while he walks toward the living room and dials.

"Hey, Trent. I saw you called. What's up?"

"What the hell are you doing, Lewis?"

"Excuse me?"

"That photo. On Instagram. What the fuck made you think that was okay to post?"

I whip around to Lewis as Trent's surround-sound voice booms through his phone.

"Maybe because it's my own social media account and I can do whatever the fuck I want with it."

A bitter laugh echoes from his phone.

"Oh, I get it. You think you know better than me, is that it? Well, my man, last time I checked, I was the one who plucked you out of obscurity. You were doing commercials and bit parts on D-list movies before I discovered you. *I* was the one who got you those big-time roles. *I* was the one who got you your very first superstar role on *The Best of It*—the role that you fucked up, remember?"

I ball my fists as I listen to Trent berate Lewis. God, this guy. He's every negative show business stereotype I can think of: rude, obscene, and callous.

"I told you to stay out of the public eye. Pulling shallow shit like this is going to ruin your comeback."

"Shallow shit?" Lewis barks.

"Yeah. S-H-A-L-L-O-W shallow. Really fucking shallow, my man. You want me to say it in a different way? You're giving that ass away for free. How do you think that makes you look? Like an attention whore who can't help but show off his body. It's brutal, but my man, it's the truth. And who's gonna wanna work with that?"

Lewis's face turns red as he swallows back what I assume is a string of profanity.

"Trent. Stop."

Muffled profanity blasts from Lewis's phone.

"I appreciate every opportunity you've helped me get, but you don't get to talk to me like that."

"Like what?"

"Like I'm a piece of garbage. You work for me, remember?"

This time muffled stammering is all I hear.

"I posted that photo because I wanted to. And it's gotten a positive response. It's a way for me to connect with fans while I'm hiding out. That's important to me."

Another bitter laugh from Trent. The muscles in my

neck and shoulders freeze at just how antagonistic this
guy is.

"What a mistake letting you stay in California was,"
Trent says. "I should have pushed harder for you to leave.
You should have listened to me. You should have gone
home to that tiny town in the boonies where your parents
live in Kansas or Colorado or wherever the fuck. But no.
You had to be a diva and do it your way, didn't you?"

Lewis's entire face and neck flare red, like he's swallowing lava.

"This would have been a million times easier if you'd
just gone and stayed with your family," Trent mutters.

"You know how I feel about my family. Don't ever
bring them up."

I jolt at the way Lewis bites out those words. Pain
flashes in his hazel eyes. For a moment I swear they go
teary, but then he blinks and it's gone.

Trent is still shouting when Lewis hangs up on him.
He tosses his phone onto the coffee table, then turns
away. All I can see is his back as he hunches over and
rests his hands on his hips.

For a few seconds, I don't say a word or try to approach him. He's clearly distraught and might need a
bit to collect himself. But I don't last long. Because even
though I can't see his expression, I can tell he's hurting.
It's in the slump of his shoulders, the shallow breaths he
takes, the way his head droops forward.

I slowly walk up to him and touch my hand to his
arm. "Hey."

He twists his head to me, like he's just now remem-
bering that I'm here.

"Are you okay?" I ask.

He opens his mouth but quickly closes it before shaking his head and staring at the floor. I step into his space and slowly slink my arms around his waist.

I pause after a second and look up at him. "Is this okay?"

Eyes closed, he nods once. I hug him tight.

I can't think of a single thing to say that would make this situation better. Clearly from what Lewis said about his family, he's not on good terms with them.

He's stiff in my embrace; even his arms remain at his sides. I start to wonder if I should let him go, but after a few seconds, he lifts his arms up, slowly wrapping them around me. When he rests his chin on top of my head, I close my eyes, breathe in, and sink into him.

We stand there for a minute, holding each other, and then he shifts slightly to nuzzle his face into my neck. A heavy sigh falls from his lips in a slow hiss. I close my eyes and hold him extra tight as I process the weight of that single breath. There's so much Lewis is holding on to, and I wish more than anything I could wave a magic wand and take his pain away.

"Thank you," he whispers into my hair.

"Always."

He starts to let go and move out of my hold, but I stop him. "It's okay if you don't feel like it, but if you want to talk or vent, I'm here for you."

He shrugs. "There's not a whole lot to say."

"You sure?"

I bite my tongue, wondering if that was too much. As much as I want Lewis to truly understand that he can say anything to me, it's a fine line to straddle. If I push too hard, it could upset him.

"You could start off with venting about how much of a douchebag your agent is."

One corner of his mouth lifts. "I really hate that guy sometimes."

"The way he spoke to you was out of line. He had no right."

Lewis nods, resting his hands on my hips as he gazes down at me. "Sometimes I get really fucking sick of working with him."

"I'm sure there are a million other agents who would kill to represent you."

He starts to shake his head, but I reach up and cup his cheek with my hand.

"I'm serious, Lewis. Whatever loyalty you think you owe Trent, there's a limit. He doesn't have a free pass to berate you just because he helped you land a job. I mean, that's what he's supposed to do. And anyway, you got yourself the role in the end."

Lewis nods slightly, like he's thinking seriously about what I've said.

He brushes a chunk of my hair away from my face. "You look like something's on your mind."

"I just want to make sure you're okay."

He studies me for a second. Then he cups his palm over my cheek. "You're wondering about what I said. About my family."

Keeping hold of his gaze, I nod. "I know it's not my business, and you're not obligated to tell me anything, of course. But I'm sorry for whatever you're going through with them."

With that he tilts my chin up and presses a light kiss to my lips. Then he drops his hands to his sides before wincing. "I might need a drink to get into that mess."

I walk back over to the freezer, pull out the bottle of vodka, grab two glasses, and pour a few splashes into both. When I turn around, I see Lewis plopping onto a stool at the island. I take the one next to him and hand him a glass.

He tells me thanks before taking a long sip. "My family sold baby pictures of me to the paparazzi years ago. It broke my trust, and I haven't spoken to them since."

My jaw drops. "Oh my god. That's awful."

He takes another sip before ruffling his hair with a hand. "Maybe it's not a big deal. A lot of people would forgive their families for doing that, but... I've always been a really private person. Kind of inconvenient, considering my passion is acting in movies and TV shows. But I've done my best to hold that boundary. I thought my family respected that about me. But I guess our issues go back way further than that."

I place my hand over his on the countertop. When he moves to lace his fingers in mine, my skin warms and my heart thunders once more. It means everything that in this moment of need, he's choosing to find comfort with me.

I squeeze his hand. "What happened?"

Another heavy sigh rockets from him. "My family has always been kind of a mess, you could say. My parents fought a lot when I was a kid. I don't get why they don't just get divorced. They clearly don't love each other."

His gaze falls to his nearly empty glass, loosening and tightening his grip on it, like he's working up the nerve to say more.

"I wasn't a planned presence in my parents' life," he says after a minute. "And it was pretty obvious."

It takes me a moment to realize what he means. "I'm so sorry."

He shrugs, almost as if he's trying to literally shrug

off the pain written in the anguished expression on his face. "I think they tried their best in a lot of ways. I mean, they didn't abuse or neglect me. But I could just feel it, like they were going through the motions with me. Taking me to school, showing up for games and events. But it never felt like they *wanted* to be there. More like they were there because they knew they had to be—because they knew that's what was expected of them."

My chest aches. I can't image my family ever treating me like that. My whole life, I've felt loved by my parents, aunts, uncles, and grandparents. The constant hugs and kisses and *I love you*s; the way they showed up for every game, recital, graduation, and award ceremony; the way they call me multiple times a week; their genuine interest and pride in everything I've ever done. It's never been a question just how much they love me.

My heart breaks knowing that Lewis never had that.

I squeeze his hand tighter. "What a loss for them, because I'm sure you were an incredible kid. Your grandpa clearly thought so, spending all that time with you and making the effort to pass along his skills."

There's a brightness behind his eyes at what I've said. "My grandpa was the best. My grandma was too, but she died when I was a teenager, so I didn't get to spend as much time with her. My favorite memories growing up were with both of them."

He swallows hard, and I scoot closer to him so I can rest my head on his shoulder. Against me I feel his body loosening, and it sends a different kind of ache to my chest.

"I was pretty detached from my parents when I moved out as an adult, but then when I started getting traction as an actor, I thought we turned a corner. They started showing an interest in my life, calling me more, asking me if they could come visit. I was so happy. Especially since my career started to take off after my grandpa passed away. His loss hit hard, because without him, it felt like I didn't have a support system anymore. But then my parents started to reach out, and I thought we were on our way to having a genuine relationship."

A sad, weak laugh spills from him as he stares straight ahead. "They were just being opportunists. The reason they were suddenly interested in me was because I was a trophy they could show off to their friends—their famous actor son. I didn't realize it until I was visiting home and happened to see my dad's phone on the dining room table. He was in a bidding war with a couple of tabloids to see which one would pay him more for personal family pictures."

I bite down so hard, I'm going to give myself a tension headache. But I don't care. A storm of anger, frustration, and pain whirls inside me as I think about just how callous Lewis's parents must be to betray their own son's trust like that.

"We got into an argument when I found out what they were trying to do," Lewis says. "They refused to apologize or even see my point. They didn't care about having a genuine relationship with me, which is all that I ever wanted from them. All they saw when they looked at me were dollar signs. We haven't spoken since."

I lift my head from his shoulder, scoop his massive hand in both of mine, then pivot on my stool to look at him.

"I haven't told many people that," he mutters.

It all makes sense now—why he's intensely private about his personal life, why he refuses to answer questions from reporters and paparazzi about his family. His own parents tried to sell him out—sell his privacy. If that happened to me, I'd be guarded too.

"It means a lot that you told me," I say. For a few seconds, I'm quiet, trying to figure out the best way to word what I want to say. "What your parents did was awful, Lewis. I'm so, so sorry they hurt you in that way. Every parent I know would trip over themselves to have a son like you—hardworking, generous, full of integrity. It's your parents' biggest loss that they chose money over a relationship with you."

When I lean up and kiss his forehead, I can feel the muscles in his face ease. I pull back and see that pained frown is gone. There's still a flash of hurt lingering in his eyes, but it fades as the seconds pass.

"Your family would never do that to you." He says it as he runs a hand through my hair, his eyes focused, his tone soft and distant.

"I'm lucky to have the loving family that I do. We're loud and emotional and fight like cats and dogs. Everyone is in each other's business, to the point that it drives me crazy sometimes. But we care about each other above anything. We'd go to battle for each other, no matter what. For that I'm grateful."

"I've always wanted that."

Emotion takes a hold at the base of my throat. I do my best to swallow it back. I don't often fall apart, but hearing how callous Lewis's parents are—and the fact that he lost the only relatives who truly cared about him—breaks me.

When I think back to how he had no one to lean on when he needed it the most—how hiding out with me, a complete stranger, was the best option he had—that urge etches deeper until I can't swallow back the tears anymore.

I blink, sending tears tumbling down my face.

His expression softens, and he cups my face with both hands. "Hey. It's okay."

"It's not. I'm so mad for you. How awful your own parents were to you. God, they didn't even care…"

When I sniffle, Lewis grabs a tissue from the box sitting at the edge of the counter and dabs my nose and face. My heart bursts at the sweetness of the gesture.

"You care about me," he says. "That's more than enough."

I kiss him lightly on the lips before we both close our eyes and rest our foreheads against one another.

I bury my face in his chest as I hug him tight. We stay like that, awkwardly hugging while perched on our stools. It's clear that today isn't going to end in hot sex, not after the emotionally charged conversation we just had. But in a way, what we just experienced is a million times more intimate than being naked together could ever be. Lewis exposed a part of himself he's never shared with anyone. We've both made it clear that we care about each other. Yeah, this is a bizarre situation. We've only known each other a few weeks, and there's an attraction neither of us can deny anymore. He's a celebrity; I'm a regular person. He's due to leave and head back to LA in just over a month, while I'm planning to split my time between Half Moon Bay and San Francisco.

But there's something between us. I feel it; he feels it. And in this moment, that's all that matters.

Chapter Sixteen

*

Lewis

My hands are shaking. I don't realize it until Harper and I break our embrace.

Shit.

I wring them out slightly. Harper frowns. "Are you okay?"

I mutter that I'm fine, but she doesn't buy it. She immediately reaches out and scoops my right hand in both of hers.

"You're shaking," she says softly. Worry creases her brow, and it feels like my heart shatters right there, inside my chest.

She's worried about me. She *cares* about me.

It's been so long since I've felt that.

"I guess I am."

It's all I can say, because I don't want to admit to her that this is a sign of just how messed up I am.

This only ever happens when I talk about my parents, which isn't often. I never even opened up about it with my ex or anyone I've dated in the past. Natalia wasn't exactly the type who cared about family. All she wanted to do when we weren't in the bedroom was go out to clubs and restaurants so we could be photographed together, with the end goal of guest starring on my old show. She wasn't interested in anything meaningful or deep. I doubt she'd even notice my shaky hands if she were standing right here, right now, looking straight at me.

But Harper noticed. She saw the physical change instantly. And as exposed and vulnerable as I feel in this moment, as terrified as I am that she might think I'm weird and weak, I'm heartened that she cares enough to notice this about me. To really *see* me in a way that no one else seems to.

It's why I told her about my parents in the first place. She's the first person I felt comfortable opening up to about that part of my life, but because it's been so long since I've talked about them, I forgot that I sometimes have a physical reaction to how distraught the whole situation makes me feel.

The touch of her hands, soft and warm, sends a wave of emotion through me. I have to close my eyes for a few seconds, it's so overwhelming.

"Are you okay?" she asks again, her voice soft and patient, like before. "Just tell me what you need. Whatever it is, I'll do it."

When I swallow, I ache from the inside out. It's almost too much, her care, her concern. But I love it. So much.

"I just need a second," I say after a moment.

"Oh. Okay."

When her grip starts to loosen, I realize I've given her the wrong idea. I squeeze my hand around hers, then I open my eyes and hope my gaze conveys just how much I need her next to me.

"No, I… Please stay."

"I'm right here."

Harper's grip turns firm against my hand, which eases

the shaking slightly. For two full minutes, she stands there holding my hand, looking at me, breathing with me. When my hands finally go still, I give her a gentle squeeze.

"Thank you."

"Of course."

She doesn't let go or even try to leave. She doesn't say a word, but her expression conveys everything. That she's here, for me, willing to listen if I want to talk.

"Sorry, I just… I get that way when I talk about my parents sometimes," I mumble. "I don't talk about them often, and it can be really upsetting. And I guess that's how my body processes it."

I brace myself for her expression to turn bewildered or curious. But it doesn't. It remains tender and understanding. And that means everything.

"That makes sense. You were recalling a traumatizing experience. That can be physically upsetting."

She asks if I want to sit down on the couch, and I tell her yes. Together, hand in hand, we sit down next to each other.

I tug my free hand through my hair, stunned at how well she's taken all this.

"It's nothing to feel bad about, Lewis," she says, as if reading my mind.

"It just feels weird when it happens. And overwhelming."

"Have you thought about talking to anyone? Like a therapist?"

I shake my head.

"I don't mean to tell you what to do," she says, her gaze flitting to her lap. "It's just that trauma can be really complicated, but there are professionals who can help you sort through it."

I'm heartened at the way she offers up help without being preachy or self-important, like some people.

"You're right. I should probably see someone about this. It's probably not normal that every time I talk about my parents, my hands shake and my heart beats like it's going to burst out of my chest."

"I talk to a therapist sometimes," she says after a moment passes. "I don't like going in person to an office. It feels like too much for some reason. But I found an online therapist who helps me sort through my feelings and emotions when I'm going through something tough. It helps a lot. That's an option."

I gaze down at her, my heart racing for an entirely different reason this time. This woman. She's unlike anyone I've ever met before. Honest and open and unafraid to talk about topics that would send most people running for the hills. Never in my life has anyone talked about therapy as casually and without judgment as she just did.

In the past, I've thought about seeing a counselor or therapist to work through the family issues I clearly have. But I had no idea how to go about finding a good doctor. I tried to ask friends and colleagues a time or two, but they made dismissive comments about mental health, so I just clammed up and told them never mind.

"Sorry if I sound like I'm trying to sell you on therapy," she says. "I used to have a pretty narrow-minded view about seeking out help, but my cousin's fiancé is a therapist, and he really changed my mind for the better."

"No, I appreciate it. I'd love to start seeing someone."

She smiles. "I can send you my therapist's info to start. She'll probably have a lot of great recommendations."

I tell her thanks, then look at our joined hands. "What a weird turn today took. I thought I'd have you writhing on top of my bedsheets, and look at us now. Holding hands and talking feelings on the couch."

"As much as I'd love to be going at it with you in bed, I don't think that's the best thing to do right now."

I deflate. It must be obvious in my expression and body language how disappointed I am, because she backtracks instantly. "Don't get me wrong. I'm ridiculously attracted to you, Lewis. There's a connection here I haven't felt with anyone before. And I'm dying to act on that. It's just that you've been through some pretty emotionally draining stuff today, so I don't want to push you into doing anything physical while you're processing everything."

I can't help the pang of disappointment that radiates through me at what she's said. But she's right. Minutes ago I couldn't stop shaking because I was so upset. I clearly need some time to settle my nerves and decompress before we dive into bed together.

"Maybe you're right," I say. "But that doesn't mean all physical stuff is off the table."

I wag an eyebrow at her, chuckling when her brow lifts slightly.

"What do you mean?" she asks.

I pull her to straddle my lap. Then I cradle her face in my hands. "I'd like to spend the next few minutes kissing the hell out of you, Harper."

The way she stammers as her mouth drops open sends a thrill surging through me.

"Are you sure?"

Her gentle tone makes me ache. "Absolutely. I've been dying to kiss you this whole time."

With that admission, she leans close, lightly pressing her lips to mine. I can tell she's being soft for my sake, because she doesn't want to push too hard, too soon. But I want it. I want *her*. I want a kiss from her more than I want air to breathe or water to drink.

With my hands gripping her hips, I pull her to slide closer to me, so that the apex of her thighs is flush with the bulge of my dick.

"Do you feel how sure I am?" I rasp against her mouth. "Do you feel just how much I want you right now?"

Any ounce of hesitation lurking inside her disappears, judging by the way she attacks me with her mouth. Her hands grip the sides of my face as she kisses so hard, so fast I can barely keep up. But then she eases, her rhythm turning slow and teasing, the tip of her tongue lapping my tongue like she's tasting the most delicious ice cream.

I groan at how smoothly she can flip from hot and heavy to slow and tantalizing. She presses harder into me until heat puddles on my lap where she's sitting. I jerk my hips up, bouncing her slightly. She giggles into my mouth, which makes me smile. But the smiles don't last for long. Soon the rhythm of our breathing turns desperate. So do our kisses. Our mouths and tongues get so filthy that I start to feel dizzy. When Harper claws at my chest, then my hair, then my chest again, I'm practically vibrating. God, I want this woman. Whatever she's willing to give me, I'll happily take.

My fingertips flirt with the hem of her shirt. She nods, and I slide my hands up the fabric, relishing the impossibly soft feel of her body.

"Your skin. Fuck. It's like silk," I say between kisses. She grins without breaking our kiss.

"Can I…" I pull her shirt up slightly.

Her response is to yank it completely over her head,

leaving her in just a lace bra. I choke at the sight of her, at the image of this flawless angel who was somehow dropped in my lap.

I cup her cheeks in my hands. "You're so beautiful."

"So are you," she says as she runs her hands up my chest. I lean up and tug the shirt off. When her gaze goes starry, it's my turn to feel shy.

"Seriously, you're stunning," she says.

I've been given a million compliments before. It comes with the territory of working in the field that I do. It's so image focused and everyone throws comments about how good you look constantly, it can sometimes feel like white noise.

But no compliment anyone has ever given me compares to what Harper has just told me. Because she's seeing me at my most raw, my most vulnerable, and she still likes what she sees.

I swallow back the emotion in my throat and try to smile.

"Stunning, huh?"

She nods quickly, her brown eyes wide, her smile cheeky. It's so damn cute.

With our gazes still locked, her expression sobers slightly. "You sure you're okay doing this?"

"Positive."

I start to shift so that I can move us to lie down on the couch, but she presses a hand on her chest, stopping me.

"I need to confess something," she says.

"Um, okay."

Her eyes scan my face before she takes a breath. "The day we bumped into each other, and I accidentally grabbed your…you know…"

"Yeah?"

"I, um… I started to masturbate, like, right after I ran

into my bedroom. I was so turned on by the sight of you. And the feel of you. I stopped myself before I could get too into it." She bites her lip. "I just felt like I needed to tell you that…so you know the kind of creep you're about to mess around with."

As soon as her expression turns sheepish, I gently grab her chin and tilt her face to look at me. I raise my eyebrow at her and try not to grin too big. "Well, you're not as much of a creep as I am, because I actually jerked off right after I closed the door to my room."

Her jaw drops. "Are you serious?"

"Dead serious. You were so sexy, I couldn't think straight. I had to do something about it."

She leans her head back and makes a squeal-groan noise. "And I thought I was such a perv."

"We're both pervs. It's a match made in heaven." I thrust my hips up, bouncing her against me again. She falls into a fit of chuckles.

I shift to move her next to me so I can stand up and take my jeans off. She reaches out and takes me in her hand. Just the silky feel of her has me rolling my eyes to the back of my head.

"I haven't done anything," she says.

"Can't help it," I say, counting out my breaths. "Your hand, your fingers, your skin…they all feel too good."

I lead her to stand up with me. "I hate being the only naked person in the room."

She giggles as I kiss her, and I bend down to pull off the skirt she's wearing. On my knees, I come to eye level to her lace panties and press a light kiss to her front. A sputtered breathing noise happens above me.

I lean back to look up at her. Her chest rises as she lifts

her eyebrow at me. "I wanna try something with you. Something dirty."

"Dirtier than everything we've done so far?"

"So much dirtier."

Her breathy words rocket pleasure straight to my dick. I'm certain I've got the smuggest, most obnoxious smirk on my face. She just said the single hottest thing anyone could ever say to me.

"What did you have in mind?"

Chapter Seventeen

Harper

Lewis's question, spoken in that growl with that smug smile on his face, has me stuttering. I have to take a second to process what's happening right now: for the second time in my life, I'm about to have sex with Lewis Prescott. He's turned on by me. He's hard for me. He's on his knees, kissing between my legs, and we're about to screw each other's brains out.

But more mind-blowing than that is the genuine connection I feel with him. The emotional bond that we've formed, the fact that he trusts me enough to open up about his past and his insecurities. The fact that I trust him enough to do the same.

This is more than just a physical attraction; what I feel with Lewis right now is unlike anything I've ever experienced before.

I'm practically shuddering at the thought, but then I swallow and refocus. I peer down at him, my heart pounding.

"Can I show you what I want?"

His eyes widen, and his smirk turns devilish as he nods. I grab him to stand up, then lead him to lie on his back on the couch. I remove my glasses and set them on the arm of the couch before I unhook my bra, drop it onto the floor, and shed my panties. I start to move to get on top of him, but he stops me with his hand on my arm.

"Wait. Can I just look at you for a second?"

I bite my lip and stand there in my birthday suit in front of one of the sexiest men in the world. I know I shouldn't be so nervous—we screwed half naked in my car, and he seemed to like the view plenty. But this is different. We were crazed with arousal in that moment. Right now we're taking things more slowly. It feels like there's a spotlight on me as Lewis's glazed-over hazel gaze takes me in. He's probably been with loads of women with perfect bodies, and I can't help but wonder how mine stacks up. I'm happy with my body, but I'm no tall and leggy Victoria's Secret model. I'm petite and busty with a plump rear end.

But any insecurities I'm harboring are zapped away when I take in the hungry look on his face. His eyes practically have stars in them. And that devilish smile is still on display.

"I look okay then?"

His brow furrows slightly as he shakes his head. "To describe you as 'okay' would be a war crime. You're fire. You're stunning. You're the hottest, sexiest, most beautiful woman I've ever been lucky enough to see naked."

A flustered laugh is all I can manage. I'm blown away by the caliber of his compliment.

"Now, why don't you show me what filthy thing you have in mind?"

He reaches his hand out and I take it, steadying myself as I climb on top of him. I maneuver to straddle my thighs over his face. When I start to lower my face between his legs, I hear him mutter, "Oh, hell yeah."

"This is good with you then?"

He growls before kissing the back of my thigh. "More than good. Do you know how long I've been wanting to do this with you?"

I lean down and kiss the tip of him, then swirl my tongue over the head. He breathes in so sharply it sounds like he's choking.

With eager hands, he grabs my hips and lowers me down to his face as I work him in my mouth. I hum and groan around him as his tongue starts slow, then swirls faster. All the muscles in my legs tremble in response to the pleasure mounting higher and higher inside me. As many times as I've done this, it's never felt as good as now, when I'm with Lewis. And judging by the grunts that emanate from him, he's enjoying this as much as I am.

Soon my thighs are shuddering around his face. The pleasure and pressure mount to an unbearable peak until I feel it everywhere. My legs, my arms, my core, my skin, my bones. Both of my calves cramp, signaling that the incoming crash of climax is imminent. When I dig my fingers into the hard flesh of his quad, Lewis takes that as his cue. He grips the backs of my thighs and moves even faster. And then, when I think I can't take it any longer, I lose it against his tongue.

I have to pull away from him when I shout. I'm thrashing so much that I don't want to hurt him. But he holds me steady the whole time. When I start to ease off my orgasm, I lower back down to finish him, but he moves to stop me.

I twist around to look at him.

"Actually, I was wondering…"

The way his eyes turn the slightest bit timid as he speaks makes me giddy.

"I'm really close, and I'd love it if I could maybe have you on your stomach. And, um, on your knees…"

I get his drift instantly.

"Absolutely. I love that. It's my favorite. Do you have a condom?"

He nods yes, and I move off him so he can grab his jeans. He fishes his wallet from the back pocket and pulls out a foil square. Then he grabs three cushions from the couch and drops them on the floor.

"I'm a tall bastard and need the extra room."

I giggle as I reposition myself on my hands and knees on top of the cushions. Lewis moves to kneel behind me, and I lower my chest all the way down, so that the side of my face and the front of my shoulders are against the plush cushions while my ass is straight up in the air.

"This okay?" I ask.

There's a grunting noise behind me. "Um, fuck yeah."

"You sound like a caveman," I say through a chuckle.

I squeal when I feel the scrape of his teeth along the back of my thigh before he gives my ass cheek a squeeze. He runs a hand along my lower back, resting his fingers on either side of my spine.

"So perfect," he hums.

"Just a warning—I get pretty loud in this position. Way louder than I was in the car."

What sounds like a scoff-laugh echoes behind me. Then he slides in, and I gasp.

"Good," he rasps, slow-thrusting into me.

I moan, gripping the cushions as he pumps into me over and over.

He leans down so that his lips are touching the shell of my ear. "I want you loud, Harper. I want you to shatter the fucking windows with how loud I make you scream."

My jaw unhinges as some animal noise I've never made before rips from inside me.

"That's my girl. Just like that."

He grips my hips tighter with each thrust. The feel of his fingers digging into my skin makes me wild. I love that I'm making him this desperate, this primal.

That familiar pressure and intensity collide inside me once more. Liquid heat pools between my legs before rushing up my spine and stomach, puddling at my chest. My entire body is flooded with lust and pleasure. I'm shouting and squealing so hard, I'd be surprised if I don't lose my voice at the end of this.

When he picks up the pace, his grunts deepen and his breath becomes more ragged. I wonder just how close he is to losing it. Then he slips a hand between my legs and starts to circle my clit. In no time that liquid heat turns to lava.

"I'm so close," I howl.

"Come for me."

A second later, I do exactly that while screaming his name. I obey his rasped command with an orgasm so intense, I lose my vision and my hearing for a moment. My entire body convulses under him. Everything is muffled and hazy. I blink furiously as the deep blue fabric of the couch cushion slowly comes into focus.

His gentle voice hits my ears. "Are you okay?"

That's when I notice his arm is braced under me. My head is so heavy I can barely keep holding it up. I'm drunk with the aftershocks of the climax Lewis just delivered to my body.

"Yeah." I take a moment to catch my breath. "Are you? Did you…"

A throaty chuckle sounds behind me before he presses his lips to my back. "Of course I came. God, you're incredible, Harper."

He slides out of me, then eases me to lie facedown on the cushions. I close my eyes to the sound of his footsteps padding down to the hallway bathroom. Thirty seconds later he's back. I fully expect him to settle next to me, but he scoops me up in his arms.

I squeal. "What are you doing?"

"Taking you to bed."

After he lays me down on his bed, he cuddles next to me.

"Are you tired?" he asks as he pulls the bedsheet over us.

Something comes over me as I take him in, skin flushed, hair mussed, eyes dilated yet fiery, that cheeky smile dancing across his lips. Suddenly I'm starving for him again.

I shake my head no.

"Good."

He leans his head to my chest and trails kisses along my breasts. Soon he's swirling his tongue around my nipples, and I'm panting. He makes an "mmm" noise before kissing down my stomach.

He nips at my hip before looking up at me. "I'm not tired either." He kisses and licks around the spot where I need to feel him most.

I tug a hand through his hair. "Lewis… Please…" I can barely get the words out.

"I want to hear you scream again, baby."

Seconds later, his tongue is right where I want it, and I'm shouting his name like it's the only word I know.

When I wake, the deep orange glow of late afternoon paints the walls of Lewis's bedroom.

I close my eyes, relishing the feel of his playing big spoon behind me, his arm draped over my stomach. He twitches slightly, and his hold around me tightens before he pulls me even closer into him. My heartbeat skids at the protective move done in his sleep. No one's ever held me like this, awake or asleep—like they can't bear to lose contact for even one second.

I decide right then and there that there's no better way on earth to wake up than being cuddled by Lewis Prescott, doting and protective even in his sleep.

Even his soft snores are endearing. I've always loathed snorers in the past, but something about the gentle rumble he makes is comforting and sweet at once.

I blink a few times, my vision blurry. When I remember I left my glasses in the living room just before our sexfest kicked off, I let out a soft groan into my pillow. I'll have to leave this comfy cocoon of Lewis's body and bedsheets to grab them. I start to lean up, but then I spot my glasses sitting on the nightstand next to my side of the bed. He must have slipped out earlier and brought them in here.

I shift as quietly as I can to face him in bed, but my careful movements fail, because he opens his eyes. I grab my glasses from the nightstand and swipe them on.

"Hey," he says through a yawn and an insanely sexy-sleepy smile.

"Hey. Thanks for getting my glasses."

He presses a kiss to my forehead, and I melt into a

puddle of goo. Good lord, this guy is freaking perfect. I want to keep him forever.

Clarity crashes through me at that moment. Lewis is going to walk out of my life in a matter of weeks after he finishes fixing up my house. He's going to go back to his A-list Hollywood life, where he'll be attending premieres, hounded by fans and press, and traveling all over to film. I'm going to go back to my regular-person life in Half Moon Bay and San Francisco, where I'll be hanging out with my family while balancing working and volunteering.

Our worlds couldn't be more different—and that means after this renovation is over, we'll probably never see each other again.

A hard swallow moves through my throat, triggering the problem-solver part of my brain. It's the part that figures out what to do when a contractor bid comes in too high or the materials for a build are on back order or a crew shows up late. I identify the issue and come up with ways to solve it quickly and efficiently. Just like I know I have to do now.

"So...that was fun," I say in a quiet voice.

The corner of his perfect pink mouth hooks up in a sleepy half smile. "It was. Which time was the most fun, though? Round one or two or three..."

He leans down and presses a whisper-soft kiss to my shoulder. His mouth moves to my breasts, which short-circuits my brain.

"To be honest, I don't know if I can pick a favorite," he says with his mouth against my stomach. "I kind of liked them all."

"'Kind of liked them'?" I lightly tug his hair while he positions himself between my legs.

The low rumble of his chuckle vibrates against the skin of my inner thigh. "What I meant to say was, I really fucking loved what we just did and would like to do it again. A lot."

"I just…wanted…to maybe…talk about…what we're… supposed…to do…now…"

I barely it make it through that sentence before my jaw falls open. Lewis's mouth is between my legs once again, turning my brain to mush and setting my entire body on fire.

But after a second, he stops and glances up at me. He rests his cheek against the inside of my thigh, lifting one of his eyebrows. "You wanna talk? Now?" he asks, his expression amused.

My chest rises as I struggle to catch my breath. "Well…yeah. Look, as much as I want to keep having amazing sex with you, we should also probably talk about it. It changes a lot about our situation."

"You're right, talking is way more fun than sex."

I give his hair another tug, this time harder.

"I'd rather have my face between your thighs when you do that."

"I'm serious, Lewis. We crossed a line here. What do we do about it?"

His mouth and eyebrows scrunch slightly at what I've said. Then he crawls back up to lie down next to me. He brushes a chunk of hair out of my face, the super-soft touch sending goose bumps all over my skin.

"It doesn't feel that way, not to me," he says. "Where we're at now feels a million times better than where we were. Because now I get to touch you. I get to kiss you. I get to do all the things that I've been fantasizing about doing to you."

He rests his palm over my heart. "All I want is more of that, Harper—more of you."

He speaks with a softness and conviction that leaves me breathless. It's enough to shut off the problem-solving part of my brain, to shove away every worry and focus on just how much I want him in this moment, in every moment.

I decide to take Maren's advice. To try living in the moment. To appreciate that I'm hooking up with a hot celebrity. To enjoy it for what it is.

I wrap my fingers around his wrist and slowly pull his hand away so I can close the space between us, and I kiss him until we're both panting and moaning. He slinks his way back down to where he started, and I lose myself in the sensations, in the pleasure, in the feel of his mouth on my body. I'll have to thank Maren the next time I see her...

"This place is really coming together," Lewis says after chugging a glass of water in the kitchen.

I stand up from the crouched position I've been in for the past few minutes while painting the bottom edges of the walls in the living room. When I take in the state of the renovation, I can't help but beam. The two of us have accomplished a ton over the past two months. The flooring is finished, the kitchen cabinets are fixed, the shower tile in the hallway bathroom has been replaced, half of the new light fixtures have been installed, and the walls in the living room and kitchen have been painted. All that's left to do is paint the bedrooms, install the rest of the light fixtures once they're delivered, and strip the white paint from the fireplace.

"I can't believe how good it looks already," I say.

Lewis walks over, grabs me by the waist, and spins me to face him. He hugs me tight against his body. "I can't believe how good *you* look."

I laugh. "I'm covered in paint and wearing your old T-shirt."

"Hot."

He leads me in a filthy kiss. This is how our days usually go ever since we jumped each other's bones. Between renovation projects, we steal kisses and grope each other, often breaking in the middle of the day to have sex. And in the morning. And in the evening.

It's the single greatest work schedule I've ever had.

When we pull apart, Lewis starts to ask what I want for dinner, but then my phone rings. Mom.

"Hey, Mom, what's up?"

I mouth "one sec" to Lewis, and he flashes a thumbs-up.

"Sweetie! It's been so long since you called. How are things going at the house?"

"Pretty good. Can't wait to show you guys what it looks like when it's done."

"Oh we're dying to see it! But hey, how about you take a break sometime? Maybe tomorrow? You could come over for dinner. We'd love to see you. It's been ages since your last visit, and Uncle Pedro misses you a lot."

Guilt radiates through me. I've been so busy working on the house and hooking up with Lewis that visiting my family has fallen to the wayside.

"I'm sorry," I say. "Dinner tomorrow night sounds perfect."

"Wonderful! We can't wait."

We end the call with *I love you*s, and I hang up. When I look up at Lewis, I feel yet another pang of guilt. We've spent every evening together ever since he moved in. Even before things got romantic between us, we shared almost every meal. It feels wrong to ditch him.

"Do you want to have dinner with my family tomorrow night?" I ask before I can think too hard and stop myself.

Lewis's brow rises slightly, and he rubs the back of his neck. "You want me to meet your family?"

"Yeah. But only if you want to," I say when I pick up on the hesitation in his body language.

But the thought of seeing Lewis with my family makes me giddy and warm all at once. I've never felt that way about having a guy meet my family before.

"I know you're worried about people recognizing you, but I promise, my parents and my great-uncle won't have any idea who you are. They don't pay attention to celebrities or pop culture. My dad only ever watches sports, and my mom only watches the news and HGTV. And the only shows my great-uncle likes are ones from the Philippines."

He grins as he walks back over to me. "So is this like a meet-the-family dinner?"

"Yeah. If you want it to be?"

"I'd like it to be."

My heart soars in my chest. For the past few weeks that we've been messing around, I haven't brought up the "what are we doing?/what are we to each other?" conversation. I wanted to focus on enjoying the moment and not put pressure on a future or expectations or anything like that. But witnessing this eagerness from him at the prospect of meeting my family sets off something inside me. When I picture Lewis with my family, laughing and chatting and joking, I feel happy and whole. I slide my arms around his waist and tiptoe up to kiss him.

"It's been a while since I've had dinner with a girl-friend's family."

I freeze on my tiptoes just as Lewis's eyes go wide, seemingly realizing what he's just said. If I'm Lewis's girlfriend, that changes things. That means our situation is more than just two people hooking up… It means we're on our way to being serious… We'd need to think about the future and what our status will be after the renovation is over. If we don't, if we keep ignoring the elephant in the room and refuse to talk about our future as a couple, one of us—or both of us—is bound to get hurt.

I quickly tell the analyzing part of my brain to shove it. That's all true, but I don't want to focus on the stress that all those questions bring about. Right now, all I want to focus on is the giddiness coursing through me at hearing Lewis call me his girlfriend.

His shoulders relax, and his expression eases. "Is it okay that I called you my girlfriend?"

My stomach does a somersault at hearing him say that word again. *Girlfriend.*

I reach up and pull his face down to me so I can kiss him breathless. "Hell yes, it's okay."

His lips stretch into a smile as he kisses me. "I've been dying to say that."

"I'm glad you finally did, boyfriend."

Chapter Eighteen

Harper

When I walk in the door of my parents' house on the outskirts of San Francisco, Lewis by my side, I hold my breath. This is the first time I've brought a guy home since… I can't even remember. College maybe?

When I see there's no one in the foyer, I exhale, relieved. That'll buy a few extra seconds of us alone before the barrage of questions starts.

Lewis peers down at me. "You seem nervous."

"Yeah, well, I haven't brought a guy home in a really, really long time. They're gonna lose their minds."

"You warned me on the drive over."

He gives my waist a light squeeze that makes me laugh.

"I know, but wait until you witness it in person."

I love my family to the moon and back, but I'm at the age where at any gathering, questions about when I'm getting married and having kids happen more frequently than "How are you?" I know they mean well, but I've always loathed just how much pressure their questions carry. I've never seen relationships as the be-all, end-all. I love the life I've built for myself as a successful single person. If I were to someday meet someone who I could envision being with long-term, that would be an awesome bonus to my already fulfilling life, but it's never been my primary focus.

Well, you met Lewis and look at you now. Pretty damn fulfilled...in more ways than one.

His confident smile doesn't budge. "I'm ready. Bring it on."

As if on cue, Mom's voice echoes from the kitchen. "Harper, honey, is that you?"

I holler back a yes, and she walks out of the kitchen.

"Oh, we're so excited to see..." Her eyes go wide when she takes in the giant handsome man standing next to me. "And who is this?"

She's beaming as she scurries over to pull me into a hug and kiss my cheek, her eyes never leaving Lewis.

"This is Lewis. My...contractor. For the remodel."

I wince at how quickly I lose my nerve, bracing myself as I hazard a look up at him. He's probably annoyed. Or hurt. But when I see that familiar amused expression on his face, my muscles instantly relax.

He reaches out a hand, but Mom shakes her head. "Oh no. Only hugs in this house."

She yanks Lewis into a hug so tight his eyes go wide. He's probably wowed that a woman as small as my mother is capable of such a powerful death grip.

"It's so good to meet you, Mrs. Ellorza," he says through a strained breath.

Seconds later she finally releases him but keeps hold of his arm. "Oh please, you call me Jules." She grips his massive arm with her tiny hands. "You have done the most incredible job with that house. Harper has been sending us photos and videos every week."

Her blue eyes sparkle as she stares up at him. When her lips start to tremble, I reach over and pat her hand.

"That house means so much to my husband's family. I remember going to family gatherings and parties there years ago, when he and I just started dating. It's so special that you're restoring it in such a beautiful way." She turns to me and scoops my hand in hers. "You both are. My brilliant architect daughter renovating her grandparents' house."

She blinks away the tears and pulls us both in to hug her.

I stretch up to glimpse over the top of Mom's head and mouth "sorry" to Lewis. He chuckles and mouths back, "It's okay."

He squeezes her back. "It's an honor to work on a house with so much love and history in it," he says to her. "And it's an absolute joy to collaborate with your daughter."

My heart explodes. He's such a good sport. Actually, no. He's more than a good sport. He's the sweetest guy ever. What am I doing hiding just how special he is to me?

"Actually, Mom, Lewis and I are together," I blurt.

Lewis bites back a chuckle as he stares at me. Mom's arms fall away from us, and she steps back, her gaze flitting between us. She covers her mouth with her hands as she gasps. When she pulls her hands away, the biggest grin stretches across her face.

"Oh my word! Oh, how romantic!" She pulls us into another hug. "So you fell for each other while working together?"

Lewis tells her yes.

"It just kind of happened," I say.

Mom lets out a squeal before clutching her hands to her chest while looking between us. "Well. This is just the most wonderful surprise!"

She grabs both of us and leads us into the kitchen. "Hope you kids are hungry. I made Harper's favorite, bacon mac and cheese."

My mouth waters. Lewis pats his stomach with his free hand. "Jules, that's my absolute favorite too."

Mom lets go of us and claps her hands once and says, "Yay," before turning back to Lewis. "You're welcome to call me Mom now if you'd like."

"Oh my god." My face heats. "That's a bit rushed, don't you think?"

She waves a hand at me, brushing off what I've said. "Not at all. It's not every day you bring someone home to us, honey. This one's gotta be special. I have a feeling."

She pats Lewis's shoulder before heading back to the oven. I wince as I make eye contact with him. Somehow, he doesn't look horrified at my mother's insistence that he call her Mom, even though they just met. In fact, judging by the soft expression on his face, he's heartened by the offer. He steps over to me and presses a kiss to my forehead.

"Mom, what I can help you with?" he asks as he walks to her. Even from the corner of my eye, I can see her light up.

"Oh, what a sweetheart you are. How about you chop up some of that lettuce on the counter? Gotta have a nice healthy salad to balance out this indulgent entrée."

"I like how you think," Lewis says as he glides a knife through two heads of romaine lettuce. "It's all about balance."

"That's what I say too!"

I watch in awe at how Lewis and Mom chat like old friends while they prep food. While I finish setting the dining table, I hear the rumble of the garage door opening.

When Dad walks in with Uncle Pedro, I run over to the door, which is right off the back of the kitchen.

"Sweetie! So good to see you!" Dad pulls me into a hug after stepping inside.

I move to give Uncle Pedro my arm, but he smiles and waves it off. "I've got this, *anak*."

I swallow back nerves as I watch him walk up the three steps faster than I expected, but he moves with ease. When he pulls me into a hug, I smile. That's the hug I grew up with, the hug I loved getting—snug with a pat on the back before letting me go. He's getting his strength back after his stint in the hospital, and it's so good to see.

Before their shoes are even off, Mom announces the exciting news.

"Look who Harper brought! This is Lewis! Her boyfriend! Isn't that wonderful?"

Dual sets of deep brown eyes go wide at the sight of Mom pulling Lewis by the arm over to them.

"He's the contractor who's been working on *Apong* Bernie and *Apong* Vivian's house for the past couple of months," I explain when I step over to stand next to him.

Uncle Pedro grins and nods at him while Dad's gaze turns a bit more thoughtful.

"It's a pleasure to meet you both," Lewis says while reaching out his hand to Dad.

While they shake hands, Dad frowns at him. "You look familiar."

Air lodges in my throat as I notice Lewis's eyes go the slightest bit wide.

Recognition flashes across Dad's face as he snaps his fingers. "I know where I've seen you! You look just like my dentist."

Lewis and I let out dual weak chuckles at the same time.

"Must be a good-looking guy then," Lewis says, quickly recovering.

Everyone laughs. Dad pats him on the back as he turns to shake Uncle Pedro's hand.

"I like him. He's funny," Dad says to me.

Dad runs upstairs to change out of his work clothes while Uncle Pedro takes a seat at the kitchen table. Mom asks him about his day at the senior center.

"Had lunch, then played some card games, then bingo. Same old, same old."

"Poker?" I ask.

"Of course."

"How much did you win?"

"Twenty-five bucks."

"Nice." I chuckle, thinking back to when I was a kid and Uncle Pedro taught me how to play his favorite card game.

I grab a glass of water along with Uncle Pedro's pill box, then walk over and set them in front of him. I sit in the chair next to him while he takes his medicine, quietly looking him over. His eyes are brighter, and his deep tan skin doesn't look pallid anymore, thankfully. I notice he even put some gel in his short-buzzed gray hair that's still as thick as it was in his heyday.

"Insurance is still covering your prescriptions, right?" I ask. "You haven't had any issues paying at the pharmacy?"

"Yes, all good."

"Well, you have the credit card I gave you just in case any unexpected expenses pop up."

"I told you before, you don't need to pay for my things, *anak*," he chides as he grabs his cloth napkin from the table to wipe his mouth.

"I want to help, Uncle Pedro."

He opens his mouth to protest but closes it while shaking his head and offering a tired smile. "I'm fine. You don't have to worry about me so much."

"I just feel bad that I left so soon right after you got home from the hospital. I should have stayed longer."

"Come on now, none of that." He pats my hand. I focus on the way his skin crinkles with the movement, like crepe paper. "You have your own life to live. I don't expect you to put it on hold just because I felt a little under the weather."

I fight the urge to explain that at his age, pneumonia isn't just some minor ailment.

"Besides, I've got your dad and mom to help look after me. I couldn't ask for a better setup than this."

"I know you miss living in your old apartment on your own."

He shrugs. "Sometimes. But I like being so close to family."

I give his hand a squeeze. "*Apong* Vivian would be pissed if we let anything happen to her little brother. That's why we take such good care of you."

His carob-brown eyes glisten. They're the same color as *Apong* Vivian's, the same color as Dad's, the same color as mine.

He blinks and smiles. "You're doing a heck of a job, *anak*."

He glances over at Lewis, who's slicing veggies for the salad as he listens to Mom chattering away.

"So he's doing a good job on the house then? And with you?"

I laugh and shake my head. "An amazing job. I have no idea how I stumbled upon someone so good."

"Sometimes it just happens like that. When you least expect it, someone comes into your life and makes you feel happier than you've ever been," Uncle Pedro says.

"It's kind of fast," I admit, careful to keep my voice low so only he can hear me. "We've only known each other a couple of months."

He shrugs like it's no big deal. "There's no set time for stuff like this. You just have to go with your gut, go with how you feel—how he makes you feel."

He nods at Lewis, who catches eyes with me and winks before turning his attention back to Mom. My stomach flips.

"He makes me feel so happy. Happier than I've ever felt." This is the first time I've said it out loud.

The crinkled corners of Uncle Pedro's mouth hook up in an amused smile. "Then I'd say he's a keeper. Plus, he's tall. Think of all the things in the house he could reach for you."

I burst out laughing as Dad strolls back into the kitchen, now dressed in jeans and a 49ers hoodie.

He pecks Mom on the lips and frowns at Lewis. "You're not charming my wife too much, are you, Lewis?"

Lewis shakes his head, stepping away from Mom and holding up a hand. "I wouldn't dare, sir."

Mom lightly smacks Dad's hand as she scolds him good-naturedly. I laugh to myself at the sight of Lewis acquiescing to my dad, who's half his size.

Lewis carries the massive casserole tray of bacon mac and cheese to the table. He sits down next to me and winks as he serves me some of the salad he made.

"I think we should do a toast!" Mom announces, glass of white wine in hand.

Dad sips from his beer bottle before holding it up. The rest of us join in and raise our glasses.

"To Harper and Lewis, for the amazing job they're doing on the Ellorza family house."

Dad nods along with Mom's toast. "Yes. Beautiful job, you two. We can't wait to see the finished product."

"And!" Mom's voice hitches up. "To finding romance in the most special place."

A flustered grin spreads across Lewis's face that I bet looks a lot like the one I'm sporting.

"Cheers!"

After we clink our glasses and sip our drinks, Mom scoops a mountain of mac and cheese onto Lewis's plate. He mumbles a thank-you.

"You're gonna lose your eight-pack," I whisper to him. "Think of all the juices you're going to have to drink after this!"

He stabs his fork into the steamy pile of cheesy bacon goodness. When he takes his first bite, he makes an "mmm" sound. "Worth it."

Chapter Nineteen

Lewis

"Welp, so long, abs. You'll be sorely missed." I pat my stomach.

Harper laughs from the passenger seat of her car as I drive us back to Half Moon Bay.

"I'm sure they'll be back soon. You spend your days doing intense physical labor for the renovation. You'll burn off those carbs and cheese in no time."

I scoop her hand in mine and press a kiss to her knuckles, still floating from the evening at her family's house. I can't believe how well it went—how amazing her family is. They welcomed me with open arms and treated me like I was one of them. Me, a total stranger. Just because I was with Harper.

An unfamiliar feeling washes over me. It's like my chest is cracking in half, but in a good way.

"Sorry again for how over-the-top my family was," Harper says, shaking her head.

"Don't apologize. They're great." I smile thinking about how Jules insisted that I call her Mom.

"You've charmed my mom. And my great-uncle thinks

you're a superhero because you're tall and can reach every shelf in the house."

I laugh.

"And you handled my dad's incessant questions about your job as a contractor like a champ."

"I get it. He wants his daughter to be with someone responsible and gainfully employed. I'd want that too for my kid. Especially if they were as amazing and accomplished as you."

I catch the expression on her face. It's joy and something else. Disbelief, maybe?

She squeezes my hand and scoffs. "You're one of the most accomplished people I've ever met. You're a talented actor. And a contractor in your spare time. And you donate to charity. You're incredible, Lewis."

I loosen my hand and gently pull out of her hold. With both hands on the steering wheel, I focus on the darkened road ahead.

"I'm hardly incredible," I mutter.

A long stretch of silence passes, and I look over at Harper. The slight frown on her face conveys concern.

"Why would you say that about yourself?" Her tone is a mix of confused and caring, and it makes me ache.

"You know how I got fired from my show?" I say after a moment.

"I mean, I know the reason that the entertainment news outlets reported. They said it was because you and the showrunner didn't get along. You got into an argument, and he fired you."

I exhale so sharply, my lungs sting. "That's not entirely true. What actually happened was the showrunner was a sexually harassing piece of shit who was going after multiple people on the crew. I found out from my makeup artist, Katie. She's a good friend of mine and was one of the people he was targeting. Apparently, he's been doing it from the beginning of the show. I had no idea."

My heart hammers at that thought of just how long that asshole got away with it—how he's still getting away with it. I clench my jaw so hard the back of my neck starts to ache.

"I asked everyone on the crew who had been targeted by him if it was okay for me to confront him about it. They all said yes. So I did."

"What happened?"

"I told him I knew what he was doing. I knew what a disgusting predator he was. I told him that his days of sexually harassing the crew were over as long as I was on that show. And he told me I was fired."

"Jesus."

"Part of me was shocked that he didn't express one ounce of shame or regret. He didn't even flinch—that's how much he didn't care about my threats. And then he got rid of me."

"God, Lewis. That's awful."

"It's nothing compared to what the crew endured from him."

I force myself to loosen my death grip on the steering wheel. Just thinking about what Darren did—what he's been able to get away with—has me wanting to rage.

I force myself to take a breath. "That's why the show's been on hiatus since I was fired. I'm guessing they're trying to figure out a way to write off or replace my character and pick up the storyline. I've been texting a bit with Katie, and she said Darren's still on the show, which means he'll be back as soon as they cast my replacement and start filming again."

I look over to see Harper's mouth half-open. It's like she's too shocked and disgusted to say anything.

"If I were actually incredible, I would have been able to do something about that sack of shit," I mutter. "But I'm not. And I don't know how to help now that I've been fired and blacklisted. I thought…" I pull at my hair. "This is gonna sound obnoxious, but I thought that since I was the lead actor on the show, I had some clout, you know? I had some power to shut down this wrong and horrible thing that was happening. But I couldn't."

Harper shakes her head. "No, I get it. I honestly would have thought the same thing, that you would have had the power to put a stop to it. But god, how messed up is it that even you couldn't do anything?"

"That's why I got drunk at Chateau Marmont after it happened. I couldn't handle the fact that this guy was gonna get away with being a criminal, that he was gonna be able to victimize even more people, and nothing would happen to him." I clench my jaw. "Well, that and the fact that my ex used me getting fired as a reason to break up with me."

Even from the corner of my eye I can see Harper's eye bulge in shock. "What?"

I rub my fist at the back of my neck to ease the knot of pain that sprang up the moment I started talking about all this.

"I'd promised to get her a guest spot on the show. She's a model and wanted to transition into acting. When I told her the reason I got fired, I thought she'd support me. Instead she got upset that I blew her chance to be a star."

Harper stammers while shaking her head. "I don't even know what to say to that. Other than she sounds like a jerk. And a callous opportunist. Good god."

"She kind of was, now that I look back on it. I'm surprised Natalia and I lasted six months."

When Harper rests her hand on my forearm, the knot at the back of my neck loosens.

"It just goes to show how many gross and horrible things go on behind the scenes in the entertainment industry—and some people don't care as long as they're benefiting," I say. "And the public has no idea."

"Maybe if you went public with the real reason you got fired?" she poses, her tone hesitant.

I swallow back the shame crawling up my throat like bile. "I want to. My agent told me not to, though, that it would jeopardize things for me when I try to make a comeback. Darren is a well-connected guy in the TV industry. I know he's made calls to other showrunners to plant the seed that I'm not worth hiring. To go public could be a death sentence for my career."

"Oh. Damn."

"And I don't know if Katie and the others are comfortable with me doing that. As much as they hate Darren and want him to face consequences for what he's done, their jobs are on the line. If he fired me, the star of the show, who knows how he could ruin them. I know how awful that sounds, like we're prioritizing jobs over human safety."

"Hey." She tugs at my hand. "I don't think that at all. I understand that this a complicated situation. There's no easy solution."

I swallow and nod. "Thanks for saying that, for understanding. I want to nail Darren's ass to the wall. We all do. We just haven't figured out how to do that without destroying everyone's careers."

She rests her hand on my leg, and I place my hand

over hers. It's such a small physical act, but it means the world. It's the greatest comfort I could have in this moment when I'm admitting my biggest secret and my biggest worry to her.

"Thank you for telling me about this," she says after a quiet minute. "I know that couldn't have been easy."

I pull into the driveway of her house, and we walk inside. As soon as I kick my shoes off, she catches my wrist, turning me to her.

"I know it didn't work out the way you wanted, but I just want you to know that you did the right thing, Lewis. You stood up for your coworkers who were being harassed. So many people wouldn't dare to do anything. At least you tried."

There's an intensity and sadness in her eyes that jolts me. I pull her into a hug.

When we crawl into bed together, she cuddles into my bare chest, just like she's done every night since we first slept together. But something about tonight feels different when I wrap my arms around her. I told Harper something I'm ashamed of, and she didn't judge me or lash out. She empathized with me. She made me feel safe and cared for.

Eyes closed, I try to commit this feeling to my memory forever. An image of Harper cuddled in my bed at my house in LA flashes behind my eyelids. She's sound asleep, tucked against my chest. And then I see her padding around the house wearing one of my shirts. I see her lounging on my couch. I see her smiling up at me as she pulls a container of leftovers from the fridge.

My heart thuds. Yeah, she's made it clear that the Bay Area is her home, but I'm falling hard for this girl—harder than I've ever fallen for anyone before—and I want to see where things go between us. Maybe after I finish up the renovations, we can talk about a serious relationship. Maybe we do long-distance before deciding who moves where...

Details may be up in the air, but one thing is clear: I want Harper in my life from this moment on.

"Are you cold? You're hugging me kind of tight tonight," she murmurs into my chest.

I press a kiss to her head. "Not cold. Just happy."

Chapter Twenty

Harper

"Ladies and gentlemen, are you ready for tonight's entertainment?"

Naomi's eyes go wide at the announcement made by one of Simon's friends from the center of the bar. She claps her hands and jumps up and down so enthusiastically that her tiara-veil nearly falls off her head. When I reach up and straighten it, she thanks me.

"Hell yes, I'm ready!" she yells. Cheers and hollers from the other attendees follow.

It's the night of Simon and Naomi's joint bachelor-bachelorette party, and they've rented the upstairs floor of a bar down the street from where they live at the edge of Nob Hill. Two dozen of their closest friends are here to celebrate the happy couple with an evening of drinks, but now it's time for the main event.

Maren trots back from the bar and drops off another tequila shot on the standing table we're perched around.

"Easy," I say to Naomi. "That's your third one tonight."

She downs it anyway. "We had barbecue for dinner, remember? I ate a ton. Three pieces of corn bread! My stomach is good and lined with fatty meats and carbs just waiting to soak up alcohol."

Even in her tipsy state she must catch my frown, because she gives me a side hug. "Promise I won't get shit-faced."

My worry melts. My cousin's a lightweight, and as much fun as I want her to have tonight, I know how miserable she's felt the few times she's ever gotten drunk enough to have a hangover. My mission as maid of honor is to make sure that she has a good time without ending up with her head in the toilet.

For a moment I take in just how much she's glowing. Ever the nontraditional bride, she rejected every white cocktail dress Maren and I suggested for the bachelor-bachelorette party, opting instead for a black-and-gold minidress. She didn't even want to wear the standard white sash with the word *bride* emblazoned on it. The silver tiara with a strip of white tulle on top of her head is the only bridal accessory she's sporting. Her other accessory? A gorgeous smile that hasn't budged the entire night.

I squeeze my arms around her. "You look so happy."

Her big brown eyes tear up. "I'm a week away from marrying my dream guy. I've never been happier."

Maren, who's on the drunker side of tipsy, joins our hug, teetering on sparkly gold stilettos. She swipes at the skirt of her long-sleeve kelly green knit minidress. I reach over and straighten the hem for her.

She makes a kissy face at me as a thanks, then sniffles when she looks at Naomi. "I'm over the moon for you. You nabbed yourself a truly good guy. And he's hot! And he's about to strip for you! Naked! Woo!"

She raises her vodka on the rocks while the crowd of Naomi and Simon's friends cheer. The dim bar lighting goes completely dark. A second later, a spotlight beams in the center of the floor. Simon's friend who hollered the announcement a minute ago waltzes over to the illuminated spot with a chair.

"Will the future Mrs. Rutler please make her way to center stage?"

A roar of whistles and cheers follows. I dig out a stack of ones from my purse and hand it to her.

"Have fun." I wink.

She grins wide before giving me one more squeeze and trotting over to the chair, only wobbling once in her black pumps. When I see her grip the hem of her dress as she plops onto the chair, I hold back a laugh.

"I hope she's wearing underwear," I say to Maren.

"Oh, she is. I made sure of it."

The opening bars of Ginuwine's "Pony" blast through the upstairs speaker system, and everyone screams. Simon emerges from a shadowy corner clad in the suit he was wearing earlier tonight, sans tie and jacket. He grooves over to Naomi, whose cheeks are on fire. She smiles wide, then opens her mouth in shock when Simon rips his shirt off and tosses it to the side while dancing in a circle around her. This time the yells are deafening.

"Naomi is one lucky wench," Maren says as she looks on.

I roll my eyes and laugh, then dart my gaze away when Simon starts to body-roll over Naomi.

"Don't get me wrong, I love my cousin and Simon to death." I cup my hand over the side of my face. "And I love that they're having a party that's so uniquely them. But I feel weird watching him strip. He's gonna be my cousin by marriage in a week. It feels kind of…incestuous…to see him get naked."

A thoughtful look crosses Maren's face. "Good point." She winces.

I check my phone, giddy when I see a text from Lewis.

Lewis: How are you holding up, DD? Have you broken down and had a shot yet?

Me: Nope, doing fine so far! It's actually not the lack of alcohol that's so bad...but I'm currently watching my cousin's fiancé give her a lap dance and...dear god, someone's gonna get pregnant by the end of the night.

He sends back a string of hysterical laughing emojis.

Lewis: Okay yeah, that sounds a bit awkward.

Lewis: When you come home will you treat me to a striptease of your own?

My heart tumbles to my feet. *Home.* He thinks of my house as home.

I take a second to put my heart back into its rightful place.

Me: I was hoping you'd give me one. This dress I'm wearing is plastered to my body, there's no sexy way to take it off.

Lewis: I disagree. Anything you do is sexy.

Lewis: But if it's a striptease from me you want, I'd be happy to give it to you.

I bite my lip, my lady bits and my heart throbbing in tandem.

"I haven't seen you smile like that in a long time."

I whip my head up and see an inquisitive look on Maren's face.

"Lewis?" she asks.

I know I'm blushing like a smitten teen when I nod at her, but I can't help it. Seeing just how well Lewis got along with my family the other night intensified the already strong feelings I have for him. And when he opened up to me about why he got fired on the car ride back to Half Moon Bay, it felt like a massive shift happened between us. In the time that I've gotten to know him, I can tell that he isn't the kind of person to let people in easily. He's not close with his family. Despite the loads of professional connections he has in LA, he doesn't seem to have many close friends. He keeps his cards close to his chest because his past history and trauma have taught him that he can't trust very many people.

Even with all that, he chose to confide in me. He chose to let me in. He chose to trust me. And that shatters me every time I think about it. Because it showed that I mean a lot to him...just like he means a lot to me.

That night after we got home from dinner with my family and we fell asleep cuddled into each other in his bed, it felt different. It's felt different every day since then. We look at each other longer. We hold each other tighter. There's something extra behind every kiss we share.

This setup doesn't feel like some temporary fling anymore. It feels deeper, more meaningful...and a lot like love.

This is the first time I've let myself think that, and it rattles me so hard, I nearly trip over my heeled feet, even as I stand in place.

"You've got it bad for him, don't you?" Maren says, interrupting my thoughts.

I open my mouth, the urge to deny it almost automatic. But no words come out. Because I can't lie to one of my best friends.

I press my eyes shut and shake my head. It's impossible to think straight with the beat of this slow jam blasting around me, all the while trying not to watch my cousin's future husband grind on her.

I pull Maren by the arm to the stairwell where it's quiet.

"I think I'm falling for Lewis."

I tell her about how I brought him over to meet my family, how we've grown closer over the past few weeks, and how he's opened up to me.

Her giddy expression softens. "Harper, that's amazing. Why do you sound so freaked-out, then? From what you just told me, you two feel the same way about each other."

I shrug and hug my arms around myself. "He's a famous TV star, Maren. When he's done renovating my house in a few weeks, he's going back to LA to kick-start his career again. I'm planning to split my time between Half Moon Bay and San Francisco to work and volunteer. How exactly can we make our two very different lifestyles work?"

"Why don't you talk to him about it?" Her tone is gentle and coaxing as she brushes away the chunk of bangs that has fallen into my eyes.

"Because it could end badly. What if I tell him I love him and I want something more—something long-term? What if he tells me he's not into it?"

"And what if he tells you that he loves you too and wants exactly what you want?"

I let out a sad laugh. "I see your point."

"You'll never know how he feels unless you talk about it. And you've always been someone who's not afraid of a tough conversation, no matter if it's work or dating or family. I've always admired that about you." She pauses, the look on her face softening as she gazes at me. "But I guess this is a testament to just how much you like this guy, huh?"

Maren gives my shoulder a squeeze. "Bold and up-front Harper can talk about anything with anyone."

"Except my mushy-gushy feelings for the guy I'm crazy about," I mumble.

"I get it. It's scary to put your heart on the line when you're really into someone."

"It is. I… I've never felt this way about anyone before."

The words linger on my tongue. That's the first time I've said this. I haven't even told Naomi.

Maren's glossy red lips curve up in a hopeful smile. "All the more reason to talk to him. You can speculate and second-guess all you want, but you won't be able to do anything unless you tell him how you really feel."

"You're right." I pull her in for a hug. "I'm so glad you moved back to the city. Don't get me wrong, I was so happy when you landed that travel nurse job. I know how much you loved it. But having one of my best friends close by again is the greatest."

"I'm so, so glad to be back. Especially now that my bestie is dating my celebrity hall pass."

I burst out laughing as we break apart. "I thought that hot Welsh actor whose name I can never remember was your hall pass?"

Maren shakes her head. "Now that I have an actual hot Welsh guy as my boyfriend, I bumped him for Lewis."

"That's fair. How's Ian doing, by the way?"

"Good. I miss him. He's still working those awful long hours, but I'm so pumped to visit him in a few months."

Even though she's still smiling, there's a gleam of sadness in her saucer eyes. She and her long-distance boyfriend, Ian, who lives in London, have been off and on for the past almost ten years. They met when she studied abroad in the UK her junior year of college and have been long-distance their entire relationship. They meet up for vacations every few months, but I know it takes a toll on Maren. She wishes they could be in the same place more than anything, but neither one of them wants to make the leap and move across the globe for the other.

"You're gonna have the best time when you see each other," I say. "He misses you like crazy too." I give her what I hope is an encouraging squeeze on the shoulder.

Doubt lingers in her stare, but then she nods once and flashes a smile that looks the slightest bit forced. "I'm gonna get another drink. Wanna come with me?"

We make our way back to the main area, both of our jaws plummeting when we see Simon kneeling between Naomi's spread legs, pressing a kiss to the inside of her thigh. Even though she's covering her face with both of her hands, I know she's sporting a wide, giddy grin. Dollar bills fall around them like confetti. Deafening hollers drown out whatever song is now playing.

"Oh my god, get a room, you two!" I yell.

Simon doesn't even look over at me as he raises his arm and gives a thumbs-up before hopping to his feet, Naomi's hand in his. His skin-fade haircut is completely mussed, and he's sporting the smuggest grin I've ever seen on him. Naomi bursts into uncontrollable giggles, likely due to the alcohol she's consumed and the hot show her husband-to-be just treated her to.

"See that? That's the smile of a man who knows he's about to experience the best lay of his life," Maren says.

"At least he's still got his pants on."

Simon nods at me. "You heard the maid of honor, everyone. I'm off to take my future wife home. Have a good night!"

He bends down and throws Naomi over his shoulder. She squeals and slaps his ass just before he starts walking toward the hallway leading to the stairs.

I shake my head. "God, those two."

"Aww, but don't you think it's so romantic how crazy they are for each other?" Maren says, pressing a palm to her chest.

"Of course I do. I just don't want to see them go at it."

I make a mock-gag noise, and Maren lightly pushes me. She grabs another drink and I check my texts.

Lewis: How much longer till you're home?

Home. There goes my heart again.

Me: Well, the groom just fireman-carried his bride out of the bar, so things are wrapping up pretty soon. I'm going to drop my friend off at her apartment when she finishes her drink, then I'll be on my way. Two hours tops.

Lewis: Can't wait ;) Get ready for the surprise of your life.

For the next hour, all I can think about is what Lewis has in store for me when I get home.

I walk in the front door to find Lewis sitting on the couch, looking at his phone, decked out in a three-piece suit.

My mouth falls open. Holy shit, he looks hot.

"Wow." I can barely get the word out, I'm so blown away at how good he looks.

He smiles as he stands up slowly and walks toward me.

"Good evening, Ms. Ellorza. Welcome to Club Lewis. You're a VIP guest, and I'm going to make sure you're taken care of tonight."

The corner of his mouth ticks up into that cheeky half smile I adore. He turns and heads to the kitchen and pulls a bottle of sparkling wine from the fridge. As he pops the cork and pours the bubbly liquid into a champagne flute, I take him in with hungry eyes. In those charcoal-gray trousers, vest, and jacket with the black tie, crisp white shirt, and black dress shoes, he looks like he walked straight off an award show red carpet.

"You just happened to pack a designer suit?" I ask, breathless.

"I always have a backup suit just in case a special occasion should arise. And make no mistake, this is a special occasion…"

He strolls back over and hands the glass to me. My throat has gone dry, so I guzzle the wine, coughing when the bubbles hit my nose.

"More?" He holds up the bottle in his hand.

"Please." He pours me another glass, and this time I sip it. "Um, you look freaking fantastic."

"Thanks. So do you."

A grunting noise rips from his throat before he takes a pull straight from the bottle. As he swallows, he does a slow scan of my body from head to toe.

"Really regret being in the shower when you left for the bachelorette party," he says, his voice a low growl.

"Really?" I drain the rest of my wine, then take the bottle from his hand and sip from it.

He nods, his eyes locked on mine. He runs the back of his hand along the curve of my hip. "This dress," he hisses.

"This old thing?" I tease, doing a little shimmy in the figure-hugging bandage dress.

He responds by squeezing my ass. He eyes fall to the hemline, which hits at the middle of my thigh.

"If I had seen you looking this hot, I wouldn't have let you leave." He runs a finger along the wine-colored fabric. He skims his hand up my body, landing at the off-the-shoulder strap.

I step forward, closing the space between us. My body presses against his, and I feel that telltale hardness against my thigh.

"What would you have done?"

"Lots and lots of filthy things."

"Show me."

Another grunt-like noise escapes from him as he grabs me by the arm and leads me into my bedroom. He sits me on the edge of the bed and stands in front of me.

"That's a nice suit," I mutter as he rips off the jacket and tosses it on the floor. "Should you hang it up? It looks expensive."

"Fuck that," he growls.

I bite my bottom lip as it curls into a massive grin. Lewis has gone full-on caveman, and I couldn't be happier. Or hornier.

I lean back and enjoy the visual of him peeling away each layer of fabric from his body. He doesn't rush, taking his time unbuttoning each button on his shirt and vest, lowering the zipper of his pants, loosening his belt. The entire time his gaze is locked on mine. I try my hardest to keep eye contact, but my stare slips below many,

many times. His body is just too beautiful. It would be a crime not to appreciate it in every state of undress.

When Lewis makes it to his gray boxer briefs, he doesn't move to take them off. He just runs his thumbs along the waistband.

"Why'd you stop?" I ask, just now realizing how short of breath I am.

"Because I want you to take over. Then I want to lie down on the bed and have you ride my face. Then I want you to ride me."

A giddy giggle works its way up my chest and throat, spilling from my lips. I sound like a drunk hyena.

"I can manage that."

A second later I'm up and lunging at him to yank down those pesky boxer briefs, revealing the most beautifully sculpted thighs I've ever seen. When I wrap my hand around his hardness, a strangled noise sounds from the base of his throat.

"Careful," he groans. "You do that for too long, I'm gonna be quite the disappointment."

"You could never."

Even in my four-inch heels, I have to tiptoe up to kiss him. But then he grips his hands around my hips, hoisting me up to wrap my legs around his waist so I'm at eye level with him. For a minute we stand just like that while we kiss, our tongues teasing each other breathless, our kiss growing filthier and filthier by the second.

"Do you ever get tired of having to lean down to kiss me? Or carry me?"

"Never. I fucking love it."

He smiles against my lips, and I catch a glimpse of that dimple in his right cheek. "Well, I really fucking love this too." I gently tap it with my index finger.

"That's convenient, since I'm a fan of your dimples."

"I don't have dimples."

He taps my lower back. "You do here."

He wags an eyebrow, and I giggle. When he drags his mouth along the side of my neck, I press my eyes shut and groan. "Lewis…"

The feel of his whiskers against the sensitive skin of my neck has me shuddering. I sink my teeth into the base of his neck. His growled and profane mutter spurs me on. I find his mouth once more and claw at his hair and shoulders.

"Bed. Now. Please," I whine.

Before I even blink, he's sitting on the edge of the bed and I'm in his lap. I slide off to stand between his legs. When I move to tug off my dress, he stills me with a hand on my arm.

"Can I?"

Biting my lip, I nod. He starts with his fingers at the hem of my dress. I raise my arms up as he slowly peels the snug fabric over my head, leaving me in just a thong.

A muttered curse is his response as he takes in the sight of my body through a dazed stare.

"God, you're so beautiful." He circles his hands around my waist before pressing a kiss right above my belly button. The whisper-soft sensation combined with the reverence in his tone has me vibrating. It ignites something raw, something unholy in me.

I shove him to lie down on the bed, slide off my thong, then do what he requested. As I climb up to his face, his hazel eyes glow amber right around the irises. When I lower myself over his mouth and feel that first lap of his heavenly tongue, the amber ring thickens. Pleasure and pressure rocket through my clit, radiating all the way up my chest, squeezing my heart and lungs.

"Lewis." I grip the headboard as my head lolls back. "Lewis…"

I chant his name as I lose myself in the sensations. When he hums against me, I gasp. The vibrations amp up the intensity of the pressure so much that I'm instantly light-headed.

I reach down and tug a hand through his hair. "Keep doing that. Please."

He licks and hums until I can barely stay upright. My entire body trembles with the need for release. When I glance down at his face, he quirks up a brow. I can't see his mouth, but I recognize the scrunch of his bearded cheeks as they crinkle upward. He's grinning. Something about seeing him devour me so openly with such smugness kicks the naughtiness of this experience up a notch. That pulse between my legs throbs fiery hot, and my chest squeezes tight.

And then he hums louder and I'm a goner.

Orgasm hits so intensely that I nearly topple over, but he grips me with both hands on my waist, propping me up as I convulse and shout.

When my screams start to fade, those powerful and sculpted arms of his slide me down so that I'm sitting on top of his waist. Eyes still on me, he swipes a condom from the top drawer of the nightstand, rips it open, and slides it on.

With a gentle hand on my chin, he pulls me down for another filthy, breathless kiss.

"Ride me," he growls before licking my bottom lip.

I mumble what sounds like "okay" in my sex-drunk haze. I slide on and groan at the delicious feel of him stretching me out. Then, for the second time tonight, I do exactly what he requests. I ride him until my legs are sore, until my voice is hoarse from shouting his name, until my body is shattered once more from the mind-blowing orgasm he gives me.

I'm shaking, clawing at his chest, thrashing my thighs against him. The whole time his gaze is locked on me, like he needs to observe my body experiencing every second of this pleasure. Then I see his eyes glaze over and the muscles in his jaw bulge as he bites down. His grip on me tightens and his thrusts into me speed up. A guttural groan escapes from his mouth, signaling his own climax.

After he leaves to get rid of the condom and crawls back into bed, I end up curled on his chest, both his arms wrapped around me. It's a minute before I manage to crawl out of the pleasure haze and formulate an actual sentence.

"Five-star rating for Club Lewis."

His throaty laugh thunders above me. "You're welcome back anytime."

I close my eyes and chuckle, then drift off to sleep.

Chapter Twenty-One

Harper

"How's it look?"

I look up from where I'm painting in the living room and spot Lewis halfway up the ladder in the dining room, right underneath the clear, half dome–shaped light fixture he just mounted. The light silver stem it hangs from glistens in the sunlight streaming in from the nearby French doors.

"Oh wow." I walk over to get a closer look. "This is perfect."

He steps off the ladder and pulls me in for a kiss.

I lean back and laugh. "You've done that every time you finish a project."

"Done what?"

"Make out with me. It's like your unofficial way of rewarding yourself for a job well done."

He wiggles his eyebrows. "I think that's a completely reasonable reward system."

He leans down for another kiss before he trots to the kitchen to guzzle some water. I pull out my phone and check my notes to cross off yet another project from the renovation to-do list. When I see there's just a handful of small-scale tasks left, my heart sinks. Only two weeks left in the renovation…which means only two weeks left living in romantic bliss with Lewis.

Maren's words from last weekend resurface yet again. *You'll never know how he feels unless you talk about it.*

In the three days since I first received Maren's sound advice, I've tried to bring up the topic of our future to Lewis a few times. I've gone over hypothetical questions and conversations in my head, what I'd do if he doesn't feel the same way, what we'd do if he does feel the same and we decide to give this a shot, how things would work long-distance and if I could handle what it would mean to date a high-profile actor who's going through a very public moment…but each time I start to say something, I've promptly lost my nerve and initiated sex instead.

I can't keep doing that. If I want to figure out where we stand, I need to just ask him.

I glance over at Lewis, who's gazing at his phone. When he looks up and sees me watching him, he winks.

I breathe in. Now's as good a time as any.

"Hey, can we—"

My phone blares, interrupting me. When I see it's Naomi, I ignore it. I'll call her back later. This conversation has waited long enough.

Lewis grabs an apple from the bowl on the island and takes a bite. "What were you saying?"

"I was going to ask if you—"

Again my phone blares with a call from Naomi. "Sorry, hang on." I answer it. "Hey, what's up?"

I can barely understand her, she's speaking so fast.

"Whoa, slow down. What happened? Are you okay?"

Her breath comes out in a shudder. "No. I'm not okay. We don't have a wedding venue anymore."

"What? How is that possible?"

She goes into panicked, fast-talking mode again, but I catch the gist of what she says. Some water main burst, flooding the San Francisco Mint and a handful of other buildings on that block. As a result, the venue sustained a ton of water damage and had to cancel all events for the next two weeks for repairs—including Naomi and Simon's wedding, which is this weekend.

"I just... I don't know what to do, Harper."

The quiver in her tone makes me want to hug her.

"Simon and I have been calling places all over the city since we got the news this morning, but it honestly seems like there are zero other venue options for us this close to our wedding date—none that we can afford anyway."

My mind races to think of something, anything comforting to say, but I can't come up with anything other than the standard, "It's gonna be okay. I promise. We'll figure something out."

She sniffles. "The wedding's in four days, Harper. I have no... I don't even... God, I can't even think straight..."

Her voice breaks just before I hear Simon's muffled voice in the background.

"Hey. Come here."

More muffled sounds echo from her end of the line, like he's hugging her.

"I'll marry you anywhere, Naomi. In the middle of a street, in a landfill, in a fast-food drive-through. I couldn't give less of a crap where we do it. All I care about is the fact that I get to be with you for the rest of my life."

My eyes tear up as I listen to Simon. Naomi sniffles, and the two of them exchange sweet words.

I tug a fist through my hair, my mind racing to figure out a solution to this impossible problem. Then I notice Lewis staring at me, concern etched in his frown.

"Everything okay?" he whispers.

"Not really," I whisper back.

I cover the mouthpiece of my phone and quickly explain the situation to him.

"Shit, that's nuts."

"I'm racking my brain, but I can't think of a single place they could do it. I mean, it's a small wedding. They're only having, like, thirty guests—just my and Naomi's family, Simon's family, and a few friends. You'd think there'd be at least one place in all of San Francisco that could host them."

Lewis's gaze turns focused as he glances around. Hands on his hips, he starts to spin in a circle, as if he's surveying the room.

He pivots to me. "What if they got married here?"

I almost laugh. "What?"

"You said it's only thirty people, right? You could easily fit that many people in this space, since it's an open-concept design."

He walks into the living room near the fireplace. "We could only fit twenty chairs in front of the fireplace, but if everyone else was okay standing for the ceremony, it could work. And I know there's a lot of tools lying around, but we can get those cleared out and do a quick clean of the space. We could even get a bunch of candles and string up some lights for decorations. That might look nice." He gestures to the ceiling.

My mouth is agape as I observe Lewis taking command of the situation like he's some sort of secret wedding planner. Naomi starts to speak again, but I tell her to hold on.

"Wait, are you serious, Lewis?"

He looks at me like I just asked him if he enjoys acting. "Of course I'm serious."

"You're okay with my cousin and her fiancé having their wedding here—in the house that you're hiding out in? You're okay with everyone seeing you?"

He takes a second, like he's rethinking what we've both said. "Yes. I'm okay with it."

"Remember when you first moved in and said you didn't want anyone coming over so they wouldn't recognize you and give away where you're staying?"

He smiles softly. "Okay, yeah, I won't lie, I'm a little nervous at the thought of being around a group of people. But meeting your family put me at ease. They haven't told anyone about me. Yeah, I know that's because they have no idea who I am, but that showed me that I can be around people if I trust them. And I trust you, Harper. If you tell the people in your life who know who I am that I'm staying with you and to keep it private, I'll be okay with this. Plus, look at me." When he shakes his head, his blond hair falls in shaggy waves around his face. He runs a hand over his short golden beard. "I haven't gotten a haircut or shaved since I've been here. I look a lot different from how everyone is used to seeing me. I bet some people won't even recognize me."

I'm speechless, so moved by his kind words and thoughtful gesture, at the same time in disbelief that he's figured out a solution to my cousin's wedding nightmare.

"If you're truly okay with this, I promise, I will do everything to protect your privacy, Lewis. Every person who comes to this wedding will be sworn to secrecy. They won't say a word about you, I swear."

He walks over and pulls me into a hug, then presses a soft kiss to my lips. For the millionth time since Lewis came into my life, my heart flutters.

"We could come up with a fake name for you. And tell them you're a celebrity look-alike or something. Just to be extra safe." I run a hand through his hair.

A smile appears in that sea of golden whiskers. "It's okay. You don't need to do all that. I trust you, Harper. If you trust your family to keep things discreet, then I trust them too."

I try to speak, but all I can do is stammer through a breath. To have Lewis's complete trust means everything. I hug him tight, then kiss him.

He smiles down at me. "Let's give your cousin the wedding of her dreams."

I'm buzzing. "We'll have to put the renovation on hold until after the wedding in order to get this place set up in time," I say.

"Totally understand." He cups his palm against my face. "Put me to work—I'll do whatever I can to help."

I tiptoe up and give him another kiss, then I bring my phone back to my ear.

"Naomi? I have an idea. Put me on speaker so Simon can hear too."

"Please tell us you've figure out some magical solution." Simon sounds exhausted.

"I have. Actually, it was my contractor's idea." I wink up at Lewis, who shakes his head, smiling.

And then I dive right in.

I watch Naomi sitting at the makeshift vanity I threw together in my bedroom: I moved the coffee table from the living room next to the full-length mirror in here. She's clad in a silky pink robe, perched on a small padded stool I found in the garage, swiping on the last of her makeup.

"How do I look?" She twists to me, and I go teary. Again. Just like every other time I've looked at my cousin today.

"You look like the most beautiful bride ever."

"I don't even have my dress on yet."

"Doesn't matter. You still look like an angel."

I fan at my eyes with both hands to stop the burn from morphing into full-blown tears. She swipes two tissues from the box next to her makeup and hands me one.

"Hold it right under your eyes, hurry! Otherwise your mascara will run."

I do exactly that, and so does she. Snotty chuckles fall from our glossed lips.

"I am sorry for what a mess I am today," I say. "But I can't help it. I love you, Naomi. I'm so happy you found your one."

I reach over and hold her hand in mine.

"I'm not used to seeing you so misty-eyed," she says, squeezing my hand. "I love it. And I love you too, Harper. Thank you for being the most wonderful cousin–slash–best friend–slash–maid of honor. You saved the day. I don't know what we would have done without you."

"Save the thanks until you see how it all looks out there," I joke.

Her lips tremble as she beams at me. "It's gonna be beautiful, I just know it."

Naomi arrived at the house early this afternoon to start getting ready in my room while Lewis was just starting to set up the living room for the sunset wedding we threw together. I smile to myself when I think about how she stared at him with wide, unblinking eyes for a solid ten seconds, stammering her own name when he introduced himself to her.

She turns back to the mirror to fix her makeup, and I move to help her. I'm in the middle of powdering her T-zone when she locks eyes with me in the mirror.

"Look, I know I was a little starstruck when I met Lewis, but I saw the way he's been looking at you. He really, really likes you, Harper."

Since I'm looking at our reflections in the mirror, I don't miss the way the skin on my neck and chest flushes.

"You think so?"

"I know so."

When I set the brush down, she gently turns my face to look at her, then dabs a Q-tip under my eyes.

"You're in love with him."

The way she says it, so surely, so definitively, feels like an accusation and a revelation all at once.

"I am." I say it so quietly I can barely hear myself.

"Have you told him?" she asks gently, like she always does when she knows she's asking me a borderline-intrusive question.

I shake my head. "I've been trying to work up the nerve."

She fixes me with a stare that's tender and determined all at once. "I know I'm especially loved up right now since it's my wedding day and all, but please tell him how you feel. I've never heard you gush about a guy like this before. I can tell he's different—he's special to you. And I know I only just met him today, but I can see the guy feels something deep for you too. His eyes turn to hearts when he looks at you. I can't wait to see his reaction when you come out in that dress."

I smooth a hand over the floor-length Grecian-style rose-gold satin dress I'm wearing.

She points to the V neckline. "Your boobs have never looked better. He's gonna notice that for sure."

I playfully shove away her hand but quietly hope that what she says is true. Because today is a special occasion, I went the extra mile with my makeup and styled my hair in loose waves. I even opted to wear contacts. He's never seen me without glasses, and I'm hoping the full-on glam look I've managed blows him away.

My stomach does a backflip in anticipation of what he'll think when he sees me. He's seen a million glammed-up people in his line of work. Will I even make an impression? Will it drive home how he feels about me? Or will it just be a blip on his radar?

Naomi cups my hand in hers, like she can tell I'm second-guessing myself.

"When he sees you, he's going to choke on his own tongue, you look so freaking stunning. He also spent the last three days busting his ass to get the house ready for your cousin's wedding, someone he doesn't even know. He gave up his hiding spot to use as a wedding venue—for you. That's love." She rests her hands on my shoulders. "You deserve to be happy, Harper. You've spent so much time working hard and looking after everyone else, making sure we're all taken care of. Now it's your turn. Go for it with him."

The bedroom door opens, and in walks Maren in a flowy long-sleeve dress with a pink-and-green floral pattern, her long hair in messy barrel curls. I tuck away Naomi's words for later and refocus on the task at hand: making sure my cousin's wedding goes off without a hitch.

Maren takes one look at Naomi and gasps. "You are freaking gorgeous." She gushes over Naomi's low side bun with a few loose waves framing her face.

"Thank God for hair and makeup tutorials on YouTube," Naomi says.

Maren points to the wedding dress, which is hanging against the back of the bedroom door. "Shall we get you dressed, Mrs. Rutler?"

Naomi nods excitedly. Together Maren and I help her into the long-sleeve, off-the-shoulder lace gown. When she's dressed, I fetch her heels. She slides into them and then turns to the mirror.

Maren and I can barely keep it together as we stand on either side of her. The three of us gaze at Naomi in the mirror, a trio of teary eyes and quivering lips.

"God, we are so pathetic," Naomi says, fanning her eyes.

We all chuckle. Then she grabs our hands. "Thank you both for being here with me. You've made this day so special."

We exchange *I love you*s just as there's a knock at the door. It's the photographer.

"Naomi, your mom wanted me to get a pic of her seeing you in your dress for the first time."

She says of course, and Maren and I step back to make room for Naomi's mom. The photographer snaps away as she bursts into tears at the sight of her only daughter in her wedding dress. They embrace, and Maren and I slip out to let them have a moment together.

In the hallway Maren turns to me. "You look so freaking stunning by the way. That dress." She whistles. "Your man is gonna have a heart attack."

I blush and chuckle. "How's he doing? I haven't had the chance to check on him in a couple of hours."

"Amazing. He's been busy setting up the decorations and chairs, so no one's really bothered him. I think some people don't even recognize him with that shaggy hair and beard he's sporting. He looks like a hot surfer more than a TV star."

We head out to the living area and my eyes bulge when I take in the space. Lewis turned the open-concept space of my grandparents' house into a rustic haven. Strings of fairy lights line the walls, creating the most beautiful mood lighting. It's the perfect amount of light—not too bright, to keep the romantic ambience, but not too dark. The photographer will be able to take good photos. Dozens of white candles dot the windowsills, the kitchen island, and the counters. White flower petals line the end of the hallway all the way to the fireplace, where Simon and Naomi will be exchanging their vows. Lewis convinced me to keep it painted white for the wedding, and I see exactly why now. It serves as the perfect blank canvas for the strings of fairy lights and white candles adorning it. Rows of white chairs line either side of the flower-petal aisle. It looks like something out of a wedding magazine.

"Holy…"

"He did good, huh?" Maren nudges me before walking off to tell Naomi's dad that she's in her wedding dress if he wants to do a first look.

I glance around to look for Lewis, but I don't see him among the few dozen people milling around. He must be in his room changing.

I snap a few pics on my phone to send to Naomi, then walk over to the corner of the living room, where the guitarist, violinist, and flutist are sitting. They've been playing soft mood music for the past hour while guests have been arriving and mingling. After making sure everything is picture-perfect for Naomi's entrance, I run over and greet my parents and Uncle Pedro as they walk through the front door.

Since Naomi and Simon wanted a small and intimate wedding ceremony, the only people attending today are their immediate family and closest friends. Simon's mom, sister, and grandma wave at me from where they're sitting at the front row of chairs. I snap their photo, then glimpse Simon standing in the kitchen sipping what looks like scotch with his friend who is the officiant. I walk over.

"Hey." I hug him. "Look at you, *GQ*." When we break apart, I swipe away a tiny piece of lint from the lapel of his black suit. His stubbled cheeks flush.

"You look beautiful, Harper," he says.

"Wait till you see your wife."

"My head's gonna explode, isn't it?"

"Right along with your heart. Seriously, though, congrats."

He pulls me into yet another hug. "Thanks again for saving the day. We owe you."

"You owe me nothing. Just be the best husband my cousin could ask for."

Eyes teary, Simon sniffles as he promises me that he will, and my heart aches. He's so, so in love with her.

When we pull apart, I pat his chest. "It's time. Go take your place."

Simon practically sprints to the altar, only stopping to quickly embrace his mom, sister, and grandma before standing in front of the fireplace. I direct everyone to either sit in the chairs or stand near the back next to the kitchen, then I run to my bedroom to tell Naomi to head out once she's ready. As I shut the door behind me, I turn and bump into a broad chest clad in a three-piece charcoal gray suit I recognize instantly. When I step back and take in Lewis, I lose all the air in my lungs.

My jaw falls open. He is the most handsome I've ever seen him.

When I make it to his face, his expression throws me. There are literal stars in his eyes.

"Holy…" A strangled noise follows.

I bite my lip at his reaction and smooth a hand over my dress.

"Harper, you…you…" He tugs a hand through his shaggy hair, as if to snap himself out of some trance. "You're breathtaking."

It feels like fireworks crackling inside me. I step forward and glide my hands up his chest and rest them on his shoulders. "You took the words right out of my mouth."

Even in my four-inch heels, I have to tiptoe up to kiss him. Before our kiss can get too filthy, I pull away. He grunts, and I chuckle.

"We gotta keep this quick and PG. This is a wedding, after all."

"Right," he mutters, that dazed look still lingering on his face. "We'll finish this later, then."

"How have the guests been? No one's being weird with you, right?"

"Everyone's been great, so polite and welcoming. Whatever talking-to you gave them is working. Though I'm pretty sure Naomi's parents and Simon's mom and grandma have no idea who I am. They've forgotten my name a few times already."

He chuckles and presses a kiss to my cheek before heading back into the living room, but I catch his wrist. "Thank you for everything you did. This place looks beyond beautiful. My cousin is gonna burst into happy tears when she sees it."

A warm look passes over his face. "It was my pleasure."

I watch him as he walks into the living room, stopping by where my parents and Uncle Pedro are seated to say a quick hello and promise to catch up after the ceremony. He stands near the kitchen island, away from everyone.

The door opens behind me, and there stands Naomi, her arm looped in the crook of her dad's elbow. She holds her bouquet in her hand; her dad hands me mine.

"Ready?" I ask her.

She beams. "So ready."

I walk out and nod to the instrumentalists. The opening bars of Pachelbel's "Canon in D" ring in the small space as I walk along the flower-petal pathway to the fireplace. Then, I turn and take in Naomi's wide-eyed reaction when she walks out and gawks at the decor. Simon is standing just a few feet away, looking like a cartoon character whose eyes have just popped out of his head as he gazes at his soon-to-be wife.

I hold in an "aww" sound. He is the definition of lovestruck.

Soon the amusement inside me morphs into an ache when I spot his chin wobble while he watches his bride walk up to him. I take Naomi's bouquet and stand off to the side. They join hands, their teary gazes glued to one another.

The photographer moves quietly around the space, snapping photos. I'm relieved that Naomi was okay with my suggestion not to have anyone take photos on their phone during the ceremony and the reception. Not only does that help protect Lewis's privacy, but she and Simon said it's perfect because they want everyone to be present in the moment and enjoy spending time together instead of being glued to their phones.

The officiant begins, and I half listen while I glance around at the small audience gazing adoringly at Simon and Naomi. But then my ears perk up when he says something that resonates.

"We're here today because Simon and Naomi decided to be brave. They decided to do one of the scariest things you can ever choose to do—make yourself vulnerable to another person, to give yourself—your heart—completely to someone else. That's terrifying, because so much could go wrong. You could get hurt. You could get your heart broken if the other person doesn't feel the same way.

"But you could also experience one of the most fulfilling and blissful things in the world—being in love. To me, that's worth all the risk. The payoff is so much greater than what you put on the line. Because the payoff is waking up every day next to the person who loves you most in the world, the person who would defend you till the end, the person who lives to make you happy, the person whose joy is wrapped in your own joy. And I hope that seeing Naomi and Simon here today declaring their love for one another inspires every one of you in this room to be brave and fight for the love you deserve."

My cynical heart pulses harder and faster at the officiant's words.

Fight for the love you deserve.

Never in my life have I ever felt the urge to fight for anyone I've been with…except for the man standing a dozen feet away from me.

I twist my head to look over at Lewis, taken aback by the intense look on his face as he gazes at me. It makes my skin tingle and my insides ache. It's even hard to breathe. But I inhale slowly, quietly. And I can't help but wonder if the officiant's words hit him as hard as they hit me.

I hope so.

It doesn't matter, really; I've already made up my mind. Tonight I'm going to be brave. I'm going to shove aside every doubt about the future, every fleeting insecurity I have. Tonight I'm going to tell Lewis that I love him.

Chapter Twenty-Two

Lewis

When I walk into the living room after changing out of my suit and see Harper passed out on the plush armchair in the corner, I chuckle to myself. She's still dressed in her gown and those sky-high heels.

I'm not surprised. It was one hell of a night she helped pull off. Now that all the guests are gone, exhaustion must have caught up with her.

After the wedding ceremony, we toasted Simon and Naomi with champagne. Everyone dined on appetizers and cupcakes. Someone's Spotify playlist played romantic songs in the background while everyone chatted. We moved the chairs into the garage and made a makeshift dance floor, where Simon and Naomi shared their first dance as a married couple. That was the only traditional wedding thing they did, opting instead to visit with guests the rest of the time. It felt more like a laidback dinner party than a wedding. I loved that. Not like I've been to a lot of weddings, but the ones I've attended have always felt so formal and stuffy.

But this crew? They blew me away with how easygoing and friendly they were about everything. I guess I'm not used to that…to being around a welcoming and loving family. Even as I opted to hang along the sidelines on my own, checking with Harper when I wasn't busy hauling away furniture or setting up food, people still went out of their way to thank me for my help and compliment me on the work I've done to the house so far. To my surprise, not a single person mentioned anything about me being an actor or my meltdown. There weren't even any curious looks thrown my way. Everyone was polite and treated me like a regular wedding guest. That honestly blew me away. Harper must have laid down the law when she talked to her family. Or maybe they're just that kind and considerate. That would make sense— that's how Harper is.

Tonight also showed me that it's worth it to let my guard down. Maybe around the right people, I don't have to be so skittish and scared of my trust being broken. I can be myself, and that'll be enough. It's an incredible feeling, this comfort, this lightness. I have Harper to thank for it.

I smile to myself again as I take in her sleeping form draped over the arm of the couch, how peaceful she looks, her chest rising and falling with each breath.

God, this woman. The longer I look at her, the harder my heart pulses. On top of the raw desire I feel for her every minute of every day, there's affection that runs deeper than I've ever felt for anyone. There's protectiveness—it hits like a punch to the gut, the realization that I'd do anything for her and fight any battle if it meant that I could keep her safe. There's contentment—I've never felt as happy as when I'm with her.

And then, just like it did during the wedding ceremony, my heart shatters on the next beat when I think about just how much I love her.

So damn much.

I think back to the moment when our stares connected while she stood next to her cousin at the makeshift fireplace altar. As the officiant spoke about being brave enough to love, I could swear I saw something different in the look in her eyes. It was like she was seeing me in a whole new light…like she could love me too, the same way that I love her.

I shoved the thought aside so I could focus on helping the wedding go off without a hitch. But I planned to talk to her about it afterward—I wanted to tell her that I love her.

That'll have to wait till morning now that she's asleep. When I scoop her into my arms and lift her up, she doesn't stir. I walk to her bedroom and set her gently on the bed before slipping her shoes off. I peel away her dress, then slip off the T-shirt I'm wearing and slide it over her head. She's sleeping so deeply that her eyes don't even flutter.

When I tuck her under the comforter and press a kiss to her forehead, she scrunches her face slightly, then lets out a soft moan. I'm still, hoping I haven't woken her up. When she doesn't move, I start to twist away, but the feel of her fingers gripping my forearm causes me to freeze. Her eyelids peel open, revealing a sliver of that beautiful carob gaze cloudy with sleep.

"I love you," she mewls before shutting her eyes.

Those three whispered words send my heart skidding. I'm grinning like a madman as her hand falls away from my arm and that heavy, steady rhythm of breathing resumes, signaling that she's fallen back to deep sleep.

But I've never felt more alive. My body feels like it's floating.

I switch off the light and crawl into bed next to her, pulling her into my chest like I do every night we're together. Even in her sleep, she curls into me. Like always.

On the inside I'm a fireworks show. I'm every color of the rainbow. I'm pulsing with joy and bliss.

I nuzzle the top of her head and close my eyes. "I love you too," I whisper.

I wake to my bladder screaming for a piss. As quietly as I can, I slip out of bed and pad to the master bathroom to relieve myself. I blink as my vision focuses, taking in the soft orange glow peeking through the cracks in the blinds. Must be just past dawn.

When I slide back into bed, Harper curls into me.

"Morning," she mumbles, her voice thick with sleep.

"Morning." I gaze down at her adorably puffy face. "You were pretty chatty in your sleep last night."

There's a recognition that flashes behind her eyes before she pulls a goofy scrunched face. And that's when I know she remembers what she said.

"I said it last night, but I'll say it again. I love you too, Harper."

The moment the words leave my mouth, her expression shifts to shock. A beat later she's beaming. "I thought I was dreaming when you said that."

"Not a dream. I mean, being with you these past couple of months has been an absolute dream. I love living with you, working with you, eating with you, joking with you, being ordered around by you."

She slides her hand up my chest. The feel of her warm-silk skin sends goose bumps across my body.

"I love you, Lewis." She says it fully awake, looking right at me, zero doubt in her eyes. "I've never felt this way about anyone before. I know there's still so much we have to work out. I mean, you're moving back to LA in a couple of weeks. You'll be on set, jetting off to whatever location you're filming next. Who knows the next time we'll—"

Gently, I press my palm over her mouth. Her chuckle rumbles against my hand.

"I know we lead very different lives," I say. "It probably won't be easy."

That glimmer in her eyes dims, but I quickly explain. "But we'll figure it out. What I want more than anything is to be with you, Harper."

She wraps her fingers around my wrist and pulls my hand away from her face. Her gaze turns pointed, serious.

"Do you really want that, Lewis? Because my life is here in the Bay Area. I want to be close to my family and volunteer and work. I don't see myself ever wanting to move to LA."

I can't deny the pang of disappointment that lands in my gut at what she says—but I also can't blame her. Her whole world is here. I know just how much this place means to her—how much it means for her to live in her grandparents' house, close to her family. I can't expect her to give that up, just for me.

"I'll figure out a way to have both you and my career," I say, hoping with everything in me that she hears the conviction in my voice, that she can feel just how much I love her.

She starts to open her mouth to say more, but I quickly kiss her. When we stop to catch our breath, she starts back up.

"How do we make this work?" she asks. "I'm serious. I love you, but you know me. I'm a planner. I'm no-nonsense. I have to think things through before I feel comfortable. I'm not saying we need to have it all mapped out right now, but I need more than just optimism to make me believe we can have a relationship in the real world."

"I love that about you," I say as I kiss the tip of her nose and brush away the hair in her face. "I'd never, ever expect you to change your life for me. I want this to work between us, and I'm willing to do whatever it takes. Whenever I'm working again, I can fly here to see you on my days off. And if you'd be up for it, I'd love for you to come and see me in LA too. You can visit me when I'm off or when I'm working. Whenever you want."

That focused expression on her face softens. "I'd love that too."

"We can take it slow, play it by ear, whatever you want," I say.

"It won't be easy."

"Nothing worthwhile ever is," I say quickly.

Grinning, she wags her eyebrow. "Well said."

"I know this isn't going to be a walk in the park. And I know that we don't have it all figured out. But I want to give this relationship with you a proper shot. I don't want to give up on us just because we're not one hundred percent certain how it'll all play out."

She nods slightly, like she's processing everything I've said.

My hands slide down to her hips. I grip the soft flesh of her curves and pull her closer to me. "I love you. Give us a chance. Please."

She makes a moaning sound against my lips that sounds a lot like "mmm, yes."

Soon she's grabbing at my body in the exact way that drives me wild: her hands start at my hair, tugging until that delicious burn jolts through my scalp. She moves lower, clawing at my shoulders and chest as our kisses turn filthy and depraved. She drags her mouth along the side of my neck and sinks her teeth into the meaty part of my shoulder. My eyes roll to the back of my head as I grunt. I sound like a fucking caveman.

With both of her palms on my stomach, she pushes me to lie down flat, trailing kisses all the way down my abdomen. When she settles between my legs, my breath hitches.

She looks up at me, her gaze cloudy and focused at once somehow. Her eye makeup from last night is smudged, but it only adds to how sexy and raw she looks in this moment.

She wraps her hand around the base of my cock, and I have to bite down just to keep from losing it. Christ, I can barely take this—my beautiful Harper looking like some devil-angel, desperate to devour me. I close my eyes and swallow, praying I last. She looks and feels so damn good I'm not sure I can.

When I open my eyes, I see her run her tongue along her full bottom lip. Pleasure rockets to my dick.

"I love you, Lewis," she says through a pant before lowering her mouth where I want her—where I *need* her.

Even though her head bobbing up and down while she works me in her mouth is the hottest sight I've ever laid eyes on, I can't watch for too long. If I do, I'll blow my load way too early for what I have planned. So I tilt my head back and stare at the ceiling while counting back from a hundred so I have a prayer of lasting.

It's no use, though. My girl is too good.

I reach down and pull her off me.

"Baby, I need you. Please." I scoot her to kneel over my mouth and run my tongue all over, savoring how she writhes over my face. Her pants and screams turn desperate as I feel her thighs squeeze the sides of my head. When she explodes, my grip on her hips tightens. I moan against her, soaking in this moment where the woman I love is losing her mind all over my face.

As her sounds and movements ease, I lean up, bracing her body with my arms. I lay her on the bed, smiling when I take in the dazed look on her face. I grab a condom from the nightstand, slide it on, and then glide into her. It's not long before she's digging her nails into my skin while thrashing and shouting my name. I know without a doubt that my back and shoulders will be shredded to hell after this, but I love it. I fucking love how wild I make this unflappable, bold-as-hell woman whenever we fall into bed together.

She shifts to touch herself while I thrust. Now it's my turn to say her name.

"Harper...fuck, that's...that's...so...hot..."

The pressure in my lower abdomen turns to fire as I watch her work herself in her own hand. I've never been more happy or turned on than right now while watching the woman I love take charge of both her pleasure and mine at the same time.

Soon she's falling apart under me as I fight with every ounce of restraint that I possess to make sure I last as long as she needs me to. When she begins to ease, I finally let go. My own orgasm hits like a freight train. The growl-yell I let loose turns my throat raw, but Harper swallows it with her kiss.

I collapse onto the mattress, careful not to put my

full weight on top of her by holding myself up on my forearms.

"No," she growls, pulling me to lie on top of her. "I want to feel all of you."

I obey her request, chuckling as I nuzzle the side of her neck.

She shivers. "We're really doing this. You and me," she whispers into my ear while running a hand through my hair.

"We are."

A quiet moment passes before I hear her beautiful voice again. "I'm all yours."

"God, hearing you say that…"

Before I can finish, she pulls me to her mouth and kisses me until I can't breathe or think. We spend the rest of the morning tangled in bed together without exchanging another word.

Chapter Twenty-Three

Harper

I gaze around the nearly finished living room. "Wow."

Lewis walks up from behind me and wraps me in a hug. He nuzzles my neck, making me shiver and moan at the same time. "You keep saying that."

"I just still can't get over how well everything turned out. I love it."

I twist my face to the side, capturing his mouth in a kiss before taking in the space once more. The hardwood floor, the walls painted the perfect shade of green-gray, the Mediterranean tile of the fireplace finally stripped free of white paint, the brass chandelier hanging in the entryway.

"I think *Apong* Bernie and *Apong* Vivian would have loved it too," I whisper, almost to myself.

Lewis squeezes me tight. "I know they would have."

I spin around so I can hug him. "And I still can't get over the fact that you did all this."

"Told you I was that good."

I laugh and try to twist out of his embrace, but his hold on me tightens before he leans down and kisses my neck.

A mewling sound escapes from my mouth while I savor the heat of his breath, the softness of his lips.

"You helped too, you know," he growls against my skin. "And now we can just focus on the two of us. We can do whatever we want."

"What did you have in mind?" I murmur.

"Other than spending every day in bed with you until I leave for LA, I hadn't planned much else."

"Sounds perfect to me."

Just the thought of Lewis heading back to LA next week sends knots to my stomach. I'm going to miss him so much. He's going to be insanely busy the moment he steps foot there. His agent called the other day to update him on what's been happening since he's been gone, and it looks like his absence accomplished exactly what he hoped: people are clamoring for a chance to meet with Lewis to discuss possible roles. He's gotten offers for more serious work, which he's pumped about. On top of that, media outlets have been blowing up his agent's phone for a chance to interview Lewis about why he left his old show, but he's made it clear he's not interested in talking—not without permission from the crew members who were targets of the harassment.

Despite everything that's on his docket, we have a plan. He's flying back to visit in two weeks to see me for the weekend, and then two weeks after that, I'm going to fly to LA and see him.

He leads me by the hand to the kitchen and tells me to sit on the bar stool. I take in the visual of my shirtless boyfriend cracking eggs at the stove as he whips up breakfast for me. I still can't believe I landed this guy. Never in a million years did I think I'd ever find myself in the healthiest, most exciting relationship of my life with a sexy-as-hell TV star.

"I can't wait to show you my favorite breakfast place in LA," Lewis says while divvying up the scrambled eggs between two plates.

"They don't just serve avocado toast, do they?" I tease.

He mock glares at me. "Just for that little quip, I'm greeting you with avocado toast when you land at LAX."

I burst out laughing. He plops on the stool next to me, and we dig into the most delicious eggs at the kitchen island, still clad in our pajamas. Between bites I glance over at him and contemplate pinching myself.

So, so perfect.

"Thank you," I say, my tone soft and shaky. "For everything."

Emotion flashes behind those mesmerizing hazel eyes. "Thank you, Harper. For letting me stay with you. For giving me a chance."

He rubs the back of his neck, the expression on his face shy all of a sudden. "I, um, have a surprise for you."

"You do? But you've done enough…"

"It's not anything big. It's just something I thought you might like."

He hops off the bar stool and heads toward the garage when there's a knock at the door. I hop off the stool, and when I open the door, I freeze. There are several dozen photographers standing on my porch and front lawn, aiming their cameras at me as I stand openmouthed in the doorway wearing pajama shorts and a tank top.

And then I hear it. The sound of a million cameras snapping as they take my photo.

Fuck.

"What's your name, honey? You shacking up with Lewis Prescott?"

The taunting tone of the random paparazzo jolts me from my shocked stupor. I stumble back and slam the door shut.

"Everything okay?" Lewis peeks inside to the house as he stands in the open doorway to the garage, cardboard box in hand.

I stare at him, stammering. My brain is struggling to figure out the best way tell him that his worst nightmare is currently standing on the front lawn.

Somehow the paparazzi found Lewis. They found my house. They're minutes—no, actually seconds—away from ruining our sense of privacy and security. This bliss bubble we've made for ourselves is about to burst.

I open my mouth to say something, anything, but all that comes out is a ragged breath. How do I explain this to him? I don't even know how they found us…

His brow furrows in concern, and he sets the box on the floor of the garage and walks over to me.

"Hey. What happened? You look like you've seen a ghost."

Muffled voices sound behind the front door.

"Who's at the door?"

I force my brain to bust through the terror fog holding it hostage. I grip his hand in both of mine. "Lewis, listen to me. The paparazzi are outside the house right now. They… I don't know how they found us, but they're here. And they know you're here too."

In a split second, his face twists from concerned to furious. His skin turns red, and his stare narrows. He jerks out of my hold. I try to swallow back the sharp pain that hits me at the sudden loss of contact as I scurry after him when he walks into the kitchen. He pulls out his phone and dials quickly.

"Trent. There's paparazzi surrounding the house where I'm staying. How the hell did that happen?"

Because of Trent's megaphone voice, I hear everything.

"Lewis, my man. I was about to call you. The news just broke here in Tinseltown. I thought I told you to lay low."

"Trent, I *was* laying low." Lewis's voice is an angry boom that makes me flinch.

"I saw the photos of you on Facebook, my man," Trent chides. "That's the exact opposite of laying low, you know. Attending a wedding and letting yourself be photographed? You blew it, man. Capital *I*, capital *T*."

My stomach plummets to my feet. Naomi's wedding. Someone must have taken photos that had Lewis in them, and when they posted them to Facebook, someone recognized him. But how? I talked to my family, to all the wedding guests... I told them photos weren't allowed and that they weren't supposed to say anything about Lewis.

Despite the dread and panic sending my heart rate to the stratosphere, I force myself to focus, to try and figure out a way to minimize this disaster. I grab my phone from the kitchen island and hit the entertainment tab on the news site that's my homepage. There I see the top headline.

Disgraced TV Star Lewis Prescott Hiding Out in Half Moon Bay

I quickly skim the article, my stomach knotting when I see a half dozen photos from that night, most of which feature Lewis smiling in the background. Then I head to Facebook to see if I can figure out who posted the photos. It only takes about ten seconds of scrolling before I see that Naomi's mom posted the album. When I read the caption, I bite my tongue so that I don't scream. She must have sneaked her phone out when no one was paying attention.

My beautiful daughter's wedding in Half Moon Bay!

She didn't tag Lewis in the photos or even mention him when she posted them, but it's clear in the images that it's him.

I do a quick skim of the comments on the photos.

Holy crap, is that Lewis Prescott???

Hey, that guy with the shaggy blond hair and beard looks kind of like Lewis Prescott!

What the heck was Lewis Prescott doing at Naomi's wedding?!

The hot veterinarian from that show was at Naomi and Simon's wedding?? OMG!!!

Panic throttles me from the inside out. I know Naomi's mom didn't mean any harm by posting the photos. I'm sure she was just so excited to share photos from her daughter's big day. But as a result, Lewis's privacy has been violated, and after successfully evading the paparazzi for nearly three months, he's in their crosshairs again. Because of my family. Because of *me*.

My stomach churns. I think I'm gonna be sick.

When I look up and see the glare on Lewis's face aimed straight at me, the panic turns to dread.

"Looks like your getaway has come to an end, my man," Trent says, interrupting our silent standoff.

Lewis blinks and glances to the side. "I'll call you back, Trent."

He hangs up and walks right past me.

"Lewis, wait." I follow him to the guest bedroom, watching in stunned silence as he starts shoving all his belongings into his suitcases. "What are you doing?"

"What does it look like I'm doing?" he bites, punching his clothing into the open slots of each bag.

I step over to him and gently place my hand on his forearm. He closes his eyes instantly.

"Lewis. Please. Can we talk about this?"

When he moves to sit on the edge of the bed, I'm heartened. He props his elbows on his knees and holds his face in his hands. I reach to touch his arm again, but he flinches. I swallow through the sudden ache in my throat.

"I'm sorry," I rasp. "My aunt—Naomi's mom—posted photos of the wedding on Facebook, and you happened to be in some of them. She didn't realize what she was doing." I pull my lips into my mouth at how pathetic that sounds. Because her intent doesn't really matter when it's created this awful situation for Lewis. For both of us. "People must have recognized you…and the post blew up."

"Yeah, I kind of figured that out," he mutters.

"I—I don't know why she did that… I told her not to. Or maybe she didn't think it would be a big deal—"

"Well, it turned out to be a pretty big fucking deal, Harper." He clamps his mouth shut and closes his eyes, like he's mad at himself for saying that. "Look, I know this isn't your fault and you didn't mean for this to happen, but I'm still really upset, okay?"

"I'm sorry, I just—"

"Saying 'sorry' doesn't magically fix this fucked-up situation."

"I know that. But I just think it's important to recognize that this was a mistake. My aunt is such a sweet and well-meaning person. She would never intentionally hurt you in this way."

"Well, she did." He goes quiet, his gaze a mix of hard and bewildered as he stares off to the side.

I can't think of a single helpful thing to say. So I stay quiet, hugging my arms around myself, and gaze at the floor until Lewis is ready to speak again.

"I can't do this."

"Can't do what?"

"We can't be together if this is what it's like to be with you."

My jaw pops as it hinges open. Did he seriously just say that?

"What do you mean, 'if this is what it's like to be with you'?"

Closing his eyes, he pinches the bridge of his nose. "I love you, Harper, but I can't be with someone whose family is gonna be a liability for me—a threat to my privacy. I've already dealt with that in my own life. I refuse to let it happen again."

There's a cold detachment to his voice that I don't recognize. It leaves me speechless.

"Lewis, what are you... You can't mean that. You

know that I'm different from your parents. So is my family. They'd never hurt you like that."

"But they did."

I tug a hand through my hair, hoping that the sudden sharp pain is a reset for the chaotic swirl of thoughts muddling my brain. It isn't.

That stony look on his face remains. He's clearly unmoved by my pleading and desperate tone.

"Lewis, my family and friends are trustworthy. For fuck's sake, I told my cousin Naomi about you the day you moved in after we bumped into each other in the hallway and I accidentally grabbed your junk. She's known about you the whole time, and she didn't peep a word. Same with my friend Maren. She's known about you almost from the get-go."

He hops to his feet. "What the hell, Harper? Did you tell everyone about me?" He mutters a curse before going back to packing. "God, no wonder the paparazzi are swarming this place."

My stomach churns at how disgusted and cruel his tone is.

"Lewis, it was your idea to have the wedding here. Don't try to put all the blame for this mess on me and my family."

He stops before slumping forward and resting his hands on his knees. "You're right." He looks so defeated.

"Look, I'm sorry I told them. You're right, I shouldn't have. But Maren and Naomi didn't rat you out. Don't you see that? They knew about you and kept you a secret because I asked them to—because they knew it was the right thing to do. Because your privacy meant something to them. And they don't even know you…"

He yanks the zippers shut on both of his suitcases and

glances up at me standing over him. When he stands to his full height and gazes down at me, his eyes glisten with unshed tears.

"We're from two different worlds. I see that now."

I recognize his muttered words as the same ones I spoke to him the morning after we exchanged *I love you*s. My chest tightens. My heart is either shattering into a billion pieces or I'm about to have a coronary.

"I made a mistake," he continues. "I let my feelings for you cloud my judgment. I shouldn't have been open about who I am to your family. I should have just left the day of the wedding."

My lips tremble as I try my hardest not to burst into tears.

"I know you didn't mean for this to happen, Harper. But I can't go through this again. My privacy means everything to me, and I can't have someone in my life who's going to compromise that, even if it wasn't intentional."

Despite the tears pooling in my eyes, I nod my understanding. For a minute we stand and look at each other.

I swallow back the sob I'm aching to let loose. "I'm sorry, Lewis."

"Me too." He clears his throat while looking down at me.

He starts to move his forearm like he's going to reach for me, but then it drops back to his side. My entire body goes cold.

"Goodbye, Harper."

When he walks past me, I don't move or speak. I stay planted in that spot while listening to Lewis's footsteps echo down the hall and out the front door. There's a blast of shouts, but the door slams shut and the noise turns muffled. A second later I break.

* * *

"How are you holding up? You can be honest. It's me, Harper."

Naomi's concerned tone as I speak to her on the phone is both a comfort and a curse. A comfort because knowing that she cares enough to call and check up on me while on her honeymoon means everything. It's a curse because every time she checks up on me, it's a reminder of what I lost.

I take a slow, quiet breath and focus on the yellow letters of the Glad You're Here sign that hangs above the office building where I'm parked. When I don't burst into tears, I count it as a win.

"You've said that every time you've called me. I'm fine, Naomi."

Even I'm surprised at how composed I sound. My tone is steady and firm. I definitely don't sound like the heartbroken mess that I am. I definitely don't sound like I spent every night of the last two weeks crying myself to sleep.

"I don't believe you," Naomi says.

"Well, I don't know what to tell you then," I mutter.

"You need to talk about your feelings. It's not good to—"

"No. I don't," I bite. "I've got a million other things on my mind. With the renovation done, I'm focused on decorating the house now. I'm upping my volunteer hours at Glad You're Here too. And I'm looking into what kind of work I want to pursue. Did I tell you I've been thinking about consulting here in the Bay Area?"

A heavy sigh rockets from her end of the line. "Harper, I mean this in the most loving way, but will you drop the act already?"

"What act?"

"The 'I'm above ever losing my shit over a guy' act. You've pulled this before and I've let it slide, but not today."

"Why not?" My voice betrays me by cracking on the last word. When my lips begin to tremble, I quickly pull them into my mouth and bite down.

"Harper." She says my name so softly and lovingly, I can feel myself inching closer to breaking completely. "You're the strongest person I know. No one keeps their cool in a crisis like you. I've always, always admired that about you. But you're allowed to be sad and cry when you get your heart broken. You're allow to hurt. You're allowed to not be fine. It doesn't make you weak or any less incredible."

Like always, my cousin knows the exact right thing to say to cut through all my defenses. Her words are like some sort of emotional trigger. Like when a dog hears a high-pitched whistle and whines in terror. Instantly my throat aches and my nose burns.

"Fine, you're right. I'm not okay, Naomi. I'm a fucking mess." When I blink, tears cascade down my cheeks.

"Oh, Harper. I wish I could be there to hug you. I wish we were at my apartment right now eating cartons of ice cream and downing our weight in vodka."

I let out a snotty chuckle while sitting in my car. "That's a terrible idea. You're such a lightweight you'd pass out after three shots."

She laughs, which makes me laugh, then sob. For a minute I alternate between the two while Naomi listens patiently on her end of the line. I wipe at my face and check the time. Ten minutes before I'm due to go in and start my volunteer shift for the day. Better get all this crying out now.

"I wish you were here too." I let out a shaky breath. "But you're on your honeymoon. You should be skinny-dipping with Simon on a secluded beach somewhere, not consoling me over the phone."

"Hey. You don't get to tell me how to spend my honeymoon."

Another watery chuckle falls from my lips. I reach over to my glove box and dig out a packet of tissues and wipe my face.

"I'm serious. You've called me every day since Lewis broke up with me. I appreciate it, but there's nothing you can do. I just need to keep living my life. And you should focus on enjoying Turks and Caicos."

"First of all, I can do both. I can have a lovely time here and still check in on you because you're my cousin and best friend. If you're not okay, then I'm not okay. I will always, always, always be here for you, whether you like it or not."

A shaky smile tugs at my lips.

"And second, don't talk like this is some average breakup. It's not. Not even close. You were having a secret relationship with a TV star. And now you're being hounded by paparazzi. That's both traumatizing and upsetting."

I glance around the parking lot, thankful that there don't appear to be any photographers trailing me. It's been two weeks since Lewis walked out on me, but paparazzi have still been camped outside my house, yelling questions every time I leave and snapping photos of me. Sometimes they trail me to the grocery store or to the Glad You're Here office. The only time I've been able to lose them is when I drive into San Francisco. Invading my privacy is one thing, but there's no way I would let them get near my family.

When they approach me, I never engage. I ignore them, but I don't know how much longer I can keep up this silent facade. I know they won't be around forever. As soon as the next juicy bit of celebrity gossip hits the news cycle, they'll ditch me. But I don't know when that'll be. And having strangers accost me with questions about my personal life and my romantic relationship with Lewis while shoving a camera in my face rockets my anxiety level to the point where I have to do breathing exercises every time I walk into or out of my house just to calm myself.

"You're right," I finally say to Naomi. "This is a nightmare. But I don't know how to fix it."

"I can't believe Lewis hung you out to dry like this. He left you to fend for yourself against the god-awful paparazzi," Naomi mutters. "I mean, he has every right to be mad at them for acting like piranhas. I swear, they are the lowest of the low. And I even understand if he's pissed at my mom for posting pics of the wedding on social media. She felt horrible for outing him when I told her what happened. But to take it out on you is so misguided. How does that make sense? You didn't do anything wrong."

"It doesn't matter." My tone now sounds as meek and defeated as I feel. "It's because of me that this all happened. Even though I didn't personally participate in exposing him, I was connected to it. I know it was an accident, but it still hurt him. Misguided or not, it's how he feels."

A long pause follows. "You're being entirely too mature and reasonable about this."

"I definitely don't feel like that. I've come so close to unblocking him and texting him, like, at least a dozen times."

She makes a sympathetic noise.

"I just feel so sad and angry and broken right now."

"Then act like it."

"What do you mean?"

"Say exactly what you're feeling, Harper. Look, I know that you've been going through the motions these past two weeks, trying to distract yourself with setting up the house and volunteering and planning your next career move," Naomi says. "That's all well and good, but you can't ignore your emotions forever. You need to express them."

"You sound like a therapist."

"I'm married to one, so I'm probably gonna sound like this a lot."

The start of a smile tugs at my lips, but it fades the moment I let myself think about just how hard I've been working to hide my emotions about my breakup with Lewis these past couple of weeks.

"I'm so fucking mad and hurt, Naomi."

"That's good. You have every right to be."

I open my mouth a half dozen times, but nothing comes out. It's like my brain is struggling to find the exact right words to express the emotions I've actively repressed for the past couple of weeks.

"I'm so pissed that he got mad at me for something that I didn't do. And I'm hurt that he left instead of staying and trying to figure out a way to work through this."

"That's good, Harper. Really good."

I pause to catch my breath. When my chest expands, it feels like my body is working to expend all this pain and sadness and anger with every word I speak, with every inhale and exhale.

"I'm mad that I let myself fall for him. I should have known better than to think I could have something lasting and meaningful with someone like him. And I'm pissed as hell that I believed him when he told me that he loved me and that we'd figure out a way for this— for us—to work. Clearly that was bullshit, given that he ditched me the second we hit a rough patch."

Tears and snot drip down my face so fast, I can barely keep up even as I dab with tissue after tissue.

"I wish I'd never let him buy me that coffee. I wish I'd never let him move into my house. I wish I'd never kissed him. I wish I'd never told him I loved him. I wish… I wish…"

I stop just to let myself sob for a second.

"I wish I'd never met him."

As the words fall from my trembling lips, my head spins. I wasn't planning to say that. I wasn't even thinking that.

But maybe there's a reason I said it. Because maybe it's true. Maybe I just didn't realize it because I was holed up in my house, hiding away in a love bubble with Lewis for the past almost three months. Maybe because we spent all that time flirting and kissing and fucking and acting like hormonal teenagers, we were immune from reality and the everyday stresses of life. And when those finally hit us, we crumbled. We just weren't meant to last outside the world we built together under that roof.

In that way, maybe Lewis was right. We're from two different worlds. We could never make a relationship work.

Naomi doesn't speak for a while. I'm guessing she's processing my crying outburst.

"How do you feel?" she finally asks.

"Like I've been hit by a truck, but emotionally. If that makes sense."

"It does."

"Sorry I sounded like a maniac just now. It felt good to get that out, though."

"Don't ever apologize for saying how you feel, Harper, least of all to me. Don't you remember how many times I've cried to you?"

"Thanks, Naomi."

"It'll get better. I promise it will."

"I hope so," I say, having zero faith that it actually will.

I check the time and see that I'm due inside in two minutes. "I have to go."

"Okay, but you're seeing Maren tonight, right?"

"Yeah, she's coming to stay with me at the house so that I won't be alone."

"Good. We'll be back in San Francisco Saturday night, and I want you come stay with us on Sunday."

I bite back a groan. "I'm not a little kid you have to keep tabs on at all times."

"That's not how I mean for this to come off. I just miss my amazing cousin and I want to see her."

My lips tremble at the sincerity in her tone, at how I can feel just how much she loves me in those few words. It makes me think of Lewis and how he doesn't have anyone in his family he can count on like I do. I wonder if he has anyone in his life to help him right now…

That thought makes me ache for him, despite the way things ended between us.

Naomi and I exchange *I love you*s and hang up. I quickly clean up my face in the mirror, take a deep breath, and walk into the office.

Chapter Twenty-Four

Lewis

"Good god. What the hell happened to you?"

The sound of Katie's voice rings like a gong in my head. Then comes the jolt of pain shooting through my skull.

I groan into my pillow.

A cracking sound echoes in my ears, and I wince. That piercing sound definitely didn't help my hangover-induced headache.

When I finally peel open my eyes, I shout into my pillow at the shock of sunlight. It burns through my eyeballs, setting my skull on fire.

"What the..."

"It's called sunlight, Lewis. You look like you could use some." Katie moves to yank open the set of blinds on the other window in my bedroom.

I mutter a string of profanities into the pillow while punching the one next to me. The mattress depresses at my feet. I roll over, thankful that I forgot to take off my shorts when I passed out last night after downing all the alcohol in my house. Katie's like my big sister, and I'd die if she saw me naked.

"You auditioning to be a zombie extra on *The Walk-*

ing Dead or something? Gotta admit, that's a bit of a step down for you. You'd for sure be an episode regular—come on now."

"You're hilarious," I mutter into my pillow.

She smacks the back of my calf.

"Ow!" I jolt up from the bed like a fish flopping on dry land. I twist around and squint at her, my eyes burning as they adjust to the sunlight. "What the hell are you hitting me for?"

Her frown is lethal, just like I remember it. Although it's been ages since she's aimed it at me.

"What the hell is going on with you? You haven't returned any of my messages or calls since you've been back in LA."

"I've been busy." I shove a pillow over my face, my head throbbing as I breathe through the thickness.

"Busy wallowing? Busy trying to drink yourself to death?"

"Sure."

"Your current state wouldn't happen to have anything to do with that woman whose house you were photographed at in Half Moon Bay, would it?"

Just the mention of Harper has my chest threatening to implode.

Harper.

For the past two weeks, ever since I walked out on her, I've been like this. Missing her so bad that it feels like my heart's been through a wood chipper. Feeling like I want to punch myself in the face when I think about how I made the biggest mistake of my life by leaving her…

I toss away the pillow, wincing when the brightness hits my face. "What are you doing here, Katie?" I ask, blatantly ignoring what she just asked me.

"See, I think that your sorry-ass condition has everything to do with your Half Moon Bay lady."

I used to chuckle in amusement every time Katie did this to whatever jerk she was telling off. I normally love how she ignores every attempt at changing the subject and simply plows through with her questions. She's like a police interrogator in the body of a makeup artist. Now that I'm on the receiving end of her pressing questions, though, I kind of hate it.

"Obviously something went down between you two, and it wasn't pretty."

My lips quiver even as I bite down to prevent the flow of tears. But it's no use. They plummet down my bearded cheeks anyway.

"Lewis." Katie's soft tone catches me off guard. I finally look up at her, her face a blur. All I can make out is the bright pink hue of her hair. "I'm your friend. I can see you're hurting. Talk to me."

I force myself to sit up and tell her everything. How I randomly met Harper and decided to hide out at her house because she was kind and trustworthy. I tell Katie how I fell for her and how when things were winding down with the renovation, we confessed our feelings for each other and decided to give a relationship a shot, that we had even scheduled visits to see each other. I tell her about meeting Harper's family and trusting them enough to tell them who I was. I tell her about the photos that Harper's aunt shared on Facebook from her cousin's wedding, outing me to the paparazzi. I tell her how ambushed and panicked I felt, how I lashed out at Harper, how I blamed her even though I knew deep down it wasn't her fault. I tell her how it reminded me of my family betraying my trust. I tell her how it led to me abruptly ending things between us. I tell her how it took less than a day of being back in LA for me to realize what a mistake I made—that I wanted Harper back in my life again. I tell her how when I tried to call her to beg for another chance, it was too late. She had blocked me, and I had no idea how to get in touch with her. I tell her how broken I've felt ever since then, because I ruined the best thing that's ever happened to me.

Katie's blue eyes go wider and wider as I reveal each detail. When I finish, her stony expression softens.

"Jesus, Lewis."

The noise I make is something between a scoff and a disgusted laugh. "I don't know what to do, Katie. Harper is the most brilliant, beautiful, badass person I've ever been with. I'm so in love with her. She actually believed in me, you know? She helped me realize I'm good enough to pursue projects I'm passionate about instead of the pretty boy/bad boy roles everyone else—even my own agent—tells me I should stick to. And it…it meant everything. She saw me for who I really am. She let me be myself without any pressure or expectation—and she actually liked that about me. And the way she treated me, the way that she welcomed me into her life…she made me feel like family…" I drift off when my voice starts to break, then quickly clear my throat. "I let my past fuck up my future with her. I can't believe I did that."

"I can."

I fall forward and rest my elbows on my knees, then cover my face with my hands. Katie puts a hand on my shoulder.

"Look, I'm not a therapist, but I've been through enough therapy to know that what likely happened is that you were triggered by what her aunt did. You trusted her family to keep quiet about your situation, and when they accidentally outed your hideout, it felt like your trust was broken again. Even though it wasn't intentional and even though you knew it wasn't Harper's fault, you blamed her because it brought you back to how your parents betrayed you. So you reacted the only way you knew how—you left and cut ties."

I nod, wiping my nose with my wrist.

"And I know this is gonna sound harsh but, Lewis, you're a famous actor. People are gonna be violating your privacy for as long as you work in this industry. It's messed up, but it's the truth. At least Harper and her family didn't try to gain anything from posting the photos. And if her family is as good-hearted as you say they are, then I think they'd do whatever it takes to apologize and respect your feelings going forward."

My head hangs as I nod my agreement. I should have realized all this sooner.

"Harper sounds like a goddamn diamond in the rough. You should try to make things right with her."

"I want to, but she blocked me."

"You can't blame her for blocking you."

"I don't. She has every right to hate me. I just wish I could tell her I'm sorry. Even if she never wants to be with me, even if she never wants to see my face again, I owe her an apology."

"Then figure it out."

I almost laugh at her pointed tone.

"I mean it. There's gotta be some way you can get in touch with her."

I start to stammer an excuse, but she holds up a hand. "You've been a drunken, hungover mess for almost two weeks. You weren't in the best state of mind."

"That's putting it kindly," I mutter.

"Now you are. Quit all this destructive, self-loathing behavior, clear your head, and figure out a way to reach out to her. She sounds like a truly genuine and honest person who has your best interests at heart, in addition to driving you wild in the best way." Katie wags an eyebrow. "That's a jackpot combination. You gotta at least try and make it right with her."

My foggy-headedness dissipates with Katie's no-nonsense advice. Even my headache is starting to fade.

"I'll figure this out."

She pats my knee and stands up. "Good. First things first, though—you gotta take a shower. You smell like a dumpster."

I let out my first genuine chuckle in almost two weeks.

I start to walk toward the master bathroom when Katie stops me.

"Don't forget about tomorrow. We've got that meeting with the crew from *The Best of It* and you're hosting it here at your house, remember?"

A fire lights within me. "Yeah, I remember."

The corner of Katie's mouth hooks up in a smile. "Good. We need you on the top of your game if we're gonna take Darren down."

I clench my fists at my sides and stand up to my full height. "We're gonna nail his ass to the wall."

I'm blown away at how many people showed up. Almost every crew member from *The Best of It* is sitting or standing in my living room, ready to do whatever it takes to take down Darren.

For an hour, we've all been catching up on what's been going on ever since the show's hiatus. None of the network higher-ups cared to get rid of Darren, even when I and the rest of the crew told them about his history of harassing crew members and extras. Because of that, everyone is refusing to return to the show when it's scheduled to start filming again. Darren is pissed, of course. No crew means no show, which is costing the network money, and that means they're breathing down his neck.

"He's threatening to blacklist every one of us who refuses to come back to work," Katie says. She runs a hand over the shaved side of her scalp, a telltale sign that she's anxious. "I have no doubt he'll do it. I mean, look what he did to Lewis, and he was the freaking star of the show."

Almost everyone murmurs their agreement.

"We have to figure out a way to hold him accountable and expose him," says Mariah, the head of wardrobe. "I don't want to work for that bastard anymore. None of us do. But we need to make money. This industry is our livelihood, and we can't let him ruin us."

When Mariah's voice shakes, Katie grabs hold of her hand.

"Are you all okay with me going public with this, then?" I ask, my gaze scanning the room. Everyone nods.

"I want to nail Darren's ass to the wall," I say. "I want everyone to know what a sack of shit he is. But I also know that it could come off the wrong way too. Like, it could rub people the wrong way to see me, the star of the show, a man who wasn't one of Darren's victims, spearhead the campaign against him. I don't want it to look like I'm taking the focus away from any of you."

Nearly everyone shakes their head.

"We want you to help us, Lewis," says Aja, the script supervisor. "A lot of times when harassment happens, male allies are hard to find, let alone celebrities with a platform and influence. They don't want to call out a fellow man for their predatory behavior. But you're willing to. And that's exactly what we need for people to take this seriously and hold Darren accountable."

Everyone voices their agreement.

"Okay. I'll do it."

The mood of the room lightens as people start to smile and chatter. I walk over to Katie and tell her what I'm planning. Her eyes go wide.

"Your agent is going to murder you."

I shrug. "I think I'm done with that guy."

I tell everyone to help themselves to whatever they want in my kitchen and to stay as long as they'd like, then I head to my office and make some calls. When I finish and walk back out over an hour later, half the people are still there.

I grab a green juice from the fridge and drain it, feeling enlivened and exhausted at once at what I'm about to do. I'm likely going to burn every bridge I've spent the last ten years building in this industry, but I don't give a shit. I want to do this—and it's the right thing to do.

"Hey." Katie walks up to me. "Thanks. For everything."

"Thank *you* and everyone else for supporting me."

She pulls me into a hug. "We're family. This is what we do for each other."

When I start to turn away, she holds me in place. "Have you figured out a way to talk to Harper?"

My stomach knots at the thought. I nod anyway. "I hope so. We'll see after I make this call."

She steps aside. "Don't let me stop you."

I walk into the hall and dial the newly saved number in my phone. I owe that IT guy a huge favor for what he did to get it. When she answers, my heart lodges in my throat, but I force myself to talk anyway.

"Hey. It's Lewis. Please don't hang up."

Chapter Twenty-Five

Harper

When Maren walks through the front door of my house, I'm speechless.

"What are you wearing?"

Instead of answering me, she spins around to face the half dozen photographers who are standing on the street in front, right along the end of the driveway. I clench my fists at the mere sight of them.

"Stay behind the line, scumbags!" she yells. "See that line where the driveway ends and the road begins? Back the hell behind that or I call the cops for trespassing."

I soften instantly. Every time she comes and visits me, she always has choice words for the paparazzi.

She flips them off with both hands raised. When I peek around her for a look at what's going on outside, I notice the photographers don't even bother to take a photo.

"There's that smile," she says after shutting the door and pulling me in for a hug.

I close my eyes, relishing the tight squeeze. "You're the best, you know that?" My voice is muffled against her shoulder since she's half a foot taller than me.

We pull away, and I take in the white T-shirt she's wearing, which boasts a cartoon hand giving the finger.

She tugs at the hem, beaming. "Paparazzi repellent. They have a harder time selling photos when there's obscene material in them."

She pulls two rolled-up T-shirts from her overnight bag along with a bottle of wine and walks with me to the kitchen. She sets the T-shirts down on top of the kitchen island. "I had some made for you so you can wear them when you go out."

"That's honestly brilliant. Thank you, Maren." I pop off the wine cork and pour her a glass. "I don't know why I didn't think to do something like that. Old me would have been all over it."

Maren swallows a sip of wine. "You're heartbroken. None of us are at the top of our game when our heart is shredded."

I nod, my eyes burning yet again. I quickly blink to keep any more tears from falling. She sidles up to me, pulling me into a side hug as we both lean against the edge of the counter.

"Thanks for coming over. I know you're so busy with work, and the drive out here can be such a pain especially when you're working all those twelve-hour shifts—"

"Hey." She tightens her arm around me. "No apologies necessary. I'm your best friend, and I want to be here for you. Always."

This time when I blink, a few tears escape. As shitty as it's been to lose Lewis, I'm so lucky to have the support system that I have with Maren and Naomi checking up on me every day.

"How about some comfort food and a Netflix binge tonight?"

I sniffle and wipe at my face. "Sounds perfect."

When she peers into the fridge, her eyes widen. "Wow. I'm guessing your mom's been by?"

"Yup. She's been trying to come every day after work, but I've negotiated her down to every other day. And she always brings something to eat. That's why I've got enough food to feed ten people for a month."

"I get it. Food is my family's love language too."

Her phone blares, and she sets the Tupperware container she just pulled from the fridge on the counter. She squints at the screen.

"Telemarketer?" I ask.

"Probably." She silences it, but then it sounds again so she answers.

I open the Tupperware and dish out *pansit* onto two plates when she stammers.

"What the... Lewis?"

I freeze at the mention of his name. The fork drops from my hand, landing on the plate with a clank. What the hell is Lewis doing calling Maren? How did he get her number?

I whip my head to Maren, who's gazing at me with bulging, unblinking eyes. "Um, yeah, I'm with her right now..." She frowns and shakes her head, like she's trying to make sense of what is happening. "Wait, how did you get my number?"

When her shocked expression turns to amused, my mouth falls open.

"An IT friend, huh? Okay then."

She's quiet again for several seconds while listening to whatever he's saying. Her expression sobers before her gaze darts to me. Her brown eyes shine with concern. "I'll ask her. Hang on."

She lowers the phone. "He wants to talk to you. He says he wants to apologize. And tell you something."

My heart has ceased beating completely. A strange mix of emotions is currently taking hold of me—shock that Lewis called one of my best friends in order to get in touch with me. Anger and annoyance that he's daring to reach out after leaving so abruptly. Longing to hear his voice just one more time. Confusion at not knowing what the hell is the right thing to do.

"It's okay if you don't want to, Harper," she says gently.

Boldness rockets through me. I'm not used to this, to being the weepy friend post-breakup who needs my girl squad to coddle me. And even though I acknowledge that it's okay—healthy, even—to allow myself to run through this gamut of messy emotions, it's also exhausting. And frustrating. And I want a break from feeling this way, even if it's just for a minute while I tell off Lewis.

I grab the phone from Maren.

"What do you want, Lewis?"

"Harper."

The brokenness of his tone catches me off guard. He sounds like someone just kicked him in the stomach.

I shove aside the feeling. His apparent sadness doesn't take away the fact that he walked out on me the moment things got complicated between us. An echo of the stabbing pain I felt in my chest radiates through me as I think back on the day that he left.

I made a mistake. I let my feelings for you cloud my judgment... I can't be with someone whose family is gonna be a liability for me—a threat to my privacy...

"Why did you call Maren?" I blurt as I refocus on the moment.

"Because I wanted to talk to you. Because I miss you. Because…"

A heavy sigh rockets from him, triggering an image of him tugging a hand through his wavy blond hair. He'd do that every time he was frustrated.

"Because I realized just how badly I fucked this up, Harper. I should never have left you. I should never have said those hurtful things about your family violating my privacy. You're right—they didn't mean to cause any harm, and I should have been more understanding. Your family was nothing but wonderful to me. They welcomed me into their lives, and I'm so sorry I said that about them. I was just so shocked and panicked to see all those photographers lurking outside your house and…"

His broken breath echoes in my ear.

"I'm so fucking sorry, Harper." His voice breaks. "You're being hounded because of me, and it kills me to think that… Look, I know I have no right to ask you to give me another chance. I know that I'm lucky to even be speaking to you right now after what I did…"

I press my eyelids shut, ignoring the fiery burn of tears, my lips trembling so hard they ache. My brain feels like someone tossed it into a blender. I can barely think, let alone process what I want in this moment. The thought of Lewis and me somehow reconciling seemed impossible even just minutes ago. But now to witness him like this—regretful and heartbroken over me—throws me off completely. I don't know how I feel or what I want.

"Meeting you was the best thing that's ever happened to me. I was the happiest I've ever been when I was with you," he says, his voice steady now. "You believed in me like no one else has before. You changed my life, Harper. And I… I know this is terrible timing, but I'm saying all this now because it's part of why I know I fucked up so badly. Leaving you was the biggest mistake of my life. I think about you every day. Every day I wish I could take back what I did. I'm a broken disaster without you. I'll never feel complete without you."

I'm speechless for a long moment before I can find the words I want to speak.

"I'm still so hurt. I'm reeling—I have been ever since you left. And I don't think I can be with someone who walks out on me the moment things get messy. But more than that…"

"More than what?" he says softly after I trail off.

I let out a shaky breath. "I meant everything I said about believing in you, Lewis. You're brilliant and talented and I want you to pursue every dream you have. But even if I could get past the way you left me—even if we tried to make a relationship between us work, I don't know how it could. You were right when you said we're from two different worlds. You're in LA. I'm in Half Moon Bay and San Francisco. You want to take your career to the next level, and I want to stay where I am." I hesitate for a few seconds, letting my thoughts take shape. "Yeah, we could visit each other for a while, but how long could we keep that up until things eventually come to a head and one of us can't take the distance anymore? It wouldn't work. I don't know how we can be together long-term. I mean, I'm two weeks into this paparazzi madness and I can barely handle it. If we were in a relationship, I'd have to deal with them hounding me every single day, and I just can't do that."

There's a long pause.

"My world is bacon mac and cheese and loud family gatherings and working a normal nine-to-five. Your world is organic pressed juices and premieres and film sets. We're just too different."

Lewis starts to stammer, but then he trails off, like he's given up on whatever he was going to say. "I understand."

I sniffle and wipe my eyes.

"I'm sorry I'm making you cry again," he says after a pause.

"I'm sorry I'm making *you* cry."

A sad, snotty chuckle sounds from his end of the line. "I deserve it, though."

Maren rests her hand on my shoulder and hands me a tissue. I mouth "thank you" to her.

"Did you ever open that box in your garage?"

It takes me a minute to figure out what Lewis is talking about. Then it dawns on me: right before we fought and broke up and he left, he mentioned surprising me with something in the garage.

"No, I never did."

"Will you please open it? You don't have to do it now, but there's something in there that I made for you. You don't have to do anything with it. And I... Honestly, now that I think about it, I probably should have asked you first before I did it. But I wanted to surprise you."

"Okay. I will."

A long silence follows.

"I'm sorry. For everything," Lewis finally says.

"Goodbye, Lewis."

"'Bye, Harper."

The second I hang up, Maren pulls me into her arms.

"It's okay," she whispers in my ear as I let out a string of weak sobs.

"He says he's sorry, that he wishes he could go back

and make things right so we can be together...but I just...
I just don't know..."

I can feel Maren nod her head in understanding in response to my snotty babble.

"I'm so confused," I mumble.

When I finally pull away, she grabs a tissue and helps
me dab at my face.

"He left me something in the garage," I mutter.

"Do you want to go see what it is?"

When I nod, she grabs my hand in hers, and together
we walk to the door leading to the garage. Just a few feet
away sits a sealed cardboard box. I point to it, and Maren
whips out her car keys to rip it open. Together we crouch
down next to it. I yank away the flaps to reveal a brass
lamp with strings of crystals as a lampshade. It takes a
few seconds of me staring at it before I recognize them
as the crystals from *Apong* Vivian's collection.

I cup my hand over my mouth as I gasp.

"This is really beautiful," Maren says. "He bought
this for you?"

I shake my head. "No, he made it. Out of my *apong*'s
crystals."

I tell Maren about the chandelier and how devastated
I was when Lewis told me that even with the ceiling reinforced it wouldn't be strong enough to support the light
fixture with all the crystals on it.

"I was pretty sad about it." I can't stop gazing at the
endless strings of crystals draped over the brass fixture
and how they look like mini prisms whenever the sunlight beaming through the garage window hits them.

I lift the lamp out of the box.

"Oh, wait." Maren picks up a small brown envelope
that was under the lamp.

She hands it to me, and I rip it open.

*I know this isn't as impressive as a chandelier, but
I hope that when you look at this, it reminds you of
your grandma. I love you, H.*
—L

This time when I cry, I'm smiling.

"Oh wow," Maren says.

For a minute I sit on the dingy garage floor and gaze at the lamp, Maren next to me, her arm wrapped around my waist. Despite the sweetness of Lewis's gift, I'm still operating in this heartbroken daze, struggling to make sense of everything. Do I move on without him like I planned before he called to apologize? Do I give things between us another chance? But how can we make this work? Things were amazing when we were hiding away together in the house, but the moment the real world started creeping in, we fell apart. Even if we were to get past all that, there's still the fact that we don't even live in the same city. I don't want to be with someone who's gone half the time.

"I don't know what to do," I finally say.

Maren rests her head on my shoulder. "Wine, *pansit*, and Netflix can't make this decision for you, but it's a good way to distract yourself."

A sad chuckle falls from my lips. Maren helps me up. I grab the lamp and follow her back into the house and set it on the end table next to the couch. I head into the kitchen, where we gather our glasses and plates, and then we plop down on the sofa. When she pulls up Netflix and starts to scroll through the options, I inhale sharply.

There's Lewis's smiling face on the promo shot for the first season of *The Best of It*.

"Shit. Sorry." Maren clicks on a random cooking show.

"It's okay," I murmur despite how thrown I am. "He's a celebrity. I'm bound to see his face."

She squeezes my hand as we watch a handsome French guy teach a group of amateur cooks about making chocolate. No matter how hard I try to focus on the screen, my mind floats back to Lewis.

I can't deny just how much I still love him and want him. I even eye my phone sitting on the coffee table. I could unblock his number, call him right now, and tell him that I want him back. But I don't move my hand from my lap to grab my phone. All I can do is stay cuddled on the couch, staring at the light dancing through the crystals, and sigh.

Chapter Twenty-Six

Harper

"*Anak*, the house looks so beautiful."

I've lost track of the number of times someone has said that this evening. This time it's Uncle Pedro.

I lean down to hug him where he's sitting on the couch. "Thanks. It came together really well with Naomi helping me decorate."

I hear Naomi in the kitchen asking Simon to watch the mini quiches in the oven before walking over to bring a glass of water to Uncle Pedro. "I just threw a bunch of pillows and paintings around," she says. "Harper was the genius who spearheaded the entire remodel. All the glory goes to you, cuz."

I pull her into a hug. Tonight I'm hosting my first gathering for family and friends to show them the completed renovation of *Apong* Bernie and *Apong* Vivian's house. My parents, Naomi's parents, Uncle Pedro, a bunch of cousins, aunts, uncles, Maren, and Simon are all here.

Everyone is milling around the open space of the kitchen, dining room, and living room while eating and chatting. Dad walks over to kiss my cheek. "My brilliant *anak*."

I laugh as he swipes the remote from the coffee table and immediately turns on the TV to search for the NBA game schedule for tonight.

Mom rolls her eyes at Dad while handing me a glass of wine. I take a long sip.

"Would it kill you to miss a game, Christian? We're here to admire the beautiful job our daughter did at renovating your parents' house, not gawk at a sports event."

"Jules, you know it would absolutely kill me," Dad says without taking his eyes off the TV. "Besides, I already saw everything." He turns and smiles at me. "The house is amazing. It's a dream come true to see it like this."

I tell him thanks, taking in the heartened look in his eyes. When he turns right back to the TV, Mom moans at him, and I chuckle to myself. As my parents continue bickering in their typical good-natured way, I do a pass around the space, making sure everyone knows that there's plenty of food on the kitchen island and counters and to eat as much as they can.

A minute later Mom walks over to me with a plate full of food and makes me sit at one of the bar stools. "Here. You've been such a great hostess running around checking on everyone, but you're gonna pass out if you don't eat. The only thing I've seen you ingest is three glasses of wine."

"And half of Simon's scotch."

She frowns. "All the more reason to make you eat some food."

"Thanks, Mom."

I've just wolfed down two *lumpia* when I notice the concern on her face.

"It's not too painful to hear everyone complimenting the house, is it?" she asks.

I stop chewing once I catch what she means. *Lewis.*

I swallow. "Um, no. I'm okay with it."

It's true…mostly. It's been almost two months since Lewis ended things, and just over a month since he called me to apologize for walking out on me. There's a tug in my chest when I think about how that's the last time that I'll ever hear his voice.

I pause to clear my throat and silently tell myself what I've been reminding myself for weeks: there's no way we can work. Even though I realized after speaking to him that I could forgive him for walking out on me, I couldn't deny the fact that we're from two completely different worlds—and we always will be.

It might work for a bit with us traveling to see each other, but long-term there's no way. I wouldn't leave San Francisco and Half Moon Bay; I know he wouldn't be able to maintain the career he wants living anywhere but LA.

End of story. Even if it was the best love story I've ever had in my life.

My appetite stalls, and I push the plate away. I reach for the glass of wine and down it.

A sad smile tugs at Mom's lips. She rests her hand on my arm. "Are you sure you're okay, honey? It's all right if you're still hurting. It takes time to get over someone you're in love with."

I grab her hand in mine. "I'll be fine, Mom."

Judging by the pinch of her eyebrows and the purse of her lips, she doesn't believe me. "I know you're a strong and capable adult, but I'll always see you as my baby." Her blue eyes turn glassy. "And I can't help but check on my baby when she's hurting."

"Mom. I promise, I'm okay. I've been busy volunteering at Glad You're Here. And I've set things up to start consulting at the beginning of next year and already have a list of firms I'm in contact with. That'll be a good boost in my finances so that I can help pay for things for Uncle Pedro and…"

Mom rests her hand on my arm. "Sweetie. Just stop for a sec, okay? I appreciate all the help you've always offered our family, but you don't have to do that. Uncle Pedro isn't your responsibility. He's staying with your dad and me, and we love looking after him. You've spent enough time taking care of everyone else around you. I don't want you to take a job you don't actually want just because you feel obligated to be a safety net for your family. That's no way to live."

It's been a while since Mom's taken such a pointed and serious tone with me. I'm thrown off for a second, but once the shock wears off, I admit to myself that she's right. I don't really want that consulting job.

"What's your dream job, honey? The thing you want to do most in the world that would make you happy?"

Her question flashes me back to months ago when Lewis and I were working on the hardwood flooring together and he asked me that same question. I still don't have an answer.

"I… I guess I'm not really sure," I say. "I mean, the thing I like doing most is volunteering at Glad You're Here, but that's not a paid position."

"Maybe it could be. Have you even looked into working for them? I bet Diana would be thrilled to know you're interested in joining her charity."

I sigh and admit that I haven't.

"Don't write things off before you give them a chance, honey."

I still as a wave of emotion washes over me. Wise words that could apply to things between Lewis and me. That ship has sailed, though.

I shake off the pang of sadness that hits and pull her into a hug. The sound of someone gasping pulls our attention to the living room.

"Hey, *anak*, isn't that the young man you brought over for dinner?" Uncle Pedro asks.

I spin around, and my eyes go wide when I see Lewis on TV. He's sitting across from an interviewer I recognize as one of the correspondents from a major entertainment news show. I can barely breathe. He looks so, so good. And not just devastatingly handsome with that freshly shaved golden stubble and his blond waves trimmed close to his scalp. But happy. Invigorated. It's even evident in his posture, how he's sitting tall, alert, yet with a relaxed expression. I don't remember seeing him like this in any interview before.

It's then that I notice the entire house has gone quiet. Maren glances up from her conversation with Naomi and Simon, a look of absolute horror on her face. Simon winces, and Naomi's eyes bulge while her gaze darts between the TV screen and me.

She quickly walks over to me. "He was interviewed for this morning's news show, and I think they're replaying it."

She starts to tell my dad to change the channel, but I stop her. As nice as it is that my family and friends care about me, I don't need to be coddled like this. It makes me feel like everyone's treating me like a fussy baby.

I start to say that I'm fine, but something the interviewer says catches my attention.

*"So tell me about this movie you're filming in the
Bay Area."*

*"I'm here in San Francisco for a project that I'm
thrilled to be the executive producer of."*

"And one of the stars."

"Supporting cast, actually," he corrects. A flustered
smile tugs at his mouth, and that dimple I love so much
appears in his right cheek.

*"I suppose that's the perk of having your own pro-
duction company,"* the interviewer says. *"You get to be
the star* and *the boss."*

He seems to ignore the cheeky look she gives him and
dives right into the project. "It's a coming-of-age romance
about a nonbinary teenager. It's our first big project, and
I've never been so excited to work on something."

Joy bursts in my chest. Lewis started his own production company and optioned that script he loved so much.
He's taking control of his career—he's making his dream
come true.

The interviewer says something about Lewis parting
ways with his old agent, and I catch myself starting to
smile. Good. That guy was the fucking worst.

*"I'm sure you're aware, but there's some news that's
leaked out about the circumstances around you getting
fired from your old show,* The Best of It. *You've employed almost all of the crew from that series, which unfortunately has been canceled. There are a lot of rumors
floating around about what actually happened and what
caused you to hide from the public eye for some months.
Care to clear that up?"*

Lewis doesn't even blink at the question. *"Absolutely.
What happened was this—the showrunner, Darren Gra-
bel, was sexually harassing multiple crew members on*

*the show. With their permission, I confronted him and
told him to stop his predatory behavior. But he refused.
And he was enraged that I called him out. In retaliation,
he fired me."*

I glance around to see all my family and friends glued
to the TV, listening intently to Lewis.

*"That's why I acted out at Chateau Marmont and left
LA for a time,"* Lewis says. *"I was angry and frustrated
because I wanted to help, but I couldn't. I needed some
time away to process things and figure out where to go
from there."*

The entire time he speaks, the interviewer nods her
head, the expression on her face thoughtful. Then she
holds up a hand and flashes a blinding smile. *"Okay,
well, I wasn't going to say it, but since you brought it up,
there were some intriguing photos taken of you leaving a
home in Half Moon Bay just over a month ago, looking
disheveled, like you had just rolled out of bed."*

Lewis is unfazed, like he was expecting her to segue
into this.

*"There were also photos of the homeowner taken later
on. She looks like a lovely young lady. What is your relationship with her? People have been speculating that
you're an item—or were an item."*

I flinch at her pointed tone before holding my breath.
In the past when Lewis has been asked about his personal
life, he shut down the interview or simply walked off.
But he stays seated in his chair, his expression focused.
The only sign that he's even slightly agitated is the slight
bulge in his jaw muscle. He's biting down.

*"I hate talking about my relationships. You know that.
But I'll make an exception just this once. The time I spent
in Half Moon Bay was life-changing. The people I spent*

*time with were incredible. I'll never, ever forget them.
And I wouldn't be here right now, pursuing my dream,
had I not met one very special person. It's why I'm here
in San Francisco, actually, hoping that maybe I'll have
the good fortune of running into her after all that we've
been through. She believed in me when no one else did.
She'll always have my heart. Always."*

I don't catch what the interviewer says in response.
My heart is thudding so hard, so fast that I can't hear
anything else. I have to rest my hand against my chest
to ground myself, it's so disorienting. Has it ever beat
like this? Frenzied and out of control, like I'm sprinting
and falling and floating all at once?

No. Never. That's because my heart belongs to Lewis.
He still loves me—enough to break his "no talking about
dating and relationships during interviews" rule. Enough
to spill his feelings on national television, something
he's never done before. Enough to film a project in San
Francisco, on the off chance that he'll run into me again.

And I realize, right then and there, that I want him.
Screw our different worlds. Screw everything that's
happened between us. Screw the mistakes we've made.
Screw what anyone else thinks or says or feels.

He's put himself out there, beating heart out in the
open for all to see—for me to see. And I know in this
moment that I want him, that he's the one for me.

I register the tightness of Naomi's grip on my arm.

"...did you hear what he said? Harper, he wants to
be with you!"

I nod quickly. "I need to get to Lewis. I need to see
him. I need to tell him how I feel about him. Right now."

I glance around for my phone, but I don't see it anywhere. "I—I could unblock his number and call..."

Loud chatter sounds around me. Mom, who's sporting teary eyes but this time with a smile, hands me my phone. I tell her thanks and quickly unblock Lewis's phone number, but when I dial him, it goes straight to voice mail.

I bite back a groan, then try again, but still nothing. My head spins. How will I get ahold of him? He's in San Francisco, but I have no idea where he's staying...

"His phone is going straight to voice mail," I mutter as I frown at my phone screen. "How am I gonna find him if he won't answer..."

Maren and Naomi chatter about driving into the city and searching every five-star hotel. Simon gently explains that Lewis is probably staying under a pseudonym and likely won't be easy to find.

"Wait! Everyone, shut up!" Naomi yells while pointing to the TV.

The interviewer closes out the segment and says something about a press conference happening this evening at the Palace Hotel in San Francisco with the cast of the upcoming movie. I wait for one of them to specify a time, but they don't. The interview ends.

"You should go see him, Harper!"

"Yes! Tell him you love him!"

"Oh my gosh! How romantic!"

"Go get 'em, *anak*!"

Adrenaline rockets through me at the same time that a million anxiety knots form in my stomach. Should I seriously crash his press conference to tell him I love him?

"I—I don't even know if the press conference is still going on," I stammer, then look at the time on my phone. "It's already past seven."

"You should at least try and go to him, *anak*."

The longer I think about it, the less insane it seems. A

long moment passes with everyone in the room quietly staring at me, clearly waiting to see what I'm going to do.

"I can't drive. I've had, like, three glasses of wine."

Naomi and Maren grab my hands. "We'll take you to him."

"Haven't you both been drinking?"

Naomi shakes her head. "I haven't. I'll drive you. We can take Simon's car."

"I'll navigate," Simon says.

"I can help. And I'll cheer you on!" Maren says.

Uncle Pedro rises from the couch. "I will too. You got room for an old guy to tag along?"

I laugh, my nerves haywire but at the same time heartened that I have so many people in my life who are willing to drop everything to help me pull off this absolutely insane stunt.

"Okay, yes. Let's do this."

Half an hour later we're minutes away from San Francisco city limits, headed to the Palace Hotel. Sitting in the passenger seat of Simon's Audi, I dial Lewis's number for the millionth time.

"He's still not answering," I mumble.

"It's okay! We're gonna help you get to him," Maren says to me from the back seat. "Naomi, when you hit the freeway, merge left."

She grips my shoulder. "It's honestly probably even better that he doesn't know you're coming. It makes this grand gesture so romantic. He'll be totally shocked when you burst into the hotel and declare your love for him."

"I appreciate your optimistic outlook, but the Palace Hotel is massive, and I have no idea where the press conference is being held—or if it's still going on."

"Wait, let me try and call the hotel."

"Remember what I said about the pseudonym, though."

Maren nods at Simon. "Take over navigating, will you?"

"Sure. Babe, take the exit for Fourth Street," he says to Naomi.

A minute later, Maren finally hangs up. "Press conference is still going on! In the ballroom on the east side of the main floor of the hotel!" she says. "But we gotta hurry, because it's supposed to wrap up in ten minutes."

"No problem." Naomi floors it.

The force of the acceleration thrusts us against our seats. I turn to check on Uncle Pedro, but he's gripping the "oh shit" handle and grinning, looking more alive than I've seen in months. Minutes later we screech to a halt at the entrance of the hotel. I hop out and admire the Beaux Arts–style exterior of this iconic hotel that takes up a good chunk of a city block. A valet appears right as we all jump out of the car. Naomi hands him the keys, and she, Maren, and I dart into the hotel entrance while Simon helps Uncle Pedro walk in behind us.

In the past when I've walked into this hotel for a business meeting, I've always taken a few seconds to gawk at the Gilded Age–inspired architecture and design. But I don't even glance at the massive marble pillars lining the lobby or the dozens of candelabra chandeliers draped in thousands upon thousands of crystals. I make a beeline for the end of the lobby and turn left for the ballroom. Behind me I hear the hurried footsteps of Naomi and Maren.

"On your right, Harper!"

I follow Maren's shouted instructions behind me and head toward the massive wooden door, but I stop when I see a menacing-looking security guard standing in the way.

"This is a closed event," he barks.

My mind races to think of how I'm going to convince this guy to let me in, but then I hear Uncle Pedro yelping behind me.

"My hip!" he shouts.

The security guard darts over and crouches down to where Uncle Pedro is lying on the floor. I start to go to him, but he winks and smiles at me before telling the security guard to run to the front desk for help. I mouth a thank-you to him and shove open the massive oak door. And then I promptly freeze. Holy shit.

It's standing room only in the ballroom with what looks like a hundred reporters and photographers. Loud chatter echoes around me. I can't even see the front of the room where I assume Lewis and his fellow cast members are sitting, answering questions. Everyone standing in front of me is taller than me. I try and maneuver around them, but people are practically shoulder to shoulder.

"Just shove your way through, *anak*!"

I spin around and see Naomi and Maren in the open doorway nodding along with Uncle Pedro's suggestion as he stands between them.

I try to push forward, but the people in front of me don't budge. "Excuse me, I need to get through…"

No one even acknowledges me. Dropping my arms to my sides, I huff out a breath just as the chatter dies down.

"Okay, everyone, there's time for one more question, but then the cast needs to get going."

Shit. Lewis will be gone before he even knows I'm here.

Simon's voice booms behind me. "Question for Lewis Prescott!"

In a flash, Simon moves to my side, hooks his arm through mine, and shoves his six-foot-plus frame through the wall of bodies in front of us. A few *oof*s and *hey*s later, the remaining people in front start parting on either side of us, like a slow-moving human sea.

I beam up at Simon right as we make it to the front of the press line. "Thank you."

He winks at me. "Anytime."

I scan the long table and find Lewis's face a second later among the dozen sitting there. He's glancing off to the side, clearly not paying attention to the commotion.

My heart rockets to my throat.

"You had a question?" says a guy sitting next to Lewis. I quickly skim the placard in front of him that reads "publicist."

"Um, yes. I do. For Lewis."

When he turns to me, his eyes go wide for a second before the corner of his mouth quirks up.

"What publication are you with?" the publicist asks.

"*Dimples* magazine," I say, zeroing in on that adorable dimple in Lewis's right cheek. His smile widens.

"Okay, great," the guy mumbles while squinting at his phone. "Ask away."

"Lewis, you did an interview this morning where you mentioned that mystery woman in Half Moon Bay. You said she'll always have your heart. Did you mean that?"

When my voice starts to tremble, I quickly swallow.

"I did. I meant every word," he says, his gaze unblinking and focused on me.

"Do you still love her?"

"Yes. I love her so much. I always will."

Soft murmurs hum around me. A few of his costars start to whisper to each other while looking over at him.

"Do you—"

"That's enough questions," the publicist says. "Thank you, *Dimples* magazine."

"No, I wanna hear what she was gonna say," Lewis practically barks at the guy. The entire room goes silent.

He turns to me, his hazel stare soft and expectant at once.

I swallow, feeling the burn of everyone's gaze on me. "Do you really think you could make a life with her? Because as much as she loves you and as much as she loves that you're choosing to film this project here in San Francisco, she knows your heart is your work. She wouldn't want you to change yourself in order to be in a relationship."

A hard swallow moves through his throat. Then his mouth curves up. He shakes his head. "She's my whole world. I want to be wherever she is. Nothing else matters."

I let out a shaky breath, my lips trembling as I smile. "Okay. That's really, really great news. One last thing— would you be okay with her running up to you right now and kissing you? She's missed you like crazy, and she's so ridiculously in love with you."

His hazel eyes flash. "Absolutely."

I don't think I've ever cleared ten feet of space so quickly. It feels like it takes less than a second to make it to Lewis. He's on his feet by the time I get to him. When I jump into his arms, he scoops me up instantly, like he was waiting for me to throw myself at him and wrap my legs around his waist. We don't bother with words; we just kiss. It's not the filthiest kiss we've ever shared, which is probably a good thing. Based on the snapping noises, flashes, and startled voices around us, this moment is being documented by everyone in this room and will make the rounds online and on TV in a matter of minutes.

But it's still amazing, earth-shattering, soul shaking, and everything good—everything I've missed and craved ever since we've been apart. The feel of his lips on mine, his arms wrapped around me, the heat of his body skimming mine—it's all heaven.

When we break our kiss, I cup my hands around his stubbly cheeks and aim a shaky smile at him.

"Hi. I love you."

My heart explodes. "Hey. I love you too."

Another kiss and more shouting happens before he finally puts me down. He doesn't let me go, though. His arms stay wrapped around me, like he's using his whole body as a shield to protect me from all this chaos.

"I know you hate all this," he says. "The cameras, the reporters, the paparazzi, the chaos—"

"No, it's okay. I can handle it as long as I have you."

He beams down at me.

"Sorry I crashed your press conference. And sorry to air our personal stuff in such a public way," I say. "I know privacy means the world to you when it comes to your personal life, but I just couldn't stand to be apart any longer. I need you in my life, Lewis. Always."

"Don't be sorry. I'm perfectly happy with the whole world knowing you're mine."

More shouting and flashes happen around us. Lewis leads me by the hand out through a side door and around the corner through another door, which leads to the stairwell. In the quiet space, we take a second to breathe before he pulls me into him once more. We stay planted in this spot as we kiss, sealed away from the chaos just feet away. Even as our lips part, we stay holding on to each other. I don't ever want to let go.

"I'll need a place to stay, now that I'm relocating to the

Bay Area. Think you can help me out?" Lewis quirks an eyebrow, and I laugh.

"Well, I have an apartment in Nob Hill that'll be vacant in a few months. But if you need something sooner, I've got this newly remodeled bungalow in Half Moon Bay that you might like."

He flashes the most beautiful smile. "I think that just might work."

Epilogue

Lewis

One year later

I shut off the water in the shower, quickly dry off, wrap the bath towel around my waist, then hop out and check the time on my phone on the bathroom counter. Already quarter to six. Shit.

"Harper, babe, we're late!"

I dart out of the bathroom, turn left into the bedroom doorway, and bump chest-first into Harper.

She lets out an *oof* noise, wobbling with the impact. I reach both hands out to steady her, dropping my towel in the process. And then it happens, like it always does every time I touch her hot-as-fuck body. My cock twitches as I take in the swell of her perfect ass and hips in that black lace thong, how her boobs are barely contained in the cups of her matching bra.

"Sorry," I rasp. "I forget how small this place is sometimes."

"*Our* place," she corrects before raising her left hand and wagging her ring finger at me. The antique cushion-cut diamond I picked out as her engagement ring months ago sparkles even in the low light. "We're married. What's mine is yours, what's yours is mine. Remember?"

I glance down at my own hand, at the silver band shining on my ring finger, before I look at her once more. "Of course. How could I forget?"

We're three months into being husband and wife, but it still feels just like yesterday that I married the woman of my dreams. This past year has been a whirlwind, what with getting married, filming a movie, Harper settling into her new job, and the two of us shuffling between the Nob Hill apartment and the house in Half Moon Bay. But I wouldn't want it any other way. I'm sharing a life with the most amazing woman I've ever met. I never knew life could feel this amazing.

Harper's stunning, saucerlike eyes drift down to my naked lower half.

Her deep brown stare turns hungry as she reaches down and palms my now rock-hard cock. The second she bites her lip, I know we're gonna be even more late. But I don't care.

I reach down and hoist her up around my waist, then pull her down for a kiss.

"We're...gonna...be...so...late," she rasps against my lips between kisses.

"Don't care. I need you now."

I walk us to the bed, then drop her onto the mattress, which makes her giggle.

I peer down at her. "Besides. What I have planned won't take long."

Smiling, she quirks her eyebrow and lies back as I press my palm against her stomach. I settle onto my knees between her legs.

"But...this is your big night," she rasps while I press

light kisses to the inside of her thighs. "I don't want to—*oh my god*!"

It doesn't take long before she's shuddering and screaming. Not even two minutes. When I finish, I hop back up on my feet and glance down at my wife, flushed and panting and beaming up at me.

"What about you?" she asks, eyeing me between my legs.

I wink at her. "I can wait till later. We've got a premiere to head to."

Harper holds my hand tight in hers as I make my way to the press line at the Castro Theatre in San Francisco. I'm still not used to maneuvering my tall self around our tiny Nob Hill apartment, even though that's where we lived while I filmed in San Francisco the past year. But one thing I love about it is how it's in the perfect location. It was a straight shot to here along Market Street, which meant that even with our little tryst, we were only fifteen minutes late tonight.

I shuffle my feet against the plush red carpet that leads to the steps of the iconic theater where my production company's very first movie will be playing in a matter of minutes. My stomach flips for the millionth time since we arrived. I honestly can't believe this is happening. It's the premiere for my dream project, the coming-of-age indie movie I thought I'd never be part of. But it happened, and filming it was the most enjoyable and fulfilling work I've ever done. Early reviews have been glowing, which is blowing my mind. Who would have thought that me, the guy who was for years typecast as the hot bimbo or the sexy bad boy, would get rave reviews for playing the troubled side character in an indie project?

If I think too hard or too long about it, my brain feels like it's going to break—in a good way. For so long I've dreamed of this, of doing work I'm passionate about. And now I'm doing exactly that.

"Hey." Harper tugs gently on my hand. "How are you holding up, superstar?"

I glance down at her, mesmerized. She's wearing a red gown that looks like it was plastered to her body. I can barely take my eyes off her—she's beyond stunning.

I let out a breath. "Pretty damn good. Just…this is all so unbelievable."

I tug at the sleeve of my tux, a sorry attempt to quell my nerves.

Harper stops me just before I walk up to the first reporter in the press line. "Just take it all in for a sec."

It's like she can read my mind. God, this woman. Absolutely incredible in every way.

I do what she says. I gaze up at the multistory pearl-hued exterior of the theater, taking in how it pops against the darkness of the nighttime sky. I glance at the dozens of photographers snapping photos of my cast mates as they make their way inside.

And then I turn around to wave at the crowd of a few thousand fans on the opposite side of Market Street, which is shut down for the premiere. The deafening cheers and screams make me grin so wide, my face aches.

"Told you your fans would love you in any role." Harper winks at me, and it feels like fireworks going off in my chest. "And they're loving your calendar."

I smile, thinking about how I just finished signing autographs and taking photos with the crowd. Most of the items I signed were copies of the nude calendar I released a few months ago. Harper was right, that was a brilliant idea. It's earned two million dollars so far, all for charity.

I pull her to me, then lean down and kiss her so long, the crowd goes wild once more.

When she pulls away, she smacks me lightly on the arm. "We're in public," she says through a flustered smile. The way her tan skin flushes as she darts her gaze around us is the most adorable thing ever.

"Good. I want everyone to see how crazy I am about you. Because none of this would be happening if you hadn't believed in me. Thank you."

Her expression turns tender, and she pulls me in for a kiss that's much more proper than the long and filthy one I planted on her just seconds ago.

"I am so, so proud of you, Lewis." The conviction in her tone has me vibrating with emotion. I swallow, steadying myself.

A publicist calls my name and gestures for me to go ahead in the press line. Harper moves to stay back, but I pull her with me.

"This is your moment," she says. "I want you to enjoy it."

"The only way I can enjoy it is with you. Always with you."

She flashes the most beautiful smile. Hand in hand, we step forward to the press line. As I answer question after question, I still can't believe this is my life right now. I've got my dream job and my dream woman. How did I get so lucky?

As we scale the steps to the theater's entrance, I feel Harper slow her pace.

"Take it all in," she says to me.

I gaze down at her, my heart swelling in my chest. "I am."

Harper

"You sure you only want one sheet pan of bacon mac and cheese, honey?" Mom asks. "I'm happy to make more so you and Lewis can have leftovers."

I give Mom's arm a gentle squeeze as I pass by her in the kitchen of the Half Moon Bay house. "Positive. We still have leftovers in the freezer in the garage from family dinner last week. We're good."

I open the door of the refrigerator and pull out the pitcher of sangria that I made. "Who wants sangria?" I call out to the crowd of friends and relatives gathered in the house. Half of them holler "yes."

While I pour, Mom hands the glasses out to everyone. Lewis hurries over to my side and plants a kiss on my cheek.

"I think we're gonna need more sangria," he says before opening up the liquor cabinet and fridge for the ingredients to make more.

"None for me, thanks," Dad says while fiddling with the remote to the flat screen. "I'll stick with beer."

"You sure, Dad?" Lewis says as he preps another pitcher beside me.

I don't miss the twinkle in my dad's eyes as he looks over at Lewis and tells him that he's good. It melts him every single time Lewis calls him Dad. He started doing it after we got engaged, and I turn to mush too whenever I witness it.

Lewis passes Dad and gives him a pat on the back on the way to drop off a sangria to Uncle Pedro, who's sitting on the couch.

Lewis starts to turn away, but Uncle Pedro stops him. "Hey." He nods to the lamp Lewis made for me using

Apong Vivian's crystal collection. "Now that's a pretty darn good lamp."

Lewis chuckles. "Thanks, Uncle Pedro."

I smile at how he says that to Lewis every time he comes over. It's a silly and cute exchange, and it makes my heart flutter every time. Everyone in my family loves Lewis to bits. You'd think he's always been part of the family based on how my parents, cousins, aunts, and uncles include him in every conversation and event, how they shower him in kisses and hugs every time they see him.

I catch Lewis smiling to himself as he walks back over to me. This is something he's always wanted, to be part of a loving and adoring family. And he finally has it—I was able to give that to him.

He pours us a glass of sangria to share, but before we can sip, Mom holds up a hand. "We should do a toast to our big star!"

She gestures at him with her glass, which prompts Lewis to blush like crazy. "It's okay, Mom," he says. "It's not a big deal."

"Nonsense! It is absolutely a big deal. My amazing son-in-law is the reason we're all here tonight, to watch your movie! We're all so proud of you, honey."

Everyone in the room raises their glasses and cheers to Lewis. Even though his movie is still in theaters, he was able to get an early release copy of it. All of our family and friends have been dying to see it, so we decided to host a family premiere at our house the day after the actual premiere.

"And the reason why we have Lewis in our family is because of Harper," Mom says, her misty gaze now fixed on me. "Now, Lewis, I know this is your big night, but

I want to take a moment to shine the light on our amazing Harper. It's because of her that we're able to gather in this beautiful house. And she's putting her architecture skills to good use in her new job. She's spearheading an affordable housing development with the charity she works for. Isn't that wonderful, everyone?"

Now it's my turn to blush as everyone claps. Being able to work for Glad You're Here as an architect has been a dream come true. I've finally figured out a way to use my professional skills to help others.

Mom uses her free hand to fan at her eyes. "Lewis. Harper. You're so wonderful together. We're blessed to have a perfect daughter, and now we have the perfect son. We're so proud of you both."

I blow her a kiss. Dad walks up to hug her.

"Jules, honey, this is sounding a lot like the toast you gave at their wedding," he jokes before kissing her cheek.

"I can't help it." She sniffles and dabs at her eyes. "I'm just a ball of emotions."

The room fills with chatter and laughter. Lewis hugs me tight against him, and the two of us watch everyone around us chat and laugh.

"Aww, you two. Making Auntie Jules cry tears of joy again." Naomi sidles next to me to refill her glass from the faucet.

"No sangria for you?" I ask.

"Nope, I'm good with just water. Honestly, the thought of alcohol makes me kind of sick."

"Spoken like a true lightweight," I tease.

When Simon walks over, I point to the end of the counter where the hard alcohol bottles are. "Don't worry, we're not gonna make you drink the fruity stuff. We got a fresh bottle of scotch for you."

"Oh. Thanks. I'm good, though."

His brow furrows slightly just before he sips from his own glass of water. He runs a hand through his light brown hair and shuffles a little.

"Well, that's a first. I don't think I've ever seen you say no to scotch."

"Yeah. Well. Just trying to cut back." He clears his throat right before exchanging a look with Naomi.

"Damn, are you pregnant, Simon? Congrats, man." After a few seconds of awkward silence at my terrible joke, I finally catch on.

"Oh shit…" I turn to Naomi. "Are you…"

"Um, maybe?" Her dark brown gaze darts around the room, but no one seems to overhear. She glances at Simon, who's trying and failing to bite back a smile. "We're not necessarily trying right now, but we're not using protection, so I'm not drinking anymore, of course, and Simon is joining in solidarity because he's a sweetheart like that. And I missed my last period by a couple of weeks, so…"

I pull her into a hug.

"Shh, we don't want to tell anyone yet. We're not even sure."

I release her from my hug and swallow back the squeal I'm aching to let loose. "Of course. Sorry," I say quietly.

I turn to Simon and pull him into a quick hug. Lewis pats him on the back, and I scoop Naomi's hand in mine.

"Does anyone else know?" I ask.

"Just Maren. She noticed Simon's no-scotch thing the other day when she was over at our apartment before she jetted off to London to visit her boyfriend."

"Promise, I won't say a word till you're ready."

Naomi is practically glowing as she hugs me.

Dad hollers that he finally figured out how to get

the movie to play. Simon and Naomi make their way to the living room while Lewis and I stay standing in the kitchen.

"You're gonna be an uncle," I whisper to him.

He tugs a hand through his gold-blond locks while shaking his head. He smiles, his eyes dazed, like he can't believe it. "I can't wait."

I move to head to the living room, but he pulls me to turn back to him.

"Hey. How do you feel about...you know..." He nods his head to Naomi and Simon, who are sitting on the floor.

"Oh. Honestly? I've never been baby crazy or anything like that, but I'm open to having kids," I say, careful to keep my voice low.

"That's exactly how I feel too."

"Does that mean we should start...not being careful?"

He beams. "I'd be good with that, if you are."

"I'd like that."

He pulls me to him once more, and I snuggle into his chest, utterly and completely content. I never thought I could feel this complete, be this happy. But here I am feeling exactly that.

"I'm so in love with you, Harper." He says it quietly with his lips pressed against my forehead.

I close my eyes and smile. "I'm so in love with you, Lewis."

* * * * *

Acknowledgments

This book wouldn't be what it is without Stefanie Simpson and Sandy Lim. Thank you for being the most amazing beta readers and friends I could ever ask for. Tova Opatrny, thanks for all the vent sessions, you help keep me sane. Stephanie Archer, thanks for being the greatest email pen pal. Thank you to my agent, Sarah Younger, and my editor, Stephanie Doig, for believing in this story and supporting me. Thank you to my family and friends for believing in me and loving me. Thanks to my cat Salem for cuddling with me during all those late-night writing sessions. And biggest thanks of all to my readers. Thank you for your kindness and support, I adore you.

About the Author

Sarah Smith is a copywriter turned author who wants to make the world a lovelier place, one kissing story at a time. Her love of romance began when she was eight and she discovered her auntie's stash of romance novels. She's been hooked ever since. When she's not writing, you can find her hiking, eating chocolate, and perfecting her *lumpia* recipe. She lives in Bend, Oregon, with her husband and adorable cat, Salem.

A new work assignment goes delightfully off script... Read on for an excerpt from The Close-Up *by Sarah Smith.*

Chapter One

Nothing good comes from a dick pic. I know that now.

It's not that I ever thought highly of them. Like so many other women, I've been sent more than my fair share of unsolicited penis photos. They're never, ever fun. It's just that tonight I discovered the kind of irreversible damage they can inflict.

Tonight I watched my year-and-a-half relationship go down the drain, all because of one ill-timed junk shot.

"Think of it this way," my cousin Harper says, pointing her martini glass at me. "At least you found out now what a gross crap-weasel Brody is. At least you weren't married. And at least you didn't have kids together."

I squint at her over the rim of my second Amaretto sour in the last half-hour. Harper is many things: my cousin, birthday twin, best friend, and a workaholic architect who earns an impressive mid-six figures in the Bay Area. One thing she's not? An emotional shoulder to cry on. She's always pragmatic and logical, even when I want to trash my cheating ex over drinks.

My cheating ex as of three hours ago.

I drain the last of my drink, then slam it on the table. "Yeah. Finding out my boyfriend cheated because he mistakenly texted a picture of his penis to me with the words, 'Miss you, Laura. General Monster Dong is aching to be inside you, baby,' is so much better."

Just speaking that heinous nickname Brody came up with for his penis makes me want to crush my empty glass in my bare hand.

"It *is* better, Naomi. Imagine how much worse it would have been if you had been home with kids and you got that text."

She's right. "Of course it's better. But it still absolutely sucks to know that I wasted the last year and a half with him. I thought he was…"

"What exactly did you think Brody would be?" Harper narrows her hickory-hued eyes.

But I can't. No matter how long I wait for the words to come, they can't hide the truth: my relationship with Brody wasn't going to last anyway. And I knew it the whole time I was with him.

I glance around this dive bar that somehow exists in the upscale Nob Hill neighborhood of San Francisco, desperate for a distraction. I try staring at the scratched-to-hell hardwood floors, the impressive layer of grime that coats every single one of the ancient light fixtures in this basement bar. When that fails, I try gazing at the handful of other bar patrons, all of whom are either enraptured by the basketball game playing on the flat-screen or staring into their drinks. Nothing works. And that's when I face the truth.

Brody was a bad habit, a go-nowhere relationship that I had gotten used to being in. We were never going to get married, buy a place together, have kids, or do any of that long-term life stuff you typically want to do with your significant other. And I knew that.

When I turn back to Harper, I expect to see her lips

pursed and one eyebrow raised, her signature "I told you so" face. She's had it ever since we were kids.

Instead a soft expression radiates from behind her thick bangs. It's pure empathy.

"Don't get me wrong," she says. "If I see Brody's smug face again, I'm going to punch it. Cheating is never, ever okay. If he was unhappy with you, he should have broken up with you. That bastard hurt you in the worst way, but you weren't right for each other in the first place."

I picture five-foot-two Harper wailing on six-foot Brody and almost laugh. She's got the no-bullshit personality of a prison guard when she's pissed off, and Brody wouldn't stand a chance.

The lump in my throat dissipates as I swallow. I was so enraged when I received the accidental dick pic this evening that I immediately marched into the bedroom where Brody was and yelled, "My name isn't Laura, you asshole." I recommended he give "General Monster Dong" a more realistic nickname, like "Private Average Sized At Best." Then I stormed out of the apartment while dialing Harper. I didn't have the time to throw on makeup before leaving like I would have on a normal night, but now I'm silently grateful. At least this way I won't have mascara streaks running down my cheeks if I end up crying.

I wait out the urge for two long seconds, thankful it doesn't take hold. "Why do you always have to be so insightful?" I let slip a joyless chuckle.

She reaches over to smooth the ends of my shoulder-blade-length hair. "Because as best friends *and* cousins, we know each other better than anyone else. You call me out on my shit, and I call you out on yours. We've been doing that since we were in diapers."

I let a small smile break free, the pain in my chest easing. "Right."

Harper looks up to thank the bartender, who drops off another gin martini for her and a bourbon for me.

"If you knew Brody wasn't right for me all along, why didn't you say something?"

As loving and protective as she is of me, she's not one to hold back her opinion. She's never mean about it, unlike some people who use honesty as a flimsy excuse to be assholes; she's just blunt. And she always, always acts with care and concern.

"Meddling's not my style. Bringing you here to Spud's Bar to drink away your post-breakup frustration is more my speed."

"Here's to that." I raise my glass in a mock toast. "And here's to no more relationships for me. Ever."

Harper frowns. "Come on, Naomi."

"Hey." I point my glass at her. "No meddling, remember?"

Her mouth twists as she sighs.

"I'm serious. I'm done with relationships. The few long-term ones I've had have brought me nothing but heartache and frustration since I started dating as a teenager. And they all ended in disaster. Brody cheated. The guy before him, Tyler, ghosted me after nearly a year together. The guy before that—Aaron—never, not once referred to me as his girlfriend for the two years we were together, only as 'the girl I'm seeing.' And what's-his-name before that broke up with me on my twenty-first birthday. While we were out having drinks with my friends. Then went home with the bartender. Remember?"

Harper winces.

"Clearly, happily-ever-afters are not in the cards for me. So from now on, it'll just be me."

This is what a lifetime of idealizing your parents' perfect marriage does to a person. When you grow up with parents like mine who never fight, who can't keep their hands off each other even after nearly forty years together, who still go out on weekly romantic date nights, it warps your expectations. It makes you think that you too will someday meet that perfect someone and have an equally perfect relationship.

But sixteen years of failed relationships have taught me one thing: it's never gonna happen.

Harper shakes her head, clearly disapproving of my relationship ban. "Fine. Keeping within my *style*, I won't say a word about your ridiculous ban. You know what else is my style? Cheering you up when you're feeling down. And you know the best way to do that?"

"No clue." I finish off the bourbon in two more gulps. I don't even stop to taste; I just guzzle and let it burn down my throat. I'm instantly light-headed. I hardly ever indulge in alcohol, so three drinks in less than forty-five minutes means I'm well on my way to drunk.

Harper signals the bartender to refill my glass. Scratch that. *Four* drinks.

"The absolute best way to cheer yourself up is to find a new hottie to cleanse your palate." Harper fixes her gaze on a guy sitting at the bar, his back to our booth.

My brow flees to my hairline. "What?! No way am I hooking up with some rando!"

She takes my shrieked response in stride, shaking her head. "For god's sake, Naomi. I'm not suggesting that. I just think you should flirt with someone a little."

"Oh." I inhale, relieved. "I'm not really in the mood."

"Come on, Miss No-More-Relationships. There's no better way to kick off a relationship ban than flirting with a hottie, zero expectations attached. You can cross it off your fuck-it list."

My fuck-it list. I haven't thought of it in years. When we were teenagers, Harper and I came up with a list of silly and crazy things we'd like to someday do, like bungee jumping and making out with a hot stranger at midnight on New Year's Eve. We joke about it whenever we feel the urge to make fun of our naive teenage selves.

"The sooner you move on—the more you look at other guys, even if it's just for a fun conversation that won't go anywhere—the easier it will be to get over Brody."

Harper's words take hold in my brain, like an anchor digging into the ocean floor. That actually makes sense.

I grip the table to steady myself. "I think I might be a tad too drunk for this."

"Flirting is always more fun when you're a bit drunk."

She says it in such a matter-of-fact way, I believe her. I stand up and smooth down the front of my flowy white blouse, which I'm wearing with a slate gray pencil skirt and black heels. I push up the sleeves, annoyed that I didn't think to change out of my work clothes before I stormed out of the apartment in a rage.

"You look amazing as always," Harper says, as if reading my mind.

I run my fingers through my hair. "I don't feel very amazing at the moment."

She pins me with you've-got-to-be-kidding-me eyes. "Naomi, you're tall with long arms and legs, perky tits, and a bubble butt. You're probably the best-looking woman that's ever walked into this dive."

"Next to you." Even though I appreciate Harper

building me up, she's a stunner. She's got an adorable girl-next-door face, and the petite and busty figure I've envied since we hit puberty together. We both share the same background—Filipino and Caucasian—as well as the same dark hair, dark eyes, and tan skin.

She winks at me. "Now go get your flirt on with Mr. Broad Muscly Back over there. He's been eyeing you since we sat down."

I turn on my heels and pause for a beat, taking extra care to make sure I don't fall.

"Wow," I mutter to myself.

Just the sight of this dude from behind is impressive. His crisp dove-gray dress shirt is an inadequate cover for the toned muscle underneath. Sculpted shoulders and thick arms highlight his broad frame perfectly. The back of his head is covered in cropped light brown hair. Judging by the slicked-back style he sports on top, he's got one of those trendy skin-fade haircuts that European soccer players and male models favor.

I lick my lips. I don't even need to see his face. There's no doubt it is just as attractive as the rest of him. No way would I ever approach a guy this hot if I were sober. He is unquestionably out of my league.

I take a breath, and the moment of insecurity passes. This is just for fun—a simple distraction.

"Fuck it. Let's do this."

Liquid courage takes hold, and I stomp up to him, leaning my hand on the bar top. "Hey!"

Judging by the way his shoulders jump to his ears, I'm way too loud. I bite my lip to stifle a laugh. Uh-oh. I've hit the giggly marker of drunk.

He turns to face me. "Hey, yourself," he chuckles.

I dry swallow the air in my throat. Just as I suspected: when this guy smiles, he is off-the-charts hot.

Gold-brown eyes, thick pouty lips, and a jawline so sharp you could cut diamonds on it. I pause at his nose. The crooked bump along the ridge tells me he must have broken it at some point. But instead of making his face look imperfect, he looks rugged. And yummy. Like a sexy caveman who broke his nose fighting off a saber-toothed tiger.

"You're hot." I immediately clamp my hand over my mouth. Not only does the alcohol have me operating at a deafening volume, it also seems to have misplaced my filter.

He bursts out laughing once more. "Oh. Uh, thanks."

He rubs the scruff on his now flushed cheek. The facial hair he sports is thick but trim. Not a beard, but more than a five o'clock shadow.

"Sorry." I hiccup. "I've had a bit too much to drink."

"You don't say?" He flashes that winning smile once more. My knees are actually weak.

"But you must hear that all the time, looking the way you do."

He doesn't answer right away. In the moment of silence that follows, I study him. Something about this guy is familiar, but I can't put my finger on it.

"I don't actually." His eyes fall to the bar top, like he's embarrassed about something.

"Well, I'm telling you. You're mega, crazy, superhot."

His expression slides to amusement. Inside I feel a ping of pride at getting this guy to laugh and smile.

A fresh bout of dizziness hits me. This time it's more intense, though. I swallow.

The handsome stranger's eyebrows knit. "Are you okay?"

I nod, even though I'm not. I grip the bar top for stability.

Gently, he steadies me with a hand on my arm. "You sure?"

The look of concern in his eyes has me feeling something familiar again. Just then a tiny bell goes off in my head. I've seen him before, but without facial hair. I just can't remember where or when...

I start to wobble, but this guy's got me upright with just his hand. He's still on the bar stool, but he's leaning on it now instead of sitting. The almost-standing position he's assumed makes it look like he's keeping guard for me. If I weren't fighting to stay up, I'd swoon.

"I'm sorry," I mumble. "It's been...kind of a rough night."

"Sorry to hear that." Sincerity radiates in his eyes and his gentle tone. Even though he's probably just being polite, it sounds like he means it.

"Do you wanna talk about it?" he asks. "Maybe over a glass of water?"

"Water? How smooth."

The corner of his mouth quirks up. "On any other night I'd offer to buy you a proper drink, but it seems like you've already had a few."

"And on any other night I'd admire you from across the bar instead of marching right up to you and calling you hot. I have two Amaretto sours and two bourbons to thank for that. Because I'm in fuck-it mode. And you are number one on my fuck-it list."

The things my liquor-laden brain comes up with. Christ.

"What's fuck-it mode? And a fuck-it list?"

"'Fuck-it mode' is me downing more alcohol in forty-five minutes than I have in the past four months combined because I found out my boyfriend cheated on me tonight. I broke up with him, of course. And now I'm chatting you up. Because fuck it. See? Fuck-it list."

"I'm still not sure I understand what a fuck-it list is, but I'm sorry you went through that. Your ex is a prick for sure. I'm kind of glad to hear that happened, though."

"Sorry, what?" I hiccup.

"I'm glad because if he hadn't screwed things up with you, I wouldn't be chatting with the most beautiful, hilarious woman I've met in a long time."

There's the slightest gleam in his eye when he speaks.

"Whoa," I say through a hot exhale. "You are smooth…"

"Simon," he says with a boyish half smile.

"Naomi."

He gives the spot on my arm where he's holding me a gentle squeeze. I pat him just above his knee and promptly salivate. My oh my, that is one firm quad.

"It's nice to meet you, Simon." I let my hand rest on his thigh, fully expecting him to politely mention that I could take my hands off him at any point.

But he doesn't. Instead his smile softens; he keeps his eyes locked on mine. That gleam in his stare sharpens, and my stomach takes a tumble. In my head, I run through everything that tells me this impromptu flirt session has gone from playful to something more.

We're openly touching.

Our faces are mere inches apart.

He's looking at me like he's starving and I'm the snack he's hungry for.

It all gives me confidence to see if I can take this exchange to the next level.

"Sorry for disrupting your quiet night," I say. "Judging by the way you're holding me and letting me touch you, though, you're into this."

"You're the kind of disruption I'm happy to have. But you're drunk."

I'm certain my cheeks and neck are as red as the letters on the exit sign above the back door. "Oh…yeah. I—I'm sorry, I…"

He pins me with those soothing gold-brown eyes. They haven't lost one ounce of intensity, despite him putting the brakes on our exchange.

"I'm definitely into this—into you. But you need to be sober for this to go anywhere. How about we exchange numbers and tomorrow you can text me where you'd like me to take you for a drink?"

His sweet offer delivered with that killer grin takes the edge off my momentary embarrassment. He whips out his phone, I give him my number, and he calls me. I make a mental note to save his number when I fetch my purse.

My eyes fall to the floor. "Sorry for my, uh…drunkenness."

He lets out the sexiest growl of a chuckle. "Don't fret about it. We've all been there."

Don't fret about it.

Those four words hit like a Mack truck to my brain. It's a phrase I remember from many, many years ago.

In a split second, I'm transported to my college dorm room. I'm alone in bed on a night when my roommate is out, my laptop propped on my pillow, my hand down the front of my pajama shorts. On my screen plays a naughty video of a gorgeous college-aged man on his knees in front of his girlfriend's bed.

The lucky lady is lying on her back, her legs hanging over the edge of the bed, her naked body open to him. The webcam recording their every move is positioned in such a way that you can't see her face.

But you sure as hell can see his. He scoots closer to her legs, rests his hands gently on the tops of her thighs, then twists his head to the camera. His mouth stretches into a smirk that somehow looks more kind than smug. He winks. Then he turns back to her open legs, lowers his face, and goes to town. Her moaning, panting, and screaming are all that can be heard for the next few minutes.

Only this isn't just some random college couple filming their bedroom escapades for thrills.

This is the most popular cam guy online at the time, someone who millions of college girls like me watched, fantasized about, and pleasured themselves to because most of the videos he streamed were of him orally pleasing whatever lady he was seeing at the time—always with her enthusiastic consent.

He was the guy we all wished our college boyfriends were more like. He was the guy our boyfriends crudely dubbed as the "pussy whisperer" because of how easily and often he could bring his partner to climax.

Those four words became his trademark. He'd make a woman screech to high heaven in record time, and she'd always giggle an apology for being loud or making a mess on his face. Every single time he'd say, "Don't fret about it," like an unofficial catchphrase.

That popular cam guy? Simon Rutler—the same

Simon standing in front of me, holding my arm, tensing under my palm, about to flirt my skirt off.

My heart thunders, transporting me back to the present. I blink through the dim lighting of the bar. This is the cam guy I pleasured myself to countless times during college. And I just made an absolute fool of myself in front of him.

"Oh my…shit."

I just drunkenly threw myself at the pussy whisperer.

I stare at him, my jaw hanging in the air, as if I just watched the Loch Ness monster trot through the bar.

"Are you okay?" he asks.

My lips purse as I almost call him the nickname, but I catch myself. I remember reading on some blog way back in the day that he hates that nickname. Saying it right now would undoubtedly piss him off, which would make this mortifying moment even worse.

Just then my stomach seizes. Of embarrassment? No, wait. That's the bourbon.

I grip the metal bar just below the bar top as my stomach lurches once more.

"Sorry, I'm…gonna be…"

I don't get to the word "sick" because hot bile shoots up my throat and out of my mouth, landing on his shoes. There's no time for apologies, though. I need to make it to the nearest toilet before I turn this entire bar into a biohazard by upchucking the contents of my stomach. I press a hand to my chest, as if that's going to somehow keep me from vomiting everywhere.

I burst through the door, ignoring Simon calling behind me as I dart to the nearest toilet and spew into the grimy bowl. My eyes burn with tears as I gag and purge. Seconds later, the putrid smell of hard alcohol mixed with the gyro I had for dinner hits my nostrils. I jolt back, crashing into a pair of legs.

"Naomi?" I register Harper's voice from above. "Holy crap...are you...are you okay?"

There's not a word that exists in the English language that fully captures this feeling of next-level humiliation. Of unknowingly hitting on my college fantasy while intoxicated, then vomiting on him.

Wiping my mouth on my sleeve, I heave a breath. "Nope. I'm definitely not okay."

Don't miss The Close-Up *by Sarah Smith,*
available wherever books are sold.
www.CarinaPress.com